The Strange Case of Mortimer Fenley

Louis Tracy

Alpha Editions

This edition published in 2024

ISBN : 9789362996183

Design and Setting By
Alpha Editions
www.alphaedis.com
Email - info@alphaedis.com

As per information held with us this book is in Public Domain.
This book is a reproduction of an important historical work. Alpha Editions uses the best technology to reproduce historical work in the same manner it was first published to preserve its original nature. Any marks or number seen are left intentionally to preserve its true form.

Contents

CHAPTER I THE WATER NYMPHS ....- 1 -

CHAPTER II "WHO HATH DONE THIS THING?" ....- 11 -

CHAPTER III THE HOUNDS ....- 22 -

CHAPTER IV BREAKING COVER ....- 34 -

CHAPTER V A FAMILY GATHERING ....- 46 -

CHAPTER VI WHEREIN FURNEAUX SEEKS INSPIRATION FROM LITERATURE AND ART ....- 59 -

CHAPTER VII SOME SIDE ISSUES ....- 72 -

CHAPTER VIII COINCIDENCES ....- 84 -

CHAPTER IX WHEREIN AN ARTIST BECOMES A MAN OF ACTION...................- 96 -

CHAPTER X FURNEAUX STATES SOME FACTS AND CERTAIN FANCIES ....- 109 -

CHAPTER XI SOME PRELIMINARY SKIRMISHING ....- 121 -

CHAPTER XII WHEREIN SCOTLAND YARD IS DINED AND WINED ....- 131 -

CHAPTER XIII CLOSE QUARTERS ....- 141 -

CHAPTER XIV THE SPREADING OF THE NET ....- 152 -

CHAPTER XV SOME STAGE EFFECTS ....- 162 -

CHAPTER XVI THE CLOSE OF A TRAGEDY ....- 172 -

CHAPTER XVII THE SETTLEMENT ....- 182 -

CHAPTER I
THE WATER NYMPHS

Does an evil deed cast a shadow in advance? Does premeditated crime spread a baleful aura which affects certain highly-strung temperaments just as the sensation of a wave of cold air rising from the spine to the head may be a forewarning of epilepsy or hysteria? John Trenholme had cause to think so one bright June morning in 1912, and he has never ceased to believe it, though the events which made him an outstanding figure in the "Strange Case of Mortimer Fenley," as the murder of a prominent man in the City of London came to be known, have long since been swept into oblivion by nearly five years of war. Even the sun became a prime agent of the occult that morning. It found a chink in a blind and threw a bar of vivid light across the face of a young man lying asleep in the front bedroom of the "White Horse Inn" at Roxton. It crept onward from a firm, well-molded chin to lips now tight set, though not lacking signs that they would open readily in a smile and perhaps reveal two rows of strong, white, even teeth. Indeed, when that strip of sunshine touched and warmed them, the smile came; so the sleeper was dreaming, and pleasantly.

But the earth stays not for men, no matter what their dreams. In a few minutes the radiant line reached the sleeper's eyes, and he awoke. Naturally, he stared straight at the disturber of his slumbers; and being a mere man, who emulated not the ways of eagles, was routed at the first glance.

More than that, he was thoroughly aroused, and sprang out of bed with a celerity that would have given many another young man a headache during the remainder of the day.

But John Trenholme, artist by profession, was somewhat of a light-hearted vagabond by instinct; if the artist was ready to be annoyed because of an imaginary loss of precious daylight, the vagabond laughed cheerily when he blinked at a clock and learned that the hour still lacked some minutes of half past five in the morning.

"By gad," he grinned, pulling up the blind, "I was scared stiff. I thought the blessed alarm had missed fire, and that I had been lying here like a hog during the best part of the finest day England has seen this year."

Evidently he was still young enough to deal in superlatives, for there had been other fine days that Summer; moreover, in likening himself to a pig, he was ridiculously unfair to six feet of athletic symmetry in which it would be difficult to detect any marked resemblance to the animal whose name is a synonym for laziness.

On the way to the bathroom he stopped to listen for sounds of an aroused household, but the inmates of the White Horse Inn were still taking life easily.

"Eliza vows she can hear that alarm in her room," he communed. "Well, suppose we assist nature, always a laudable thing in itself, and peculiarly excellent when breakfast is thereby advanced a quarter of an hour."

Eliza was the inn's stout and voluble cook-housekeeper, and her attic lay directly above Trenholme's room. He went back for the clock, crept swiftly upstairs, opened a door a few inches, and put the infernal machine inside, close to the wall. He was splashing in the bath when a harsh and penetrating din jarred through the house, and a slight scream showed that Eliza had been duly "alarmed."

A few minutes later came a heavy thump on the bathroom door.

"All right, Mr. Trenholme!" cried an irate female voice. "You've been up to your tricks, have you? It'll be my turn when I make your coffee; I'll pepper an' salt it!"

"Why, what's the matter, Eliza?" he shouted.

"Matter! Frightenin' a body like that! I thought a lot o' suffrigettes were smashin' the windows of the snug."

Eliza was still touchy when Trenholme ventured to peep into the kitchen.

"I don't know how you dare show your face," she cried wrathfully. "The impidence of men nowadays! Just fancy you comin' an' openin' my door!"

"But, *chérie*, what have I done?" he inquired, his brown eyes wide with astonishment.

"I'm not your cherry, nor your peach, neither. Who put that clock in my room?"

"What clock, *ma belle*?"

Eliza picked up an egg, and bent so fiery a glance on the intruder that he dodged out of sight for a second.

"Listen, *carissima*," he pleaded, peering round the jamb of the door again. "If the alarm found its way upstairs I must have been walking in my sleep. While you were dreaming of suffragettes I may have been dreaming of you."

"Stop there a bit longer, chatterin' and callin' me names, an' your bacon will be frizzled to a cinder," she retorted.

"But I really hoped to save you some trouble by carrying in the breakfast tray myself. I hate to see a jolly, good-tempered woman of your splendid physique working yourself to a shadow."

Eliza squared her elbows as a preliminary to another outburst, when the stairs creaked. Mary, the "help," was arriving hurriedly, in curl papers.

"Oh, *you*'ve condescended to get up, have you?" was the greeting Mary received.

"Why, it's on'y ten minutes to six!" cried the astonished girl, gazing at a grandfather's clock as if it were bewitched.

"You've never had such a shock since you were born," went on the sarcastic Eliza. "But don't thank *me*, my girl. Thank Mr. Trenholme, the gentleman stannin' there grinnin' like a Cheshire cat. Talk to him nicely, an' p'raps he'll paint your picter, an' then your special butcher boy will see how beautiful you reelly are."

"Jim don't need tellin' anything about that," said the girl, smiling, for Eliza's bark was notoriously worse than her bite.

"Jim!" came the snorting comment. "The first man who ever axed me to marry him was called Jim, an' when, like a wise woman, I said 'No,' he went away an' 'listed in the Royal Artillery an' lost his leg in a war—that's what Jim did."

"What a piece of luck you didn't accept him!" put on Trenholme.

"An' why, I'd like to know?"

"Because he began by losing his head over you. If a leg was missing, too, there wasn't much of Jim left, was there?"

Mary giggled, and Eliza seized the egg again; so Trenholme ran to his sitting-room. Within half an hour he was passing through the High Street, bidding an affable "Good morning" to such early risers as he met, and evidently well content with himself and the world in general. His artist's kit revealed his profession even to the uncritical eye, but no student of men could have failed to guess his bent were he habited in the garb of a costermonger. The painter and the poet are the last of the Bohemians, and John Trenholme was a Bohemian to the tips of his fingers.

He carried himself like a cavalier, but the divine flame of art kindled in his eye. He had learned how to paint in Julien's studio, and that same school had taught him to despise convention. He looked on nature as a series of exquisite pictures, and regarded men and women in the mass as creatures that occasionally fitted into the landscape. He was heart whole and fancy free. At twenty-five he had already exhibited three times in the Salon, and was spoken of by the critics as a painter of much promise, which is the critical method of waiting to see how the cat jumps when an artist of genius and originality arrests attention.

He had peculiarly luminous brown eyes set well apart in a face which won the prompt confidence of women, children and dogs. He was splendidly built for an out-door life, and moved with a long, supple stride, a gait which people mistook for lounging until they walked with him, and found that the pace was something over four miles an hour. Add to these personal traits the fact that he had dwelt in Roxton exactly two days and a half, and was already on speaking terms with most of the inhabitants, and you have a fair notion of John Trenholme's appearance and ways.

There remains but to add that he was commissioned by a magazine to visit this old-world Hertfordshire village and depict some of its beauties before a projected railway introduced the jerry-builder and a sewerage scheme, and his presence in the White Horse Inn is explained. He had sketched the straggling High Street, the green, the inn itself, boasting a license six hundred years old, the undulating common, the church with its lych gate, the ivy-clad ruin known as "The Castle," with its square Norman keep still frowning at an English countryside, and there was left only an Elizabethan mansion, curiously misnamed "The Towers," to be transferred to his portfolio. Here, oddly enough, he had been rebuffed. A note to the owner, Mortimer Fenley, banker and super City man, asking permission to enter the park of an afternoon, had met with a curt refusal.

Trenholme, of course, was surprised, since he was paying the man a rare compliment; he had expressed in the inn his full and free opinion concerning all money grubbers, and the Fenley species thereof in particular; whereupon the stout Eliza, who classed the Fenley family as "rubbish," informed him that there was a right of way through the park, and that from a certain point near a lake he could sketch the grand old manor house to his heart's content, let the Fenleys and their keepers scowl as they chose.

The village barber, too, bore out Eliza's statement.

"A rare old row there was in Roxton twenty year ago, when Fenley fust kem here, an' tried to close the path," said the barber. "But we beat him, we did, an' well he knows it. Not many folk use it nowadays, 'coss the artful ole dodger opened a new road to the station; but some of us makes a point of strollin' that way on a Sunday afternoon, just to look at the pheasants an' rabbits, an' it's a treat to see the head keeper's face when we go through the lodge gates at the Easton end, for that is the line the path takes."

Here followed a detailed description, for the Roxton barber, like every other barber, could chatter like a magpie; it was in this wise that Trenholme was able to defy the laws forbidding trespass, and score off the seemingly uncivil owner of a historical dwelling.

He little imagined, that glorious June morning, that he was entering on a road of strange adventure. He had chosen an early hour purposely. Not only were the lights and shadows perfect for water color, but it was highly probable that he would be able to come and go without attracting attention. He had no wish to annoy Fenley, or quarrel with the man's myrmidons. Indeed, he would not have visited the estate at all if the magazine editor had not specially stipulated for a full-page drawing of the house.

Now, all would have been well had the barber's directions proved as bald in spirit as they were in letter.

"After passin' 'The Waggoner's Rest,' you'll come to a pair of iron gates on the right," he had said. "On one side there's a swing gate. Go through, an' make straight for a clump of cedars on top of a little hill. There mayn't be much of a path, but that's it. It's reelly a short cut to the Easton gate on the London road."

Yet who could guess what a snare for an artist's feet lay in those few words? How could Trenholme realize that "a pair of iron gates" would prove to be an almost perfect example of Christopher Wren's genius as a designer of wrought iron? Trenholme's eyes sparkled when he beheld this prize, with its acanthus leaves and roses beaten out with wonderful freedom and beauty of curve. A careful drawing was the result. Another result, uncounted by him, but of singular importance in its outcome was the delay of forty minutes thus entailed.

He crossed an undulating park, and had no difficulty in tracing an almost disused path in certain grass-grown furrows leading past the group of cedars. On reaching this point he obtained a fair view of the mansion; but the sun was directly behind him, as the house faced southeast, and he decided to encroach some few yards on private property. A brier-laden slope fell from the other side of the trees to a delightful-looking lake fed by a tiny cascade on the east side. An ideal spot, he thought.

This, then, was the stage setting: Trenholme, screened by black cedars and luxuriant brushwood, was seated about fifty feet above the level of the lake and some forty yards from its nearest sedges. The lake itself, largely artificial, lay at the foot of the waterfall, which gurgled and splashed down a miniature precipice of moss-covered bowlders. Here and there a rock, a copper beech, a silver larch, or a few flowering shrubs cast strong shadows on the dark, pellucid mirror beneath. On a cunningly contrived promontory of brown rock stood a white marble statue of Venus Aphrodite, and the ripples from the cascade seemed to endow with life the shimmering reflection of the goddess.

Beyond the lake a smooth lawn, dotted with fine old oaks and chestnuts, rose gently for a quarter of a mile to the Italian gardens in front of the house. To the left, the park was bounded by woods. To the right was another wood, partly concealing a series of ravines and disused quarries. Altogether a charming setting for an Elizabethan manor, pastoral, peaceful, quite English, and seeming on that placid June morning so remote from the crowded mart that it was hard to believe the nearest milestone, with its "London, 30 miles."

Had Trenholme glanced at his watch he would have discovered that the hour was now half past seven, or nearly an hour later than he had planned. But Art, which is long-lived, recks little of Time, an evanescent thing. He was enthusiastic over his subject. He would make not one sketch, but two. That lake, like the gates, was worthy of immortality. Of course, the house must come first. He unpacked a canvas hold-all, and soon was busy.

He worked with the speed and assured confidence of a master. By years of patient industry he had wrested from Nature the secrets of her tints and tone values. Quickly there grew into being an exquisitely bright and well balanced drawing, impressionist, but true; a harmony of color and atmosphere. Leaving subtleties to the quiet thought of the studio, he turned to the lake. Here the lights and shadows were bolder. They demanded the accurate appraisement of the half closed eye. He was so absorbed in his task that he was blithely unconscious of the approach of a girl from the house, and his first glimpse of her was forthcoming when she crossed the last spread of velvet sward which separated a cluster of rhododendrons in the middle distance from the farther edge of the lake.

It was not altogether surprising that he had not seen her earlier. She wore a green coat and skirt and a most curiously shaped hat of the same hue, so that her colors blended with the landscape. Moreover, she was walking rapidly, and had covered the intervening quarter of a mile in four minutes or less.

He thought at first that she was heading straight for his lofty perch, and was perhaps bent on questioning his right to be there at all. But he was promptly undeceived. Her mind was set on one object, and her eyes did not travel beyond it. She no more suspected that an artist was lurking in the shade of the cedars than she did that the man in the moon was gazing blandly at her above their close-packed foliage. She came on with rapid, graceful strides, stood for a moment by the side of the Venus, and then, while Trenholme literally gasped for breath, shed coat, skirt and shoes, revealing a slim form clad in a dark blue bathing costume, and dived into the lake.

Trenholme had never felt more surprised. The change of costume was so unexpected, the girl's complete ignorance of his presence so obvious, that he regarded himself as a confessed intruder, somewhat akin to Peeping Tom of Coventry. He was utterly at a loss how to act. If he stood up and essayed a hurried retreat, the girl might be frightened, and would unquestionably be annoyed. It was impossible to creep away unseen. He was well below the crest of the slope crowned by the trees, and the nymph now disporting in the lake could hardly fail to discover him, no matter how deftly he crouched and twisted.

At this crisis, the artistic instinct triumphed. He became aware that the one element lacking hitherto, the element that lent magic to the beauty of the lake and its vivid environment of color, was the touch of life brought by the swimmer. He caught the flash of her limbs as they moved rhythmically through the dark, clear water, and it seemed almost as if the gods had striven to be kind in sending this naiad to complete a perfect setting. With stealthy hands he drew forth a small canvas. Oil, not mild water color, was the fitting medium to portray this Eden. Shrinking back under cover of a leafy brier, he began a third sketch in which the dominant note was the contrast between the living woman and the marble Venus.

For fifteen minutes the girl disported herself like a dolphin. Evidently she was a practiced swimmer, and had at her command all the resources of the art. At last she climbed out, and stood dripping on the sun-laved rock beside the statue. Trenholme had foreseen this attitude—had, in fact, painted with feverish energy in anticipation of it. The comparison was too striking to be missed by an artist. Were it not for the tightly clinging garments, the pair would have provided a charming representation of Galatea in stone and Galatea after Pygmalion's frenzy had warmed her into life.

Trenholme was absolutely deaf now to any consideration save that of artistic endeavor. With a swift accuracy that was nearly marvelous he put on the canvas the sheen of faultless limbs and slender neck. He even secured the spun-gold glint of hair tightly coifed under a bathing cap—a species of head-dress which had puzzled him at the first glance—and there was more than a suggestion of a veritable portrait of the regular, lively and delicately beautiful features which belonged to a type differing in every essential from the cold, classic loveliness of the statue, yet vastly more appealing in its sheer femininity.

Then the spell was broken. The girl slipped on her shoes, dressed herself in a few seconds, and was hurrying back to the house, almost before Trenholme dared to breathe normally.

"Well," he muttered, watching the swaying of the green skirt as its owner traversed the park, "this is something like an adventure! By Jove, I've been lucky this morning! I've got my picture for next year's Salon!"

He had got far more, if only he were gifted to peer into the future; but that is a privilege denied to men, even to artists. Soon, when he was calmer, and the embryo sketch had assumed its requisite color notes for subsequent elaboration, he smiled a trifle dubiously.

"If that girl's temperament is as attractive as her looks I'd throw over the Salon for the sake of meeting her," he mused. "But that's frankly impossible, I suppose. At the best, she would not forgive me if she knew I had watched her in this thievish way. I could never explain it, never! She wouldn't even listen. Well, it's better to have dreamed and lost than never to have dreamed at all."

And yet he dreamed. His eyes followed the fair unknown while she entered the garden through a gateway of dense yews, and sped lightly up the steps of a terrace adorned with other statues in marble and bronze. No doorway broke the pleasing uniformity of the south front, but she disappeared through an open window, swinging herself lightly over the low sill. He went with her in imagination. Now she was crossing a pretty drawing-room, now running upstairs to her room, now dressing, possibly in white muslin, which, if Trenholme had the choosing of it, would be powdered with tiny *fleurs de lys*, now arranging her hair with keen eye for effect, and now tripping down again in obedience to a gong summoning the household to breakfast.

He sighed.

"If I had the luck of a decent French poodle, this plutocrat Fenley would eke have invited me to lunch," he grumbled.

Then his eyes sought the sketch, and he forgot the girl in her counterfeit. By Jove, this *would* be a picture! "The Water Nymphs." But he must change the composition a little—losing none of its character; only altering its accessories to such an extent that none would recognize the exact setting.

"Luck!" he chortled, with mercurial rise of spirits. "I'm the luckiest dog in England today. Happy chance has beaten all the tricks of the studio. O ye goddesses, inspire me to heights worthy of you!"

His visions were rudely dispelled by a gunshot, sharp, insistent, a tocsin of death in that sylvan solitude. A host of rooks arose from some tall elms near the house; a couple of cock pheasants flew with startled chuckling out of the wood on the right; the white tails of rabbits previously unseen revealed their owners' whereabouts as they scampered to cover. But Trenholme was sportsman enough to realize that the weapon fired was a rifle; no toy, but of high velocity, and he wondered how any one dared risk its dangerous use in such a locality. He fixed the sound definitely as coming from the wood to the right—the cover quitted so hurriedly by the pheasants—and instinctively his glance turned to the house, in the half formed thought that some one there might hear the shot, and look out.

The ground floor window by which the girl had entered still remained open, but now another window, the most easterly one on the first floor, had been raised slightly. The light was peculiarly strong and the air so clear that even at the distance he fancied he could distinguish some one gesticulating, or so it seemed, behind the glass. This went on for a minute or more. Then the window was closed. At the same time he noticed a sparkling of glass and brasswork behind the clipped yew hedge which extended beyond the east wing. After some puzzling, he made out that a motor car was waiting there.

That was all. The clamor of the rooks soon subsided. A couple of rabbits skipped from the bushes to resume an interrupted meal on tender grass shoots. A robin trilled a roundelay from some neighboring branch. Trenholme looked at his watch. Half past nine! Why, he must have been mooning there a good half hour!

He gathered his traps, and as the result of seeing the automobile, which had not moved yet, determined to forego his earlier project of walking out of the park by the Easton gate.

He had just emerged from the trees when a gruff voice hailed him.

"Hi!" it cried. "Who're you, an' what are you doin' here!"

A man, carrying a shotgun and accompanied by a dog, strode up with determined air.

Trenholme explained civilly, since the keeper was clearly within his rights. Moreover, the stranger was so patently a gentleman that Velveteens adopted a less imperative tone.

"Did you hear a shot fired somewhere?" he asked.

"Yes. Among those trees." And Trenholme pointed. "It was a rifle, too," he added, with an eye at the twelve-bore.

"So *I* thought," agreed the keeper.

"Rather risky, isn't it, firing bullets in a place like this?"

"I just want to find out who the ijiot is that did it. Excuse me, sir, I must be off." And man and dog hurried away.

And Trenholme, not knowing that death had answered the shot, took his own departure, singing as he walked, his thoughts altogether on life, and more especially on life as revealed by the limbs of a girl gleaming in the dark waters of a pool.

CHAPTER II
"WHO HATH DONE THIS THING?"

Trenholme's baritone was strong and tuneful—for the Muses, if kind, are often lavish of their gifts—so the final refrain of an impassioned love song traveled far that placid morning. Thus, when he reached the iron gates, he found the Roxton policeman standing there, grinning.

"Hello!" said the artist cheerily. Of course he knew the policeman. In a week he would have known every man and dog in the village by name.

"Good mornin', sir," said the Law, which was nibbling its chin strap and had both thumbs stuck in its belt. "That's a fine thing you was singin'. May I arsk wot it was? I do a bit in that line meself."

"It's the *cantabile* from Saint-Saëns' *Samson et Dalila*," replied Trenholme. "Mon cœur s'ouvre à ta voix!"

"Is it now? An' wot may that be, sir?"

The policeman's humor was infectious. Trenholme laughed, too. Realizing that the words and accent of Paris had no great vogue in Hertfordshire, he explained, and added that he possessed a copy of the song, which was at the service of the force. The man thanked him warmly, and promised to call at the inn during the afternoon.

"By the way, sir," he added, when Trenholme had passed through the wicket, "did you hear a shot fired while you was in the park?"

"Yes."

"Jer see anybody?"

"A keeper, who seemed rather annoyed about the shooting. Some one had fired a rifle."

"It sounded like that to me, sir, and it's an unusual thing at this time of the year."

"A heavy-caliber rifle must sound unusual at any time of the year in an enclosed estate near London," commented Trenholme.

"My idee exactly," said the policeman. "I think I'll go that way. I may meet Bates."

"If Bates is a bandy-legged person with suspicious eyes, a red tie, many pockets, brown leggings, and a yellow dog, you'll find him searching the wood beyond the lake, which is the direction the shot came from."

The policeman laughed.

"That's Bates, to a tick," he said. "If he was 'wanted,' your description would do for the *Police Gazette*."

They parted. Since Trenholme's subsequent history is bound up more closely with the policeman's movements during the next hour than with his own unhindered return to the White Horse Inn, it is well to trace the exact course of events as they presented themselves to the ken of a music-loving member of the Hertfordshire constabulary.

Police Constable Farrow did not hurry. Why should he? A gunshot in a gentleman's park at half past nine on a June morning might be, as he had put it, "unusual," but it was obviously a matter capable of the simplest explanation. Such a sound heard at midnight would be sinister, ominous, replete with those elements of mystery and dread which cause even a policeman's heart to beat faster than the regulation pace. Under the conditions, when he met Bates, he would probably be told that Jenkins, underkeeper and Territorial lance corporal, had resolved to end the vicious career of a hoodie crow, and had not scrupled to reach the wily robber with a bullet.

So Police Constable Farrow took fifteen minutes to cover the ground which Trenholme's longer stride had traversed in ten. Allow another fifteen for the artist's packing of his sketching materials, his conversation with gamekeeper and policeman, and the leisurely progress of the latter through the wood, and it will be found that Farrow reached the long straight avenue leading from the lodge at Easton to the main entrance of the house about forty minutes after the firing of the shot.

He halted on the grass by the side of the well-kept drive, and looked at the waiting motor car. The chauffeur was not visible. He had seen neither Bates nor Jenkins. His passing among the trees had not disturbed even a pheasant, though the estate was alive with game. The door of The Towers was open, but no stately manservant was stationed there. A yellow dog sat in the sunshine. Farrow and the dog exchanged long-range glances: the policeman consulted his watch, bit his chin strap, and dug his thumbs into his belt.

"Mr. Fenley is late today," he said to himself. "He catches the nine forty-five. As a rule, he's as reliable as Greenwich. I'll wait here till he passes, an' then call round an' see Smith."

Now, Smith was the head gardener; evidently Police Constable Farrow was not only well acquainted with the various inmates of the mansion, but could have prepared a list of the out-door employees as well. He stood there, calm and impassive as Fate, and, without knowing it, represented Fate in her most inexorable mood; for had he betaken himself elsewhere, the shrewdest brains of Scotland Yard might have been defeated by the enigma they were asked to solve before Mortimer Fenley's murderer was discovered.

Indeed, it is reasonable to suppose that if chance had not brought the village constable to that identical spot, and at that very hour, the precise method of the crime might never have been revealed. Moreover, Farrow himself may climb slowly to an inspectorship, and pass into the dignified ease of a pension, without being aware of the part he played in a tragedy that morning. Of course, in his own estimation, he filled a highly important rôle as soon as the hue and cry began, but a great deal of water would flow under London Bridge before the true effect of his walk through the wood and emergence into sight in the avenue began to dawn on other minds.

His appearance there was a vital fact. It changed the trend of circumstances much as the path of a comet is deflected by encountering a heavy planet. Presumably, neither comet nor planet is aware of the disturbance. That deduction is left to the brooding eye of science.

Be that as it may, Police Constable Farrow's serenity was not disturbed until a doctor's motor car panted along the avenue from Easton and pulled up with a jerk in front of him. The doctor, frowning with anxiety, looked out, and recognition was mutual.

"Have you got the man?" he asked, and the words were jerked out rather than spoken.

"What man, sir?" inquired Farrows, saluting.

"The man who shot Mr. Fenley."

"The man who shot Mr. Fenley!" Farrow could only repeat each word in a crescendo of amazement. Being a singer, he understood the use of a crescendo, and gave full scope to it.

"Good Heavens!" cried the doctor. "Haven't you been told? Why are you here? Mr. Fenley was shot dead on his own doorstep nearly an hour ago. At least that is the message telephoned by his son. Unfortunately I was out. Right ahead, Tom!"

The chauffeur threw in the clutch, and the car darted on again. Farrow followed, a quite alert and horrified policeman now. But it was not ordained that he should enter the house. He was distant yet a hundred yards, or more, when three men came through the doorway. They were Bates, the keeper, Tomlinson, the butler, and Mr. Hilton Fenley, elder son of the man now reported dead. All were bareheaded. The arrival of the doctor, at the instant alighting from his car, prevented them from noticing Farrow's rapid approach. When Hilton Fenley saw the doctor he threw up his hands with the gesture of one who has plumbed the depths of misery. Farrow could, and did, fit in the accompanying words quite accurately.

"Nothing can be done, Stern! My father is dead!"

The two clasped each other's hand, and Hilton Fenley staggered slightly. He was overcome with emotion. The shock of a terrible crime had taxed his self-control to its uttermost bounds. He placed a hand over his eyes and said brokenly to the butler:

"You take Dr. Stern inside, Tomlinson. I'll join you in a few minutes. I must have a breath of air, or I'll choke!"

Doctor and butler hurried into the house; then, but not until then, Hilton Fenley and the keeper became aware of Farrow, now within a few yards. At sight of him, Fenley seemed to recover his faculties; the mere possibility of taking some definite action brought a tinge of color to a pallid and somewhat sallow face.

"Ah! Here is the constable," he cried. "Go with him, Bates, and have that artist fellow arrested!"

"Meaning Mr. Trenholme, sir?" inquired the policeman, startled anew by this unexpected reference to the man he had parted from so recently.

"I don't know his name; but Bates met him in the park, near the lake, just after the shot was fired that killed my father."

"But I met him, too, sir. He didn't fire any shot. He hadn't a gun. In fact, he spoke about the shootin', and was surprised at it."

"Look here, Farrow, I am incapable of thinking clearly; so you must act for the best. Some one fired that bullet. It nearly tore my father to pieces. I never saw anything like it. It was ghastly—oh, ghastly! The murderer must be found. Why are you losing time? Jump into the car, and Brodie will take you anywhere you want to go. The roads, the railway stations, must be scoured, searched. Oh, do something, or I shall go mad!"

Hilton Fenley did, indeed, wear the semblance of a man distraught. Horror stared from his deep-set eyes and lurked in the corners of his mouth. His father had been struck dead within a few seconds after they had separated in the entrance hall, both having quitted the breakfast room together, and the awful discovery which followed the cry of an alarmed servant had almost shaken the son's reason.

Farrow was hardly fitted to deal with a crisis of such magnitude, but he acted promptly and with fixed purpose—qualities which form the greater part of generalship.

"Bates," he said, turning a determined eye on the keeper, "where was you when you heard the shot?"

"In the kennels, back of the lodge," came the instant answer.

"And you kem this way at once?"

"Straight. Didn't lose 'arf a minute."

"So no one could have left by the Easton gate without meeting you?"

"That's right."

"And you found Mr. Trenholme—where?"

"Comin' away from the cedars, above the lake."

"What did he say?"

"Tole me about the shot, an' pointed out the Quarry Wood as the place it kem from."

"Was he upset at all in his manner?"

"Not a bit. Spoke quite nateral-like."

"Well, between the three of us, you an' me an' Mr. Trenholme, we account for both gates an' the best part of two miles of park. Where is Jenkins?"

"I left him at the kennels."

"Ah!"

The policeman was momentarily nonplussed. He had formed a theory in which Jenkins, that young Territorial spark, figured either as a fool or a criminal.

"What's the use of holding a sort of inquiry on the doorstep?" broke in Hilton Fenley shrilly. His utterance was nearly hysterical. Farrow's judicial calm appeared to stir him to frenzy. He clamored for action, for zealous scouting, and this orderly investigation by mere words was absolutely maddening.

"I'm not wastin' time, sir," said Farrow respectfully. "It's as certain as anything can be that the murderer, if murder has been done, has not got away by either of the gates."

- 15 -

"If murder has been done!" cried Fenley. "What do you mean? Go and look at my poor father's corpse———"

"Of course, Mr. Fenley is dead, sir, an' sorry I am to hear of it; but the affair may turn out to be an accident."

"Accident! Farrow, you're talking like an idiot. A man is shot dead at his own front door, in a house standing in the midst of a big estate, and you tell me it's an accident!"

"No, sir. I on'y mentioned that on the off chance. Queer things do happen, an' one shouldn't lose sight of that fact just because it's unusual. Now, sir, with your permission, I want Brodie, an' Smith, an' all the men servants you can spare for the next half hour."

"Why?"

"Brodie can motor to the Inspector's office, an' tell him wot he knows, stoppin' on the way to send Jenkins here. Some of us must search the woods thoroughly, while others watch the open park, to make sure no one escapes without bein' seen. It's my firm belief that the man who fired that rifle is still hidin' among those trees. He may be sneakin' off now, but we'd see him if we're quick in reachin' the other side. Will you do as I ask, sir?"

Farrow was already in motion when Fenley's dazed mind recalled something the policeman ought to know.

"I've telephoned to Scotland Yard half an hour ago," he said.

"That's all right, sir. The main thing now is to search every inch of the woods. If nothing else, we may find footprints."

"And make plenty of new ones."

"Not if the helpers do as I tell 'em, sir."

"I can't argue. I'm not fit for it. Still, some instinct warns me you are not adopting the best course. I think you ought to go in the car and put the police into combined action."

"What are they to do, sir? The murderer won't carry a rifle through the village, or along the open road. I fancy we'll come across the weapon itself in the wood. Besides, the Inspector will do all that is necessary when Brodie sees him. Reelly, sir, I *know* I'm right."

"But should that artist be questioned?"

"Of course he will, sir. He won't run away. If he does, we'll soon nab him. He's been stayin' at the White Horse Inn the last two days, an' is quite a nice-spoken young gentleman. Why should *he* want to shoot Mr. Fenley?"

"He is annoyed with my father, for one thing."

"Eh? Wot, sir?"

Farrow, hitherto eager to be off on the hunt, stopped as if he heard a statement of real importance.

Hilton Fenley pressed a hand to his eyes.

"It was nothing to speak of," he muttered. "He wrote asking permission to sketch the house, and my father refused—just why I don't know; some business matter had vexed him that day, I fancy, and he dashed off the refusal on the spur of the moment. But a man does not commit a terrible crime for so slight a cause.... Oh, if only my head would cease throbbing!... Do as you like. Bates, see that every assistance is given."

Fenley walked a few paces unsteadily. Obviously he was incapable of lucid thought, and the mere effort at sustained conversation was a torture. He turned through a yew arch into the Italian garden, and threw himself wearily into a seat.

"Poor young fellow! He's fair off his nut," whispered Bates.

"What can one expect?" said Farrow. "But we must get busy. Where's Brodie? Do go an' find him."

Bates jerked a thumb toward the house.

"He's in there," he said. "He helped to carry in the Gov'nor. Hasn't left him since."

"He must come at once. He can't do any good now, an' we've lost nearly an hour as it is."

The chauffeur appeared, red-eyed and white-faced. But he understood the urgency of his mission, and soon had the car in movement. Others came—the butler, some gardeners, and men engaged in stables and garage, for the dead banker maintained a large establishment. Farrow explained his plan. They would beat the woods methodically, and the searcher who noted anything "unusual"—the word was often on the policeman's lips—was not to touch or disturb the object or sign in any way, but its whereabouts should be marked by a broken branch stuck in the ground. Of course, if a stranger was seen, an alarm should be raised instantly.

The little party was making for the Quarry Wood, when Jenkins arrived on a bicycle. The first intimation he had received of the murder was the chauffeur's message. There was a telephone between house and lodge, but no one had thought of using it.

"Now, Bates," said Farrow, when the squad of men had spread out in line, "you an' me will take the likeliest line. You ought to know every spot in the covert where it's possible to aim a gun at any one stannin' on top of the steps at The Towers. There can't be many such places. Is there even one? I don't suppose the barefaced scoundrel would dare come out into the open drive. Brodie said Mr. Fenley was shot through the right side while facin' the car, so he bears out both your notion an' Mr. Trenholme's that the bullet kem from the Quarry Wood. What's *your* idea about it? Have you one, or are you just as much in the dark as the rest of us?"

Bates was sour-faced with perplexity. The killing of his employer was already crystallizing in his thoughts into an irrevocable thing, for the butler had lifted aside the dead man's coat and waistcoat, and this had shown him the ghastly evidences of a wound which must have been instantly fatal. Now, a shrewd if narrow intelligence was concentrated on the one tremendous question, "Who hath done this thing?" He looked so worried that the yellow dog, watching him, and quick to interpret his moods, slouched warily at heel; and Farrow, though agog with excitement, saw that his crony was ill at ease because of some twinge of fear or suspicion.

"Speak out, Jim," he urged, dropping his voice to a confidential pitch, lest one of the others might overhear. "Gimme the straight tip, if you can. It need never be known that it kem from you."

"I've a good berth here," muttered the keeper, with seeming irrelevance.

"Tell me something fresh," said Farrow, quickening with grateful memories of many a pheasant and brace of rabbits reposing a brief space in his modest larder.

"So, if I tell you things in confidence like———"

"I've heard 'em from any one but you."

Bates drew a deep breath, only to expel it fiercely between puffed lips.

"It's this way," he growled. "Mr. Robert an' the ol' man didn't hit off, an' there was a deuce of a row between 'em the other day, Saturday it was. My niece, Mary, was a-dustin' the banisters when the two kem out from breakfast, an' she heerd the Gov'nor say: 'That's my last word on the subjec'. I mean to be obeyed this time.'

"'But, look here, pater,' said Mr. Robert—he always calls his father pater, ye know—'I reelly can't arrange matters in that offhand way. You must give me time.' 'Not another minute,' said Mr. Fenley. 'Oh, dash it all,' said Mr. Robert, 'you're enough to drive a fellow crazy. At times I almost forget that I'm your son. Some fellows would be tempted to blow their brains out, an' yours, too.'

"At that, Tomlinson broke in, an' grabbed Mr. Robert's arm, an' the Gov'nor went off in the car in a fine ol' temper. Mr. Robert left The Towers on his motor bike soon afterward, an' he hasn't been back since."

Although the fount of information temporarily ran dry, Farrow felt that there was more to come if its secret springs were tapped.

"Did Mary drop a hint as to what the row was about?" he inquired.

"She guessed it had something to do with Miss Sylvia."

"Why Miss Sylvia?"

"She an' Mr. Robert are pretty good friends, you see."

"I see." The policeman saw little, but each scrap of news might fit into its place presently.

"Is that all?" he went on. They were nearing that part of the wood where care must be exercised, and he wanted Bates to talk while in the vein.

"No, not by a long way," burst out the keeper, seemingly unable to contain any longer the deadly knowledge weighing on his conscience. "Don't you try an' hold me to it, Farrow, or I'll swear black an' blue I never said it; but I knew the ring of the shot that killed my poor ol' guv'nor. It was fired from an express rifle, an' there's on'y one of the sort in Roxton, so far as *I've* ever seen. An' it is, or ought to be, in Mr. Robert's sittin'-room at this very minute. There! Now you've got it. Do as you like. Get Tomlinson to talk, or anybody else, but keep me out of it—d'ye hear?"

"I hear," said Farrow, thrilling with the consciousness that when some dandy detective arrived from the "Yard," he would receive an eye-opener from a certain humble member of the Hertfordshire constabulary. Not that he quite brought himself to believe Robert Fenley his father's murderer. That was going rather far. That would, indeed, be a monstrous assumption as matters stood. But as clues the quarrel and the rifle were excellent, and Scotland Yard must recognize them in that light.

Certainly, this *was* an unusual case; most unusual. He was well aware of the reputation attached to Robert Fenley, the banker's younger son, who differed from his brother in every essential. Hilton was steady-going, business-like, his father's secretary and right hand in affairs, both in the bank and in matters affecting the estate. Robert, almost unmanageable as a youth, had grown into an exceedingly rapid young man about town. But Roxton folk feared Hilton and liked Robert; and local gossip had deplored Robert's wildness, which might erect an insurmountable barrier against an obviously suitable match between him and Mr. Mortimer Fenley's ward, the rich and beautiful Sylvia Manning.

These things were vivid in the policeman's mind, and he was wondering how the puzzle would explain itself in the long run, when an exclamation from Bates brought his vagrom speculations sharply back to the problem of the moment.

The keeper, of course, as Farrow had said, was making straight for the one place in the Quarry Wood which commanded a clear view of the entrance to the mansion. The two men were skirting the disused quarry, now a rabbit warren, which gave the locality its name; they followed the rising edge of the excavation, treading on a broad strip of turf, purposely freed of encroaching briers lest any wandering stranger might plunge headlong into the pit. Near the highest part of the rock wall there was a slight depression in the ground; and here, except during the height of a phenomenally dry Summer, the surface was always moist.

Bates, who was leading, had halted suddenly. He pointed to three well marked footprints.

"Who's been here, an' not so long ago, neither?" he said, darting ferret eyes now at the telltale marks and now into the quarry beneath or through the solemn aisle of trees.

"Stick in some twigs, an' let's hurry on," said Farrow. "Footprints are first rate, but they'll keep for an hour or two."

Thirty yards away, and somewhat to the right, a hump of rock formed the Mont Blanc of that tiny Alp. From its summit, and from no other part of the wood, they could see the east front of The Towers. In fact, while perched there, having climbed its shoulder with great care lest certain definite tokens of a recent intruder should be obliterated, they discovered a dusty motor car ranged between the doctor's runabout and the Fenley limousine, which had returned.

The doctor and Miss Sylvia Manning were standing on the broad mosaic which adorned the landing above the steps, standing exactly where Mortimer Fenley had stood when he was stricken to death. With them were two strangers: one tall, burly and official-looking; the other a shrunken little man, whose straw hat, short jacket, and clean-shaven face conveyed, at the distance, a curiously juvenile aspect.

Halfway down the steps were Hilton Fenley and Brodie, and all were gazing fixedly at that part of the wood where the keeper and the policeman had popped into view.

"Hello!" said Bates. "Who is that little lot?"

Clearly, he meant the big man and his diminutive companion. Farrow coughed importantly.

"That's Scotland Yard," he said.

"Who?"

"Detectives from the Yard. Mr. Hilton telephoned for 'em. An' wot's more, they're signalin' to us."

"They want us to go back," said Bates.

"Mebbe."

"There can't be any doubt about it." And, indeed, only a blind man could have been skeptical as to the wishes of the group near the door.

"I'm goin' through this wood first," announced Farrow firmly. "Mind how you get down. Them marks may be useful. I'm almost sure the scoundrel fired from this very spot."

"Looks like it," agreed Bates, and they descended.

Five minutes later they were in the open park, where their assistant scouts awaited them. None of the others had found any indication of a stranger's presence, and Farrow led them to the house in Indian file, by a path.

"Scotland Yard is on the job," he announced. "Now we'll be told just wot we reelly ought to have done!"

He did not even exchange a furtive glance with Bates, but, for the life of him he could not restrain a note of triumph from creeping into his voice. He noticed, too, that Tomlinson, the butler, not only looked white and shaken, which was natural under the circumstances, but had the haggard aspect of a stout man who may soon become thin by stress of fearsome imaginings.

Farrow did not put it that way.

"Bates is right," he said to himself. "Tomlinson has something on his chest. By jingo, this affair *is* a one-er an' no mistake!"

At any rate, local talent had no intention of kowtowing too deeply before the majesty of the "Yard," for the Chief of the Criminal Investigation Department himself could have achieved no more in the time than Police Constable Farrow.

CHAPTER III
THE HOUNDS

Superintendent James Leander Winter, Chief of the Criminal Investigation Department at Scotland Yard, had just opened the morning's letters, and was virtuously resisting the placid charms of an open box of cigars, when the telephone bell rang. The speaker was the Assistant Commissioner.

"Leave everything else, and motor to Roxton," said the calm voice of authority. "Mr. Mortimer Fenley, a private banker in the City, was shot dead about nine thirty at his own front door. His place is The Towers, which stands in a park between the villages of Roxton and Easton, in Hertfordshire. His son, who has just telephoned here, believes that a rifle was fired from a neighboring wood, but several minutes elapsed before any one realized that the banker was shot, the first impression of the servants who ran to his assistance when he staggered and fell being that he was suffering from apoplexy. By the time the cause of death was discovered the murderer could have escaped, so no immediate search was organized. Mr. Hilton Fenley, a son, who spoke with difficulty, explained that he thought it best to 'phone here after summoning a doctor. The dead man is of some importance in the City, so I want you to take personal charge of the inquiry."

The voice ceased. Mr. Winter, while listening, had glanced at a clock.

"Nine thirty this morning, sir?" he inquired.

"Yes. The son lost no time. The affair happened a quarter of an hour ago."

"I'll start in five minutes."

"Good. By the way, who will go with you?"

"Mr. Furneaux."

"Excellent. I leave matters in your hands, Superintendent. Let me hear the facts if you return to town before six."

Evidently the Roxton murder was one of the year's big events. It loomed large already in the official mind. Winter called up various departments in quick succession, gave a series of orders, sorted his letters hastily, thrusting some into a drawer and others into a basket on the table, and was lighting a cigar when the door opened and his trusted aide, Detective Inspector Furneaux, entered.

"Ha!" cackled the newcomer; for Winter had confided to him, only the day before, certain reasons why the habit of smoking to excess was injurious, and his (Winter's) resolve to cut down the day's cigars to three, one after each principal meal.

"Circumstances alter cases," said the Superintendent blandly, scrutinizing the Havana to make sure that the outer leaf was burning evenly. "You and I are off for a jaunt in the country, Charles, and the sternest disciplinarian unbends during holiday time."

"Scotland Yard, as well as the other place, is paved with good intentions," said Furneaux.

Winter stooped, and took a couple of automatic pistols from a drawer in the desk at which he was seated.

"Put one of those in your pocket," he said.

Again did his colleague smile derisively.

"So it is only a 'bus driver's holiday?" he cried.

"One never knows. Some prominent banker, name of Fenley, has been shot. There may be more shooting."

"Fenley? Not Mortimer Fenley?"

"Yes. Do you know him?"

"Better than I know you; because you often puzzle me, whereas he struck me as a respectable swindler. Don't you remember those bonds which disappeared so mysteriously two months ago from the safe of the Mortgage and Discount Bank, and were all sold in Paris before the loss was discovered?"

"By Jove! Is that the Fenley?"

"None other. Of course, you were hob-nobbing with royalty at the time, so such a trifle as the theft of ten thousand pounds' worth of negotiable securities didn't trouble you a bit. I see you're wearing the pin today."

"So would you wear it, if an Emperor deigned to take notice of such a shrimp."

"Shrimp you call me! Imagine a lobster sticking rubies and diamonds into a heliotrope tie!"

Winter winked solemnly.

"I picked up some wrinkles in color blends at the Futurist Exhibition," he said. "But here's Johnston to tell us the car is ready."

The oddly assorted pair followed the constable in uniform, now hurrying ahead to ring for the elevator. The big, bluff, bullet-headed Superintendent was physically well fitted for his responsible position, though he combined with the official demeanor some of the easy-going characteristics of a country squire; but Charles François Furneaux was so unlike the detective of romance and the stage that he often found it difficult to persuade strangers that he was really the famous detective inspector they had heard of in connection with many a celebrated trial.

On the other hand, if one were told that he hailed from the Comédie Française, the legend would be accepted without demur. He had the clean-shaven, wrinkled face of the comedian; his black eyes sparkled with an active intelligence; an expressive mouth bespoke clear and fluent speech; his quick, alert movements were those of the mimetic actor. Winter stood six feet in height, and weighed two hundred and ten pounds; Furneaux was six inches shorter and eighty pounds lighter. The one was a typical John Bull, the other a Channel Islander of pure French descent, and never did more curiously assorted couple follow the trail of a criminal.

Yet, if noteworthy when acting apart, they were almost infallible in combination. More than one eminent scoundrel had either blown out his brains or given himself up to the law when he knew that the Big 'Un and Little 'Un of the Yard were hot on his track. Winter seldom failed to arrive at the only sound conclusion from ascertained facts, whereas Furneaux had an almost uncanny knowledge of the kinks and obliquities of the criminal mind. In the phraseology of logic, Winter applied the deductive method and Furneaux the inductive; when both fastened on to the same "suspect" the unlucky wight was in parlous state.

It may be taken for granted, therefore, that the Assistant Commissioner knew what he was about in uttering his satisfaction at the Superintendent's choice of an assistant. Possibly he had the earlier bond robbery in mind, and expected now that another "mystery" would be solved. Scotland Yard guards many secrets which shirk the glare of publicity. Some may never be explained; but by far the larger proportion are cleared up unexpectedly by incidents which may occur months or years afterward, and whose connection with the original crime is indiscernible until some chance discovery lays bare the hidden clue.

One queer feature of the partnership between the two was their habit of chaffing and bickering at each other during the early stages of a joint hunt. They were like hounds giving tongue joyously when laid on the scent; dangerous then, they became mute and deadly when the quarry was in sight. In private life they were firm friends; officially, Furneaux was Winter's subordinate, but that fact neither silenced the Jersey man's sarcastic tongue nor stopped Winter from roasting his assistant unmercifully if an opportunity offered.

Their chauffeur took the line through the parks to the Edgware Road, and they talked of anything save "shop" until the speed limit was off and the car was responding gayly to the accelerator. Then Winter threw away the last inch of a good cigar, involuntarily put his hand to a well-filled case for its successor, sighed, and dropped his hand again.

"Force of habit," he said, finding Furneaux's eye on him.

"I didn't even think evil," was the reply.

"I really mustn't smoke so much," said Winter plaintively.

"Oh, for goodness' sake light up and be happy. If you sit there nursing your self-righteousness you'll be like a bear with a sore head before we pass Stanmore. Besides, consider me. I like the smell of tobacco, though my finer nervous system will not endure its use."

"Finer fiddlesticks," said Winter, cutting the end off a fresh Havana. "Now tell me about Fenley and the ten thousand. What's his other name? I forget—Alexander, is it?"

"No, nor Xenophon. Just Mortimer. He ran a private bank in Bishopsgate Street, and that, as you know, generally hides a company promoter. Frankly, I was bothered by Fenley at first. I believe he lost the bonds right enough, for he gave the numbers, and was horribly upset when it was found they had been sold in Paris. But, to my idea, he either stole them himself and was relieved of them later or was victimized by one of his sons.

"The only other person who could have taken them was the cashier, a hoary-headed old boy who resides at Epping, and has not changed his method of living since he first wore a silk hat and caught the eight-forty to the City one morning fifty years ago. I followed him home on a Saturday afternoon. The bookstall clerk at Liverpool Street handed him *The Amateur Gardener*, and the old boy read it in the train. Five minutes after he had reached his house he was out on the lawn with a daisy fork. No; the cashier didn't arrange the Paris sale."

"What of the sons?"

"The elder, Hilton Fenley, is a neurotic, like myself, so he would shine with equal luster as a saint, or a detective, or a dyed-in-the-wool thief. The younger, Robert, ought to be an explorer, or a steeplechase jockey, or an airman. In reality, he is a first-rate wastrel. In my distress I harked back to the old man, to whom the loss of the bonds represented something considerably less than a year's expenditure. He is mixed up in all sorts of enterprises—rubber, tea, picture palaces, breweries and automobile finance. He lent fifty thousand pounds on five per cent. first mortgage bonds to one firm at Coventry, and half that amount to a rival show in West London. So he has the stuff, and plenty of it. Yet——"

Winter nodded.

"I know the sort of man. Dealing in millions today; tomorrow in the dock at the Old Bailey."

"The point is that Fenley has never dealt in millions, and has kept his head high for twenty years. Just twenty years, by the way. Before that he was unknown. He began by the amalgamation of some tea plantations in Assam. Fine word, 'amalgamation.' It means money, all the time. Can't we amalgamate something, or somebody?"

"In Fenley's case it led to assassination."

"Perhaps. I have a feeling in my bones that if I knew who touched the proceeds of those bonds I might understand why some one shot Fenley this morning."

"I'll soon tell you a trivial thing like that," said Winter, affecting a close interest in the landscape.

"I shouldn't be at all surprised if you did," said Furneaux. "You have the luck of a Carnegie. Look at the way you bungled that affair of Lady Morris's diamonds, until you happened to see her maid meeting Gentleman George at the White City."

Winter smoked complacently.

"Smartest thing I ever did," he chortled. "Fixed on the thief within half an hour, and never lost touch till I knew how she had worked the job."

"The Bow Street method."

"Why didn't you try something of the sort with regard to Fenley's bonds?"

"I couldn't be crude, even with a City financier. I put it gently that the money was in the family; he blinked at me like an owl, said that he would give thought to the suggestion, and shut down the inquiry by telephone before I reached the Yard from his office."

"Oh, he did, did he? It seems to me you've made a pretty good guess in associating the bonds and the murder. You've seen both sons, of course?"

"Yes, often."

"Are there other members of the family?"

"An invalid wife, never away from The Towers; and a young lady, Miss Sylvia Manning—a ward, and worth a pile. By the way, she's twenty. Mortimer Fenley, had he lived, was appointed her guardian and trustee till she reached twenty-one."

"Twenty!" mused Winter.

"Yes, twice ten," snapped Furneaux.

"And Fenley has cut a figure in the City for twenty years."

"I was sure your gray matter would be stimulated by its favorite poison."

"Charles, this should be an easy thing."

"I'm not so sure. Dead men tell no tales, and Fenley himself could probably supply many chapters of an exciting story. They will be missing. Look at the repeated failures of eminent authors to complete 'Edwin Drood.' How would they have fared if asked to produce the beginning?"

"Still, I'm glad you attended to those bonds. Who had charge of the Paris end?"

"Jacques Faure."

"Ah, a good man."

"Pretty fair, for a Frenchman."

Winter laughed.

"You born frog!" he cried.... "Hello, there's a Roxton sign post. Now let's compose our features. We are near The Towers."

The estate figured on the county map, so the chauffeur pulled up at the right gate. A woman came from the lodge to inquire their business, and admitted the car when told that its occupants had been summoned by Mr. Hilton Fenley.

"By the way," said Furneaux carelessly, "is Mr. Robert at home?"

"No, sir."

"When did he leave?"

"I'm sure I don't know, sir."

Mrs. Bates knew quite well, and Furneaux knew that she knew.

"The country domestic is the detective's aversion," he said as the car whirred into the avenue. "The lady of the lodge will be a sufficiently tough proposition if we try to drag information out of her, but the real tug of war will come when we tackle the family butler."

"Her husband is also the head keeper," said Winter.

"Name of Bates," added Furneaux.

"Oh, you've been here before, then?"

"No. While you were taking stock of the kennels generally, I was deciphering a printed label on a box of dog biscuit."

"I hardly feel that I've begun this inquiry yet," said Winter airily.

"You'd better pull yourself together. The dead man's limousine is still waiting at the door, and the local doctor is in attendance."

"Walter J. Stern, M.D."

"Probably. That brass plate on the Georgian house in the center of the village positively glistened."

They were received by Hilton Fenley himself, all the available men servants having been transferred to the cohort organized and directed by Police Constable Farrow.

"Good morning, Mr. Furneaux," said Fenley. "I little thought, when last we met, that I should be compelled to seek your help so soon again, and under such dreadful circumstances."

Furneaux, whose face could display at will a Japanese liveliness of expression or become a mask of Indian gravity, surveyed the speaker with inscrutable eyes.

"This is Superintendent Winter, Chief of my Department," he said.

"The Assistant Commissioner told me to take charge of the inquiry without delay, sir," explained Winter. He glanced at his watch. "We have not been long on the road. It is only twenty minutes to eleven."

Fenley led them through a spacious hall into a dining-room on the left. On an oak settee at the back of the hall the outline of a white sheet was eloquent of the grim object beneath. In the dining-room were an elderly man and a slim, white-faced girl. Had Trenholme been present he would have noted with interest that her dress was of white muslin dotted with tiny blue spots—not *fleurs de lys*, but rather resembling them.

"Dr. Stern, and Miss Sylvia Manning," said Fenley to the newcomers. Then he introduced the Scotland Yard men in turn. By this time the young head of the family had schooled himself to a degree of self-control. His sallow skin held a greenish pallor, and as if to satisfy some instinct that demanded movement he took an occasional slow stride across the parquet floor or brushed a hand wearily over his eyes. Otherwise he had mastered his voice, and spoke without the gasping pauses which had made distressful his words to Farrow.

"Ours is a sad errand, Mr. Fenley," began Winter, after a hasty glance at the table, which still bore the disordered array of breakfast. "But, if you feel equal to the task, you might tell us exactly what happened."

Fenley nodded.

"Of course, of course," he said quietly. "That is essential. We three, my father, Miss Manning and myself, breakfasted together. The second gong goes every morning at eight forty-five, and we were fairly punctual today. My father and Sylvia, Miss Manning, came in together—they had been talking in the hall previously. I saw them entering the room as I came downstairs. During the meal we chatted about affairs in the East; that is, my father and I did, and Syl—Miss Manning—gave us some news of a church bazaar in which she is taking part.

"My father rose first and went to his room, to collect papers brought from the City overnight. I met him on the stairs, and he gave me some instructions about a prospectus. (Let me interpolate that I was going to Victoria by a later train, having an appointment at eleven o'clock with Lord Ventnor, chairman of a company we are bringing out.) I stood on the stairs, saying something, while my father crossed the hall and took his hat and gloves from Harris, the footman. As I passed along the gallery to my own room I saw him standing on the landing at the top of the steps.

"He was cutting the end off a cigar, and Harris was just behind him and a little to the left, striking a match. Every fine morning my father lighted a cigar there. In rain or high wind he would light up inside the house. By the way, my mother is an invalid, and dislikes the smell of tobacco, so unless we have guests we don't smoke indoors.

"Well, I had reached my room, a sitting-room adjoining my bedroom, when I heard a gunshot. Apparently it came from the Quarry Wood, and I was surprised, because there is no shooting at this season. A little later—some few seconds—I heard Sylvia scream. I did not rush out instantly to discover the cause. Young ladies sometimes scream at wasps and caterpillars. Then I heard Tomlinson say, 'Fetch Mr. Hilton at once,' and I ran into Harris, who blurted out, 'Mr. Fenley has been shot, sir.'

"After that, I scarcely know what I said or how I acted. I remember running downstairs, and finding my father lying outside the front door, with Sylvia supporting his head and Tomlinson and Brodie trying to lift him. I think—in fact, I am sure now from what Dr. Stern tells me—that my father was dead before I reached him. We all thought at first that he had yielded to some awfully sudden form of paralysis, but some one—Tomlinson, I believe—noticed a hole through the right side of his coat and waistcoat. Then Sylvia—oh, perhaps that is matterless———"

"Every incident, however slight, is of importance in a case of this sort," Winter encouraged him.

"Well, she said—what was it, exactly? Do you remember, Sylvia?"

"Certainly," said the girl, unhesitatingly. "I said that I thought I recognized the sound of Bob's .450. Why shouldn't I say it? Poor Bob didn't shoot his father."

Her voice, though singularly musical, had a tearful ring which became almost hysterical in the vehemence of the question and its disclaimer.

Fenley moved uneasily, and raised his right hand to his eyes, while the left grasped the back of a chair.

"Bob is my brother Robert, who is away from home at this moment," he said, and his tone deprecated the mere allusion to the rifle owned by the absentee. "I only mentioned Miss Manning's words to show how completely at a loss we all were to account for my father's wound. I helped Tomlinson and Brodie to carry him to the settee in the hall. Then we—Tomlinson, that is—opened his waistcoat and shirt. Tomlinson cut the shirt with a scissors, and we saw the wound. Dr. Stern says there are indications that an expanding bullet was used, so the injuries must have been something appalling.... Sylvia, don't you think———"

"I'll not faint, or make a scene, if that is what you are afraid of, Hilton," said the girl bravely.

"That is all, then, or nearly all," went on Fenley, in the same dreary, monotonous voice. "I telephoned to Dr. Stern, and to Scotland Yard, deeming it better to communicate with you than with the local police. But it seems that Bates, our head keeper hurrying to investigate the cause of the shot, met some artist coming away from the other side of the wood. The Roxton police constable too, met and spoke with the same man, who told both Bates and the policeman that he heard the shot fired. The policeman, Farrow, refused to arrest the artist, and is now searching the wood with a number of our men———"

"Can't they be stopped?" broke in Furneaux, speaking for the first time.

"Yes, of course," and Hilton Fenley became a trifle more animated. "I wanted Farrow to wait till you came, but he insisted—said the murderer might be hiding there."

"When did Farrow arrive?"

"Oh, more than half an hour after my father was shot. I forgot to mention that my mother knows nothing of the tragedy yet. That is why we did not carry my poor father's body upstairs. She might overhear the shuffling of feet, and ask the cause."

"One thing more, Mr. Fenley," said Winter, seeing that the other had made an end. "Have you the remotest reason to believe that any person harbored a grievance against your father such as might lead to the commission of a crime of this nature?"

"I've been torturing my mind with that problem since I realized that my father was dead, and I can say candidly that he had no enemies. Of course, in business, one interferes occasionally with other men's projects, but people in the City do not shoot successful opponents."

"No private feud? No dismissed servant, sent off because of theft or drunkenness?"

"Absolutely none, to my knowledge. The youngest man on the estate has been employed here five or six years."

"It is a very extraordinary crime, Mr. Fenley."

For answer, the other sank into a chair and buried his face in his hands.

"How can we get those clodhoppers out of the wood?" said Furneaux. His thin, high-pitched voice dispelled the tension, and Fenley dropped his hands.

"Bates is certain to make for a rock which commands a view of the house," he said. "Perhaps, if we go to the door, we may see them."

He arose with obvious effort, but walked steadily enough. Winter followed with the doctor, and inquired in an undertone—

"Are you sure about the soft-nosed bullet, doctor?"

"Quite," was the answer. "I was in the Tirah campaign, and saw hundreds of such wounds."

Furneaux, too, had something to say to Miss Manning.

"How were you seated during breakfast?" he asked.

She showed him. It was a large room. Two windows looked down the avenue, and three into the garden, with its background of timber and park. Mr. Mortimer Fenley could have commanded both views; his son sat with his back to the park; the girl had faced it.

"I need hardly put it to you, but you saw no one in or near the trees?" said Furneaux.

"Not a soul. I bathe in a little lake below those cedars every morning, and it is an estate order that the men do not go in that direction between eight and nine o'clock. Of course, a keeper might have passed at nine thirty, but it is most unlikely."

"Did you bathe this morning?"

"Yes, soon after eight."

"Did you see the artist of whom Mr. Fenley spoke?"

"No. This is the first I have heard of any artist. Bates must have mentioned him while I was with Dr. Stern."

When Farrow arrived at the head of his legion he was just in time to salute his Inspector, who had cycled from Easton after receiving the news left by the chauffeur at the police station. Farrow was bursting with impatience to reveal the discoveries he had made, though resolved to keep locked in his own breast the secret confided by Bates. He was thoroughly nonplussed, therefore, when Winter, after listening in silence to the account of the footprints and scratches on the moss-covered surface of the rock, turned to Hilton Fenley.

"With reference to the rifle which has been mentioned—where is it kept?" he said.

"In my brother's room. He bought it nearly a year ago, when he was planning an expedition to Somaliland."

"May I see it?"

Fenley signed to the butler, who was standing with the others at a little distance.

"You know the .450 Express which is in the gun rack in Mr. Robert's den?" he said. "Bring it to the Superintendent."

Tomlinson, shaken but dignified, and rather purple of face as the result of the tramp through the trees, went indoors. Soon he came back, and the rich tint had faded again from his complexion.

"Sorry, sir," he said huskily, "but the rifle is not there."

"Not there!"

It was Sylvia Manning who spoke; the others received this sinister fact in silence.

"No, miss."

"Are you quite sure?" asked Fenley.

"It is not in the gun rack, sir, nor in any of the corners."

There was a pause. Fenley clearly forced the next words.

"That's all right. Bates may have it in the gun room. We'll ask him. Or Mr. Robert may have taken it to the makers. I remember now he spoke of having the sight fitted with some new appliance."

He called Bates. No, the missing rifle was not in the gun room. Somehow the notion was forming in certain minds that it could not be there. Indeed, the keeper's confusion was so marked that Furneaux's glance dwelt on him for a contemplative second.

CHAPTER IV
BREAKING COVER

Winter drew the local Inspector aside. "This inquiry rests with you in the first instance," he said. "Mr. Furneaux and I are here only to assist. Mr. Fenley telephoned to the Commissioner, mainly because Scotland Yard was called in to investigate a bond robbery which took place in the Fenley Bank some two months ago. Probably you never heard of it. Will you kindly explain our position to your Chief Constable? Of course, we shall work with you and through you, but my colleague has reason to believe that the theft of the bonds may have some bearing on this murder, and, as the securities were disposed of in Paris, it is more than likely that the Yard may be helpful."

"I fully understand, sir," said the Inspector, secretly delighted at the prospect of joining in the hunt with two such renowned detectives. The combined parishes of Easton and Roxton seldom produced a crime of greater magnitude than the theft of a duck. The arrest of a burglar who broke into a villa, found a decanter of whisky, and got so hopelessly drunk that he woke up in a cell at the police station, was an event of such magnitude that its memory was still lively, though the leading personage was now out on ticket of leave after serving five years in various penal settlements.

"You will prepare and give the formal evidence at the inquest, which will be opened tomorrow," went on Winter. "All that is really necessary is identification and a brief statement by the doctor. Then the coroner will issue the burial certificate, and the inquiry should be adjourned for a fortnight. I would recommend discretion in choosing a jury. Avoid busybodies like the plague. Summons only sensible men, who will do as they are told and ask no questions."

"Exactly," said the Inspector; he found Machiavellian art in these simple instructions. How it broadened the horizon to be brought in touch with London!

Winter turned to look for Furneaux. The little man was standing where Mortimer Fenley had stood in the last moment of his life. His eyes were fixed on the wood. He seemed to be dreaming, but his friend well knew how much clarity and almost supernatural vision was associated with Furneaux's dreams.

"Charles!" said the Superintendent softly.

Furneaux awoke, and ran down the steps. In his straw hat and light Summer suit he looked absurdly boyish, but the Inspector, who had formed an erroneous first impression, was positively startled when he met those blazing black eyes.

"Mr. Fenley should warn all his servants to speak fully and candidly," said Winter. "Then we shall question the witnesses separately. What do you think? Shall we start now?"

"First, the boots," cried Furneaux, seemingly voicing a thought. "We want a worn pair of boots belonging to each person in the house and employed on the estate, men and women, no exceptions, including the dead man's. Then we'll visit that wood. After that, the inquiry."

Winter nodded. When Furneaux and he were in pursuit of a criminal they dropped all nice distinctions of rank. If one made a suggestion the other adopted it without comment unless he could urge some convincing argument against it.

"Mr. Fenley should give his orders now," added Furneaux.

Winter explained his wishes to the nominal head of the household, and Fenley's compliance was ready and explicit.

"These gentlemen from Scotland Yard are acting in behalf of Mrs. Fenley, my brother and myself," he said to the assembled servants. "You must obey them as you would obey me. I place matters unreservedly in their hands."

"And our questions should be answered without reserve," put in Winter.

"Yes, of course. I implied that. At any rate, it is clear now."

"Brodie," said Furneaux, seeming to pounce on the chauffeur, "you were seated at the wheel when the shot was fired?"

"Ye—yes, sir," stuttered Brodie, rather taken aback by the little man's suddenness.

"Were you looking at the wood?"

"In a sort of a way, sir."

"Did you see any one among the trees?"

"No, sir, that I didn't." This more confidently.

"Place your car where it was stationed then. Take your seat, and try to imagine that you are waiting for your master. Start the engine, and behave exactly as though you expected him to enter the car. Don't watch the wood. I mean that you are not to avoid looking at it, but just throw yourself back to the condition of mind you were in at nine twenty-five this morning. Can you manage that?"

"I think so, sir."

"No chatting with others, you know. Fancy you are about to take Mr. Fenley to the station. If you should happen to see me, wave your hand. Then you can get down and stop the engine. You understand you are not to keep a sharp lookout for me?"

"Yes, sir."

The butler thought it would take a quarter of an hour to collect sample pairs of boots from the house and outlying cottages. Police Constable Farrow was instructed to bring the butler and the array of boots to the place where the footprints were found, and Bates led the detectives and the Inspector thither at once.

Soon the four men were gazing at the telltale marks, and the Inspector, of course, was ready with a shrewd comment.

"Whoever it was that came this way, he didn't take much trouble to hide his tracks," he said.

The Scotland Yard experts were so obviously impressed that the Inspector tried a higher flight.

"They're a man's boots," he continued. "We needn't have worried Tomlinson to gather the maids' footgear."

Furneaux left two neat imprints in the damp soil.

"Bet you a penny whistle there are at least two women in The Towers who will make bigger blobs than these," he said.

A penny whistle, as a wager, is what Police Constable Farrow would term "unusual."

"Quite so," said the Inspector thoughtfully.

Winter caught Furneaux's eye, and frowned. There was nothing to be gained by taking a rise out of the local constabulary. Still, he gave one sharp glance at both sets of footprints. Then he looked at Furneaux again, this time with a smile.

The party passed on to the rock on the higher ground. Bates pointed out the old scratches, and those made by Farrow and himself.

"Me first!" cried Furneaux, darting nimbly to the summit. He was not there a second before he signaled to some one invisible from beneath. Winter joined him, and the east front of the house burst into view. Brodie was in the act of descending from the car. The doctor had gone. A small group of men were gazing at the wood, but Hilton Fenley and Sylvia Manning were not to be seen.

Neither man uttered a word. They looked at the rock under their feet, at the surrounding trees, oak and ash, elm and larch, all of mature growth, and towering thirty to forty feet above their heads, while the rock itself rose some twelve feet from the general level of the sloping ground.

Bates was watching them.

"The fact is, gentlemen, that if an oak an' a couple o' spruce first hadn't been cut down you wouldn't see the house even from where you are," he said. "Mr. Fenley had an idee of buildin' a shelter on this rock, but he let it alone 'coss o' the birds. Ladies would be comin' here, an' a-disturbin' of 'em."

The detectives came down. Furneaux, meaning to put the Inspector in the right frame of mind, said confidentially—

"Brodie saw me instantly."

"Did he, now? It follows that he would have seen any one who fired at Mr. Fenley from that spot."

"It almost follows. We must guard against assuming a chance as a certainty."

"Oh, yes."

"And we must also try to avoid fitting facts into preconceived notions. Now, while the butler is gathering old boots, let us spend a few profitable minutes in this locality."

After that, any trace of soreness in the inspectorial breast was completely obliterated.

Both Winter and Furneaux produced strong magnifying-glasses, and scrutinized the scratches and impressions on the bare rock and moss. Bates, skilled in wood lore, was quick to note what they had discerned at a glance.

"Beg pardon, gentlemen both, but may I put in a word?" he muttered awkwardly.

"As many as you like," Winter assured him.

"Well, these here marks was made by Farrow an' meself, say about ten forty, or a trifle over an hour after the murder; an' I have no sort o' doubt as these other marks are a day or two days older."

"You might even put it at three days," agreed Winter.

"Then it follows——" began the Inspector, but checked himself. He was becoming slightly mixed as to the exact sequence of events.

"Come, now, Bates," said Furneaux, "you can tell us the day Mr. Robert Fenley left home recently? There is no harm in mentioning his name. It can't help being in our thoughts, since it was discovered that his gun was missing."

"He went off on a motor bicycle last Saturday mornin', sir."

"Can you fix the hour?"

"About half past ten."

"You have not seen him since?"

"No, sir."

"You would be likely to know if he had returned?"

"Certain, sir, unless he kem by the Roxton gate."

"Oh, is there another entrance?"

"Yes, but it can't be used, 'cept by people on foot. The big gates are always locked, and the road has been grassed over, an' not so many folk know of a right of way. Of course, Mr. Robert knows."

Bates was disturbed. He expected to be cross-examined farther, but, to his manifest relief, the ordeal was postponed. Winter and Furneaux commenced a careful scrutiny of the ground behind the rock. They struck off on different paths, but came together at a little distance.

"The trees," murmured Winter.

"Yes, when we are alone."

"Have you noticed——"

"These curious pads. They mean a lot. It's not so easy, James."

"I'm growing interested, I admit."

They rejoined the others.

"Did you tell me that only you and Police Constable Farrow visited this part of the wood?" said Furneaux to Bates.

"I don't remember tellin' you, sir, but that's the fact," said the keeper.

"Well, warn all the estate hands to keep away from this section during the next few days. You will give orders to Farrow to that effect, Inspector?"

"Yes. If they go trampling all over, you won't know where you are when it comes to a close search," was the cheerful answer. "Now, about that gun—it must be hidden somewhere in the undergrowth. The man who fired it would never dare to carry it along an open road on a fine morning like this, when everybody is astir."

"You're undoubtedly right," said Winter. "But here come assorted boots. They may help us a bit."

Tomlinson was a man of method. He and Farrow had brought two wicker baskets, such as are used in laundry work. He was rather breathless.

"House—and estate," he wheezed, pointing to each basket in turn.

"Go ahead, Furneaux," said Winter. "Because I ought to stoop, I don't."

The little man choked back some gibe; the presence of strangers enforced respect to his chief. He took a thin folding rule of aluminum from a waistcoat pocket, and applied it to the most clearly defined of the three footprints. Then beginning at the "house" basket, he ran over the contents rapidly. One pair of boots he set aside. After testing the "estate" basket without success, he seized one of the selected pair, and pressed it into the earth close to an original print. He looked up at Tomlinson, who was in a violent perspiration.

"Whose boot is this?" he asked.

"God help us, sir, it's Mr. Robert's!" said Tomlinson in an agonized tone.

The Inspector, Farrow and Bates were visibly thrilled; but Furneaux only sank back on his heels, and peered at the boot.

"I don't understand why any one should feel upset because these footprints (which, by the way, were not made by this pair of boots) happen to resemble marks which may have been made by Mr. Robert Fenley," he said, apparently talking to himself. "These marks are three or four days old. Mr. Robert Fenley went away on Saturday. Today is Wednesday. He may have been here on Saturday morning. What does it matter if he was? The man who murdered his father must have been here two hours ago."

Sensation! Tomlinson mopped his forehead with a handkerchief already a wet rag; Farrow, not daring to interfere, nibbled his chin strap; Bates scowled with relief. But the Inspector, after a husky cough, spoke.

"Would you mind telling me, Mr. Furneaux, why you are so sure?" he said.

"Now, Professor Bates, you tell him," cackled Furneaux.

The keeper dropped on his knees by the side of the detective, and gazed critically at the marks.

"At this time o' year, gentlemen, things do grow wonderful," he said slowly. "In this sort o' ground, where there's wet an' shade, there's a kind o' constant movement. This here new print is clean, an' the broken grass an' crushed leaves haven't had time to straighten themselves, as one might say. But, in this other lot, the shoots are commencin' to perk up, an' insec's have stirred the mold. It's just the difference atween a new run for rabbits and an old 'un."

"Thank you, Bates," broke in Winter sharply. "Now, we must not waste any more time in demonstrations. Mr. Furneaux explained this thing purposely, to show the folly of jumping at conclusions. Innocent men have been hanged before today on just such evidence as this. We should deem ourselves lucky that these footprints were found so soon after the crime was committed. Tomorrow, or next day, there might have been a doubt in our minds. Luckily there is none. The man who shot Mr. Fenley this morning—" he paused; Furneaux alone appreciated his difficulty—"could not possibly have left those marks today."

It was a lame ending, but it sufficed. Four of his hearers took him to mean that the unknown, whose feet had left their impress in the soil could not have been the murderer; but Furneaux growled in French—

"You tripped badly that time, my friend. You need another cigar!"

Seemingly, he was soliloquizing, and none understood except the one person for whose benefit the sarcasm was intended.

Winter felt the spur, but because he was a really great detective it only stimulated him. Nothing more was said until the little procession reached the avenue. During their brief disappearance in the leafy depths two cars and three motor cycles had arrived at The Towers. A glance sufficed. The newspapers had heard of the murder; this was the advance guard of an army of reporters and photographers. Winter buttonholed the Inspector.

"I'll tell you the most valuable service you can render at this moment," he said. "Arrange that a constable shall mount guard at the rock till nightfall. Then place two on duty. With four men you can provide the necessary reliefs, but I want that place watched continuously, and intruders warned off till further notice. This man who happens to be here might go on duty immediately. Then you can make your plans at leisure."

Thus, by the quaint contriving of chance, Police Constable Farrow, whose stalwart form and stubborn zeal had blocked the path to the Quarry Wood since a few minutes after ten o'clock, was deputed to continue that particular duty till a comrade took his place.

His face fell when he heard that he was condemned to solitude, shut out from all the excitement of the hour, debarred even, as he imagined, from standing on the rock and watching the comings and goings at the mansion. But Winter was a kindly if far-seeing student of human nature.

"It will be a bit slow for you," he said, when the Inspector had given Farrow his orders. "But you can amuse yourself by an occasional peep at the landscape, and there is no reason why you shouldn't smoke."

Farrow saluted.

"Do you mean, sir, that I can show myself?"

"Why not? The mere fact that your presence is known will warn off priers. Remember—no one, absolutely no one except the police, is to be allowed to pass the quarry, or approach from any side within hailing distance."

"Not even from the house, sir?"

"Exactly. Mr. Fenley and Miss Manning may be told, if necessary, why you are there, and I am sure they will respect my wishes."

Farrow turned back. It was not so bad, then. These Scotland Yard fellows had chosen him for an important post, and that hint about a pipe was distinctly human. Odd thing, too, that Mr. Robert Fenley was not expected to put in an appearance, or the Superintendent would have mentioned him with the others.

On reaching the house there were evidences of disturbance. Hilton Fenley stood in the doorway, and was haranguing the newspaper men in a voice harsh with anger. This intrusion was unwarranted, illegal, impudent. He would have them expelled by force. When he caught sight of the Inspector he demanded fiercely that names and addresses should be taken, so that his solicitors might issue summonses for trespass.

All this, of course, made excellent copy, and Winter put an end to the scene by drawing the reporters aside and giving them a fairly complete account of the murder. Incidentally, he sent off the Inspector post haste on his bicycle to station a constable at each gate, and stop the coming invasion. The house telephone, too, closed the main gate effectually, so when the earliest scouts had rushed away to connect with Fleet Street order was restored.

Winter was puzzled by Fenley's display of passion. It was only to be expected that the newspapers would break out in a rash of black headlines over the murder of a prominent London financier. By hook or by crook, journalism would triumph. He had often been amazed at the extent and accuracy of news items concerning the most secret inquiries. Of course the reporters sometimes missed the heart of an intricate case. In this instance, they had never heard of the bond robbery, though the numbers of the stolen securities had been advertised widely. Moreover, he was free to admit that if every fact known to the police were published broadcast, no one would be a penny the worse; for thus far the crime was singularly lacking in motive.

Meanwhile Furneaux had fastened on to Brodie again.

"You saw me at once?" he began.

"I couldn't miss you, sir," said the chauffeur, a solid, stolid mechanic, who understood his engine and a road map thoroughly, and left the rest to Providence. "I wasn't payin' particular attention, yet I twigged you the minute you popped up."

"So it is reasonable to suppose that if any one had appeared in that same place this morning and taken steady aim at Mr. Fenley, you would have twigged him, too."

"It strikes me that way, sir."

"Did you see nothing—not even a puff of smoke? You must certainly have looked at the wood when you heard the shot."

"I did, sir. Not a leaf moved. Just a couple of pheasants flew out, and the rooks around the house kicked up such a row that I didn't know the Guv'nor was down till Harris shouted."

"Where did the pheasants fly from?"

"They kem out a bit below the rock; but they were risin' birds, an' may have started from the ground higher up."

"No birds were startled before the shot was fired?"

"Not to my knowledge, sir. But June pheasants are very tame, and they lie marvelous close. A pheasant would just as soon run as fly."

The detectives began a detailed inquiry almost at once. It covered the ground already traversed, and the only new incident happened when Hilton Fenley, at the moment repeating his evidence, was called to the telephone.

"If either of you cares to smoke there are cigars and Virginia cigarettes on the sideboard," he said. "Or, if you prefer Turkish, here are some," and he laid a gold case on the table. Furneaux grabbed it when the door had closed.

"All neurotics use Turkish cigarettes," he said solemnly. "Ah, I guessed it! A strong, vile, scented brand!"

"Sometimes, my dear Charles, you talk rubbish," sighed Winter.

"Maybe. I never think or smoke it. 'Language was given us to conceal our thoughts,' said Talleyrand. I have always admired Talleyrand, 'that rather middling bishop but very eminent knave,' as de Quincey called him. '*Cré nom!* I wonder what de Quincey meant by 'middling.' A man who could keep in the front rank under the Bourbons, during the Revolution, with Napoleon, and back again under the Bourbons, and yet die in bed, must have been superhuman. St. Peter, in his stead, would have lost his napper at least four times."

Winter stirred uneasily, and gazed out across the Italian garden and park, for the detectives were again installed in the dining-room.

"What about that artist, Trenholme?" he said after a pause.

"We'll look him up. Before leaving this house I want to peep into various rooms. And there's Tomlinson. Tomlinson is a rich mine. Do leave him to me. I'll dig into him deep, and extract ore of high percentage—see if I don't."

"Do you know, Charles, I've a notion that we shall get closer to bed-rock in London than here."

Furneaux pretended to look for an invisible halo surrounding his chief's close-cropped bullet head.

"Sometimes," he said reverently, "you frighten me when you bring off a brilliant remark like that. I seem to see lightning zigzagging round Jove's dome."

Fenley returned.

"It was a call from the bank," he announced. "They have just seen the newspapers. I told them I would run up to town this afternoon."

"Then you did not telephone Bishopsgate Street earlier?" inquired Winter, permitting himself to be surprised.

"No. I had other things to bother me."

"Now, Mr. Fenley, can you tell me where your brother is?"

"I can not."

He placed a rather unnecessary emphasis on the negative. The question seemed to disturb him. Evidently, if he could consult his own wishes, he would prefer not to discuss his brother.

"I take it he has not been home since leaving here on Saturday?" persisted Winter.

"That is so."

"Had he quarreled with your father?"

"There was a dispute. Really, Mr. Winter, I must decline to go into family affairs."

"But the probability is that the more we know the less our knowledge will affect your brother."

The door opened again. Mr. Winter was wanted on the telephone. Then there happened one of those strange coincidences which Furneaux's caustic wit had christened "Winter's Yorkers," being a quaint play on the lines:

Now is the Winter of our discontent Made glorious Summer by this sun of York.

For the Superintendent had scarcely squeezed his big body into the telephone box when he became aware of a mixup on the line; a querulous voice was saying:

"I insist on being put through. I am speaking from Mr. Fenley's bank, and it is monstrous that I should be kept waiting. I've been trying for twenty minutes——"

Buzz. The protest was squelched.

"Are you there?" came the calm accents of the Assistant Commissioner.

"Yes, sir," said Winter.

"Any progress?"

"A little. Oddly enough, you are in the nick of time to help materially. Will you ring off, and find out from the exchange who 'phoned here two minutes ago? I don't mean Fenley's Bank, which is just trying to get through. I want to know who made the preceding call, which was effective."

"I understand. Good-by."

Winter explained in the dining-room that the Assistant Commissioner was anxious for news. He had hardly finished when the footman reappeared. A call for Mr. Hilton Fenley.

"Confound the telephone," snapped Fenley. "We won't have a moment's peace all day, I suppose."

Winter winked heavily at Furneaux. He waited until Fenley's hurried footsteps across a creaking parquet floor had died away.

"This is the bank's call," he murmured. "The other was from the Lord knows who. I've put the Yard on the track. I wonder why he lied about it."

"He's a queer sort of brother, too," said Furneaux. "It strikes me he wants to put Robert in the cart."

CHAPTER V
A FAMILY GATHERING

Fenley was frowning when he reappeared.

"Another call from the Bank," he said gruffly. "Everything there is at sixes and sevens since the news was howled through the City. That is why I really must go to town later. I'm not altogether sorry. The necessity of bringing my mind to bear on business will leaven the surfeit of horrors I've borne this morning...."

"Now, about my brother, Mr. Winter. While listening to Mr. Brown's condolences—you remember Brown, the cashier, Mr. Furneaux—I was thinking of more vital matters. A policy of concealment often defeats its own object, and I have come to the conclusion that you ought to know of a dispute between my father and Robert. There's a woman in the case, of course. It's a rather unpleasant story, too. Poor Bob got entangled with a married woman some months ago. He was infatuated at first, but would have broken it off recently were it not for fear of divorce proceedings."

"Would you make the position a little clearer, sir?" said Winter, who also was listening and thinking. He was quite certain that when he met Mr. Brown he would meet the man who had been worrying a telephone exchange "during the last twenty minutes."

"I—I can't." And Fenley's hand brushed away some imaginary film from before his eyes. "Bob and I never hit it off very well. We're only half brothers, you see."

"Was your father married twice?"

"Am I to reopen a forgotten history?"

"Some person, or persons, may not have forgotten it."

"Well, you must have the full story, if at all. My father was not a well-born man. Thirty years ago he was a trainer in the service of a rich East Indian merchant, Anthony Drummond, of Calcutta, who owned racehorses, and one of Drummond's daughters fell in love with him. They ran away and got married, but the marriage was a failure. She divorced him—by mutual consent, I fancy. Anyhow, *I* was left on his hands.

"He went to Assam, and fell in with a tea planter named Manning, who had a big estate, but neglected it for racing. My father suddenly developed business instincts and Manning made him a partner. Unfortunately—well,

- 46 -

that is a hard word, but it applies—my father married again—a girl of his own class; rather beneath it, in fact. Then Bob was born.

"The old man made money, heaps of it. Manning married, but lost his wife when Sylvia came into the world. That broke him up; he drank himself to death, leaving his partner as trustee and guardian for the infant. There was a boom in tea estates; my father sold on the crest of the wave and came to London. He progressed, but Mrs. Fenley—didn't. She was just a Tommy's daughter, and never seemed to try and rise above the level of 'married quarters'.

"I had to mind my p's and q's as a boy, I can assure you. My mother was always thrown in my teeth. Mrs. Fenley called her 'black.' It was a —— lie. She was dark-skinned, as I am, but there are Cornish and Welsh folk of much darker complexion. My father, too, shared something of the same prejudice. I had to be the good boy of the family. Otherwise, I should have been turned out, neck and crop.

"As I behaved well, he was forced to depend on me, because Bob did as he liked, with his mother always ready to aid and abet him. Then came this scrape I've spoken of. I believe Bob was being blackmailed. That's the long and the short of it. Now you know the plain, ungarbled facts. Better that they should come from me than reach you with the decorations of gossip and servants' tittle-tattle."

The somewhat strained and metallic voice ceased. Fenley was seated at the corner of the table near the door. Seemingly yielding to that ever-present desire for movement, he pushed with his foot an armchair out of its place at the head of the table.

Sylvia Manning had pointed out that chair to Furneaux as the one occupied by Mortimer Fenley at breakfast.

"Is the first Mrs. Fenley dead?" said Furneaux suddenly.

"I don't think so," said Fenley, after a pause.

"You are not sure?"

"No."

"Have you ever tried to find out?"

"No, I dare not."

"May I ask why?"

"If it were discovered that my mother and I were in communication I would have been given short shrift in the bank."

"Did she marry again?"

"I don't know."

Again there was silence. Furneaux seemed to be satisfied that he was following a blind alley, and Winter became the inquisitor.

"What is the name of the woman with whom your brother is mixed up?"

"I can not tell you, but my father knew."

"What leads you to form that opinion?"

"Some words that passed between Bob and him last Saturday morning."

"Where? Here?"

"Yes, in the hall. Tomlinson heard more distinctly than I. I saw there was trouble brewing, and kept out of it—hung back, on the pretense of reading a newspaper."

"As to the missing rifle—can you help us there?"

"Not in the least. I wish to Heaven Bob had gone to Africa, as he was planning. Then all this misery would have been avoided."

"Do you mean your father's death?"

Fenley started. He had not weighed his words.

"Oh, no, no!" he cried hurriedly. "Don't try to trip me into admissions, Mr. Winter. I can't stand that, damned if I can."

He jumped up, went to the sideboard and mixed himself a weak brandy and soda, which he swallowed as if his throat were afire with thirst.

"I am not treating you as a hostile witness, sir," answered Winter calmly. "Mr. Furneaux and I are merely clearing the ground. Soon we shall know, or believe that we know, what line to avoid and what to follow."

"Is Miss Sylvia Manning engaged to be married?" put in Furneaux. Fenley gave him a fiendish look.

"What the devil has Miss Manning's matrimonial prospects got to do with this inquiry?" he said, and the venom in his tone was hardly to be accounted for by Furneaux's harmless-sounding query.

"One never knows," said the little man, taking the unexpected attack with bland indifference. "You don't appreciate our position in this matter. We are not judges, but guessers. We sit in the stalls of a theater, watching people on the stage of real life playing four acts of a tragedy, and it is our business to construct the fifth, which is produced in court. Let me give you a wildly supposititious version of that fifth act now. Suppose some neurotic fool was in love with Miss Manning, or her money, and Mr. Mortimer Fenley opposed the project. That would supply a motive for the murder. Do you take the point?"

"I'm sorry I blazed out at you. Miss Manning is not engaged to be married, nor likely to be for many a day."

Now, the obvious question was, "Why, she being such an attractive young lady?" But Furneaux never put obvious questions. He turned to Winter with the air of one who had nothing more to say. His colleague was evidently perplexed, and showed it, but extricated the others from an awkward situation with the tact for which he was noted.

"I am much obliged to you for your candor in supplying such a clear summary of the family history, Mr. Fenley," he said. "Of course, we shall be meeting you frequently during the next few days, and developments can be discussed as they arise."

His manner, more than his words, conveyed an intimation that when the opportunity served he would trounce Furneaux for an indiscretion. Fenley was mollified.

"Command me in every way," he said.

"There is one more question, the last and the gravest," said Winter seriously. "Do you suspect any one of committing this murder?"

"No! On my soul and honor, no!"

"Thank you, sir. We'll tackle the butler now, if you please."

"I'll send him," said Fenley. Probably in nervous forgetfulness, he lighted a cigarette and went out, blowing two long columns of smoke through his nostrils. He might, or might not, have been pleased had he heard the reprimanding of Furneaux.

"Good stroke, that about the stage, Charles," mumbled Winter. Furneaux threw out his hands with a gesture of disgust.

"What an actor the man is!" he almost hissed, owing to the need there was of subduing his piping voice to a whisper. "Every word thought out, but allowed to be dragged forth reluctantly. Putting brother Bob into the tureen, isn't he? 'On my soul and honor,' too! Don't you remember, some French blighter said that when an innocent man was being made a political scapegoat?... Of course, the mother is a Eurasian, and he has met her. A nice dish he served up! A salad of easily ascertainable facts with a dressing of lying innuendo. Name of a pipe! If Master Hilton hadn't been in the house——"

A knock, and the door opened.

"You want me, gentlemen, I am informed by Mr. Hilton Fenley," said Tomlinson.

There spoke the butler, discreet, precise, incapable of error. Tomlinson had recovered his breath and his dignity. He was in his own domain. The very sight of the Mid-Victorian furniture gave him confidence. His skilled glance traveled to the decanter and the empty glass. He knew to a minim how much brandy had evaporated since his last survey of the sideboard.

"Sit down, Tomlinson," said Winter pleasantly. "You must have been dreadfully shocked by this morning's occurrence."

Tomlinson sat down. He drew the chair somewhat apart from the table, knowing better than to place his elbows on that sacred spread of polished mahogany.

"I was, sir," he admitted. "Indeed, I may say I shall always be shocked by the remembrance of it."

"Mr. Mortimer Fenley was a kindly employer?"

"One of the best, sir. He liked things done just so, and could be sharp if there was any laxity, but I have never received a cross word from him."

"Known him long?"

"Ever since he come to The Towers; nearly twenty years."

"And Mrs. Fenley?"

"Mrs. Fenley leaves the household entirely under my control, sir. She never interferes."

"Why?"

"She is an invalid."

"Is she so ill that she can not be seen?"

"Practically that, sir."

"Been so for twenty years?"

Tomlinson coughed. He was prepared with an ample statement as to the catastrophe which took place at nine thirty A. M., but this delving into bygone decades was unexpected and decidedly distasteful, it would seem.

"Mrs. Fenley is unhappily addicted to the drug habit, sir," he said severely, plainly hinting that there were bounds, even for detectives.

"I fancied so," was the dry response. "However, I can understand and honor your reluctance to reveal Mrs. Fenley's failings. Now, please tell us exactly what Mr. Fenley and Mr. Robert said to each other in the hall last Saturday morning."

How poor Farrow, immured in his jungle, would have gloated over Tomlinson's collapse when he heard those fatal words! To his credit be it said, the butler had not breathed a word to a soul concerning the scene between father and son. He knew nothing of an inquisitive housemaid, and his tortured brain fastened on Hilton Fenley as the Paul Pry. Unconsciously, he felt bitter against his new master from that moment.

"Must I go into these delicate matters, sir?" he bleated.

"Most certainly. The man whom you respected so greatly has been killed, not in the course of a heated dispute, but as the outcome of a brutal and well-conceived plan. Bear that in mind, and you will see that concealment of vital facts is not only unwise but disloyal."

Winter rather let himself go in his earnestness. He flushed slightly, and dared not look at Furneaux lest he should encounter an admiring glance.

The butler, however, was far too worried to pay heed to his questioner's florid turn of speech. He sighed deeply. He felt like a timid swimmer in a choppy sea, knowing he was out of his depth yet compelled to struggle blindly.

So, with broken utterance, he repeated the words which a rabbit-eared housemaid had carried to Bates. Nevertheless, even while he labored on, he fancied that the detectives did not attach such weight to the recital as he feared. He anticipated that Winter would write each syllable in a notebook, and show an exceeding gravity of appreciation. To his great relief, nothing of the kind happened. Winter's comment was distinctly helpful.

"It must have been rather disconcerting for you to hear father and son quarreling openly," he said.

"Sir, it was most unpleasant."

"Now, did you form any opinion as to the cause of this bickering? For instance, did you imagine that Mr. Fenley wished his son to break off relations with an undesirable acquaintance?"

"I did, sir."

"Is either Mr. Hilton or Mr. Robert engaged to be married? Or, I had better put it, had their father expressed any views as to either of his sons marrying suitably?"

"We, in the house, sir, had a notion that Mr. Fenley would like Mr. Robert to marry Miss Sylvia."

"Exactly. I expected that. Were these two young people of the same way of thinking?"

"They were friendly, sir, but more like brother and sister. You see, they were reared together. It often happens that way when a young gentleman and young lady grow up from childhood in each other's company. They never think of marriage, whereas the same young gentleman would probably fall head over heels in love with the same young lady if he met her elsewhere."

"Good!" broke in Furneaux. "Tomlinson, do you drink port?"

The butler looked his astonishment, but answered readily enough—

"My favorite wine, sir."

"I thought so. Taken in moderation, port induces sound reasoning. I have some Alto Douro of '61. I'll bring you a bottle."

Tomlinson was mystified, a trifle scandalized perhaps; but he bowed his acknowledgments.

"Sir, I will appreciate it greatly."

"I know you will. My Alto Douro goes down no gullet but a connoisseur's."

Even in his agitation, Tomlinson smiled.

What a queer little man this undersized detective was, to be sure, and how oddly he expressed himself!

"I ask this just as a matter of form, but did Mr. Robert Fenley take his .450 Express rifle when he went away on Saturday?" said Winter.

"No, sir. He had only a valise strapped to the carrier. But I do happen to know that the gun was in his room on Friday, because Friday is my day for house inspection."

"Any cartridges?"

"I can't say, sir. They would be in a drawer, or, more likely, in the gun room."

"Where is this gun room?"

"Next to the harness room, sir—second door to the right in the courtyard."

"Speaking absolutely in confidence, have you formed a theory as to this murder?"

"No, sir. But if any sort of evidence is piled up against Mr. Robert I shall not credit it. No power on earth could make me believe that he would kill his father in cold blood. He respected his father, sir. He's a bit wild, as young men with too much money are apt to be, but he was good-hearted and genuine."

"Yet he did speak of blowing his own brains out, and his father's."

"That was his silly way of talking, sir. He would say, 'Tomlinson, if you tell the pater what time I came home last night I'll stab you to the heart.' When there was a bit of a family squabble he would threaten to mix a gallon of weed-killer and drink every drop. Everything was rotten, or beastly, or awfully ripping. He was not so well educated as he ought to have been—Mrs. Fenley's fault entirely; and he hadn't the—the words——"

"The vocabulary."

"That's it, sir. I see you understand."

"Tomlinson," interrupted Furneaux, "a famous American writer, Oliver Wendell Holmes, described adjectives of that class as the blank checks of intellectual bankruptcy. You have hit on the same great thought."

The butler smiled again. He was beginning to like Furneaux.

"You have never heard, I suppose, of Mr. Fenley receiving any threatening letters?" continued Winter.

"No, sir. Some stupid postcards were sent when he tried to close a right of way through the park; but they were merely ridiculous, and that occurred years ago."

"So you, like the rest of us, feel utterly unable to assign a motive for this crime?"

"Sir, it's like a thunderbolt from a clear sky."

"Were the brothers, or half brothers, on good terms with each other?"

Tomlinson started at those words, "or half brothers." He was not prepared for the Superintendent's close acquaintance with the Fenley records.

"They're as different as chalk and cheese, sir," he said, after a pause to collect his wits. "Mr. Hilton is clever and well read, and cares nothing about sport, though he has a wonderful steady nerve. Yes, I mean that——" for Winter's prominent eyes showed surprise at the statement. "He's a strange mixture, is Mr. Hilton. He's a fair nailer with a revolver. I've seen him hit a

- 53 -

penny three times straight off at twelve paces, and, when in the mind, he would bowl over running rabbits with a rook rifle. Yet he never joined the shooting parties in October. Said it made him ill to see graceful birds shattered by clumsy folk. All the same, he would ill-treat a horse something shameful. I——"

The butler bethought himself, and pulled up with a jerk. But Winter smiled encouragingly.

"Say what you had in mind," he said. "You are not giving evidence. You may rely on our discretion."

"Well, sir, he's that sort of man who must have his own way, and when things went against him at home, he'd take it out of any servant or animal that vexed him afterwards."

"It was not an ideally happy household, I take it?"

"Things went along very smoothly, sir, all things considered. They have been rather better since Miss Sylvia came home from Brussels. She was worried about Mrs. Fenley at first, but gave it up as a bad job; and Mr. Fenley and the young gentlemen used to hide their differences before her. That was why Mr. Fenley and Mr. Robert blazed up in the hall on Saturday. They couldn't say a word in front of Miss Sylvia at the breakfast table."

"The four always met at breakfast, then?"

"Almost without fail, sir. On Monday and Tuesday mornings Mr. Hilton breakfasted early, and his father was joking about it, for if any one was late it would be him—or should I say 'he', sir?"

Furneaux cackled.

"I wouldn't have you alter your speech on any account," he grinned. "Why did Mr. Hilton turn over these new leaves on Monday and Tuesday?"

"He said he had work to do. What it was I don't know, sir. But he managed to miss the nine forty-five, and Mr. Fenley was vexed about it. Of course, I don't know why I am telling you these small things. Mr. Hilton might be angry——"

Some one knocked. Harris, the footman, entered, a scared look on his face.

"Can you come a moment, Mr. Tomlinson?" he said. "The undertaker is here for the body."

"What is that?" cried Winter sharply.

The butler arose.

"Didn't Mr. Hilton mention it, sir?" he said. "Dr. Stern must hold a post mortem before the inquest, and he suggested that it could be carried through more easily in the mortuary attached to the Cottage Hospital. Isn't that all right, sir?"

"Oh, yes, I'm sorry. I didn't understand. Go, by all means. We'll wait here."

When they were alone, the two detectives remained silent for a long minute. Winter arose and looked through a window at the scene outside. A closed hearse had arrived; some men were carrying in a rough coffin and three trestles. There was none of the gorgeous trappings which lend dignity to such transits in public. Polished oak and gleaming brass and rare flowers would add pageantry later; this was the livery of the dissecting-room.

"Queer case!" growled Winter over his shoulder.

"If only Hilton had breakfasted early *this* morning!" said Furneaux.

"If the dog hadn't stopped to scratch himself he would have caught the hare," was the irritable answer.

"Aren't you pleased with Tomlinson, then?"

"The more he opened up the more puzzled I became. By the way, you hardly asked him a thing, though you were keen on tackling him yourself."

"James, I'm an artist. You handled him so neatly that I stood by and appreciated. It would be mean to suggest that the prospect of a bottle of Alto Douro quickened his imagination. I——"

Winter's hands were crossed behind his back, and his fingers worked in expressive pantomime. Furneaux was by his side in an instant. Hilton Fenley was standing on the steps, a little below and to the left of the window. He was gazing with a curiously set stare at the bust of Police Constable Farrow perched high among the trees to the right. The observers in the room had then an excellent opportunity to study him at leisure.

"More of Asia than of Europe in that face and figure," murmured Furneaux.

"The odd thing is that he should be more interested in our sentinel than in the disposal of his father's body," commented Winter.

"A live donkey is always more valuable than a dead lion."

"We shall have to go to that wood soon, Charles."

"Your only failing is that you can't see the forest for the trees."

They were bickering, an ominous sign for some one yet unknown. Suddenly, far down the avenue, they saw a motor bicycle traveling fast. Hilton Fenley saw it at the same moment and screened his eyes with a hand, for he was bareheaded and the sun was now blazing with noonday intensity.

"Brother Bob!" hissed Furneaux.

Winter thought the other had recognized the man crouched over the handlebar.

"Gee!" he said. "Your sight must be good."

"I'm not using eyes, but brains. Who else can it be? This is the psychological moment which never fails. Bet you a new hat I'm right."

"I'm not buying you any new hats," said Winter. "Look at Hilton. He knows. Now, I wonder if the other one telephoned. No. He'd have told us. He'd guess it would crop up in talk some time or other. Yes, the motorist is waving to him. There! You can see his face. It *is* Robert, isn't it?"

"O sapient one!" snapped Furneaux.

The meeting between the brothers was orthodox in its tragic friendliness. The onlookers could supply the words they were unable to hear. Robert Fenley, bigger, heavier, altogether more British in build and semblance than Hilton, was evidently asking breathlessly if the news he had read in London was true, and Hilton was volubly explaining what had happened, pointing to the wood, the doorway, the hearse, emphasizing with many gestures the painful story he had to tell.

Then the two young men mounted the steps, the inference being that Robert Fenley wished to see his father's body before it was removed. A pallor was spreading beneath the glow on the younger Fenley's perspiring face. He was obviously shocked beyond measure. Grief and horror had imparted a certain strength to somewhat sullen features. He might be a ne'er-do-well, a loose liver, a good deal of a fool, perhaps, but he was learning one of life's sharpest lessons; in time, it might bring out what was best in his character. The detectives understood now why the butler, who knew the boy even better than his own father, deemed it impossible that he should be a parricide. Some men are constitutionally incapable of committing certain crimes. At least, the public thinks so; Scotland Yard knows better, and studies criminology with an open mind.

The brothers had hardly crossed the threshold of the house when an eldritch scream rang through the lofty hall. The detectives hastened from the dining-room, and forthwith witnessed a tableau which would have received the envious approval of a skilled producer of melodrama. The hall measured some thirty-five feet square, and was nearly as lofty, its ceiling forming the second floor. The staircase was on the right, starting from curved steps in the inner right angle and making a complete turn from a half landing to reach a gallery which ran around three sides of the first floor. The fourth contained the doorway, with a window on each hand and four windows above.

The stairs and the well of the hall were of oak, polished as to parquet and steps, but left to age and color naturally as to wainscot, balusters and rails. The walls of the upper floor were decorated in shades of dull gold and amber. The general effect was superb, either in daylight or when a great Venetian luster in the center of the ceiling blazed with electric lights.

The body of the unfortunate banker had not been removed from the oaken settee at the back of the hall, and was still covered with a white sheet. An enormously stout woman, clothed in a dressing-gown of black lace, was standing in the cross gallery and resisting the gentle efforts of Sylvia Manning, now attired in black, to take her away. The stout woman's face was deathly white, and her distended eyes were gazing dully at the ominous figure stretched beneath. Two podgy hands, with rings gleaming on every finger, were clutching the carved railing, and the tenacity of their grip caused the knuckles to stand out in white spots on the ivory-tinted skin.

This, then, was Mrs. Fenley, in whom some vague stirring of the spirit had induced a consciousness that all was not well in the household with which she "never interfered."

It was she who had uttered that ringing shriek when some flustered maid blurted out that "the master" was dead, and her dazed brain had realized what the sheet covered. She lifted her eyes from that terrifying object when her son entered with Hilton Fenley.

"Oh, Bob!" she wailed. "They've killed your father! Why did you let them do it?"

Even in the agony of the moment the distraught young man was aware that his mother was in no fit state to appear thus openly.

"Mother," he said roughly, "you oughtn't to be here, you know. Do go to your room with Sylvia. I'll come soon, and explain everything."

"Explain!" she wailed. "Explain your father's death! Who killed him? Tell me that, and I'll tear them with my nails. But is he dead? Did that hussy lie to me? You all tell me lies because you think I am a fool. Let me alone, Sylvia. I *will* go to my husband. Let me alone, or I'll strike you!"

By sheer weight she forced herself free from the girl's hands, and tottered down the stairs. At the half landing she fell to her knees, and Sylvia ran to pick her up. Then Hilton Fenley seemed to arouse himself from a stupor. Flinging a command at the servants, he rushed to Sylvia's assistance, and, helped by Tomlinson and a couple of footmen, half carried the screaming and fighting woman up the stairs and along a corridor.

Thus it happened that Robert Fenley was left in the hall with the dead body of his father. He stood stock still, and seemed to follow with disapproval the manner of the disappearance of the poor creature whom he called mother. Her shrieks redoubled in volume as she understood that she would not be allowed to see her husband's corpse, and her son added to the uproar by shouting loudly:

"Hi, there! Don't ill-treat her, or I'll break all your —— necks! Confound you, be gentle with her!"

He listened till a door slammed, and a sudden cessation of the tumult showed that some one, in sheer self-defense, had given her morphia, the only sedative that could have any real effect. Then he turned, and became aware of the presence of the two detectives.

"Well," he said furiously, "who are you, and what the blazes do you want here? Get out, both of you, or I'll have you chucked out!"

CHAPTER VI
WHEREIN FURNEAUX SEEKS INSPIRATION FROM LITERATURE AND ART

The head of the Criminal Investigation Department was not the sort of man to accept meekly whatsoever coarse commands Robert Fenley chose to fling at him. He met the newcomer's angry stare with a cold and steady eye.

"You should moderate your language in the presence of death, Mr. Fenley," he said. "We are here because it is our duty. You, on your part, would have acted more discreetly had you gone to your mother's assistance instead of swearing at those who were acting for the best under trying conditions."

"Damn your eyes, are you speaking to me?" came the wrathful cry.

"Surely you have been told that your father is lying there dead!" went on Winter sternly. "Mrs. Fenley might have yielded readily to your persuasion, but your help took the form of threatening people who adopted the only other course possible. Calm yourself, sir, and try to remember that the father from whom you parted in anger has been murdered. My colleague and I represent Scotland Yard; we were brought here by your brother. See that you meet us in the dining-room in a quarter of an hour. Come, Furneaux!"

And, stirred for once to a feeling of deep annoyance, the big man strode out into the open air, with a sublime disregard for either the anger or the alarm struggling for mastery in Robert Fenley's sullen face.

"Phew!" he said, drawing a deep breath before descending the steps. "What an unlicked cub! And they wanted to marry that girl to him!"

"It sha'n't be done, James," said Furneaux.

"I actually lost my temper," puffed the other.

"Tell you what! Let's put the Inspector on to him. Tell the local sleuths half what we know, and they'll run him in like a shot."

"Pooh! He's all talk. Tomlinson is right. The neurotic Hilton has more nerve in his little finger than that dolt in the whole of his body."

"What did you think of his boots?"

"I shall be surprised if they don't fit those footprints exactly."

"They will. The left heel is evenly worn, but the right bears on the outer edge. Let's cool our fevered brows under the greenwood tree till this hearse is out of the way."

The butler, who had asked the undertaker's assistants to suspend operations when Robert Fenley arrived, now appeared at the door and signaled the men that they were free to proceed with their work. The detectives strolled into the wood, and soon were bending over some curious blotchy marks which somehow suggested the passage of a pad-footed animal rather than a human being. Bates, of course, would have noted them had he not been on the alert for footprints alone, but they had stared at Winter and Furneaux from the instant their regularity became apparent. They represented a stride considerably shorter than the average length of a man's pace, and were strongly marked when the surface was spongy enough to receive an impression. Except, however, in the slight hollow already described, the ground was so dry that traces of every sort were lost. In the vicinity of the rock, too, the only marks left were the scratches in the moss adhering to the steep sides of the bowlder itself.

"What do you make of 'em, Charles?" inquired Winter, when both had puzzled for some minutes over the uncommon signs.

"Some one has thought out the footprint as a clue pretty thoroughly," said Furneaux. "He not only took care to leave a working model of one set, but was extremely anxious not to provide any data as to his own tootsies, so he fastened a bundle of rags under each boot, and walked like a cat on walnut shells."

Winter nodded.

"When we find the gun, too—it's somewhere in this wood—you'll see that the fingerprints won't help," he replied thoughtfully. "The man who remembered to safeguard his feet would not forget his hands. We're up against a tough proposition, young fellow-me-lad."

"Your way of thinking reminds me of Herbert Spencer's reason for not learning Latin grammar as a youth," grinned Furneaux.

"It would be a pity to spoil one of your high-class jokes; so what was the reason?"

"He refused to accept any statement unaccompanied by proof. The agreement of an adjective with its noun displeased him, because an arbitrary rule merely said it was so."

"An ingenious excuse for not learning a lesson, but I don't see———"

"Consider. Mortimer Fenley was shot dead at nine thirty this morning, and the bullet which killed him came from the neighborhood of the rock above our heads. One shot was fired. It was so certain, so true of aim, that the murderer made sure of hitting him—at a fairly long range, too. How many men were there in Roxton and Easton this morning—was there even one woman?—capable of sighting a rifle with such calm confidence of success? Mind you, Fenley had to be killed dead. No bungling. A severe wound from which he might recover would not meet the case at all. Again, how many rifles are there in the united parishes of Roxton and Easton of the type which fires expanding bullets?"

"Of course, those vital facts narrow down the field, but Hilton Fenley was unquestionably in the house."

Furneaux cackled shrilly.

"You're in Herbert's class, Charles," he cried, delighted at having trapped his big friend.

"Pardon me, gentlemen," said a voice from among the leaves, "but I thought you might like to know that Mr. Robert Fenley is starting off again on his motor bike."

Even as Police Constable Farrow spoke they heard the loud snorting of an exhaust, marking the initial efforts of a motor bicycle's engine to get under way. In a few seconds came the rhythmic beat of the machine as it gathered speed; the two men looked at each other and laughed.

"Master Robert defies the majesty of the law," said Winter dryly. "Perhaps, taking one consideration with another, it's the best thing he could have done."

"He is almost bound to enter London by the Edgware Road," said Furneaux instantly.

"Just so. I noticed the make and number of his machine. A plain-clothes man on an ordinary bicycle can follow him easily from Brondesbury onwards. Time him, and get on the telephone while I keep Hilton in talk. If we're mistaken we'll ring up Brondesbury again."

Winter was curtly official in tone when Hilton Fenley came downstairs at his request.

"Why did your brother rush off in such an extraordinary hurry?" he asked.

"How can I tell you?" was the reply, given offhandedly, as if the matter was of no importance. "He comes and goes without consulting my wishes, I assure you."

"But I requested him to meet me here at this very hour. There are questions he has to answer, and it would have been best in his own interests had he not shirked them."

"I agree with you fully. I hadn't the least notion he meant going until I looked out on hearing the bicycle, and saw him racing down the avenue."

"Do you think, sir, he is making for London?"

"I suppose so. That is where he came from. He says he heard of his father's death through the newspapers, and it would not surprise me in the least if I did not see him again until after the funeral."

"Thank you, sir. I'm sorry I bothered you, but I imagined or hoped he had given you some explanation. His conduct calls for it."

The Superintendent's manner had gradually become more suave. He realized that these Fenleys were queer folk. Like the Pharisee, "they were not as other men," but whether the difference between them and the ordinary mortal arose from pride or folly or fear it was hard to say.

Hilton Fenley smiled wanly.

"Bob is adopting the supposed tactics of the ostrich when pursued," he said.

"But no one is pursuing him."

"I am speaking metaphorically, of course. He is in distress, and hides behind the first bush. He has no moral force—never had. Physically he doesn't know what fear is, but the specters of the mind loom large in his eyes. And now, Superintendent, I am just on the point of leaving for London. I shall return about six thirty. Do you remain?"

"No, sir. I shall return to town almost immediately. Mr. Furneaux will stop here. Can he have a bedroom in the house?"

"Certainly. Tomlinson will look after him. You are not going cityward, I suppose?"

"No, sir. But if you care to have a seat in my car——"

"No, thanks. The train is quicker and takes me direct to London Bridge. Much obliged."

Fenley hurried to the cloakroom, which was situated under the stairs, but on a lower level than the hall. The telephone box was placed there, and

Furneaux emerged as the other ran down a few steps. The little man hailed him cheerfully.

"I suppose, now," he said, "that hot headed brother of yours thinks he has dodged Scotland Yard till it suits his convenience to be interviewed. Strange how people insist on regarding us as novices in our own particular line. Now you wouldn't make that mistake, sir."

"What mistake? I wouldn't run away, if that is what you mean."

"I'm sure of that, sir. But Mr. Robert has committed the additional folly, from his point of view, of letting us know why he was so desperately anxious to get back to London."

"But he didn't say a word!"

"Ah, words, idle words!

"Words are like leaves; and where they most abound
Much fruit of sense beneath is rarely found.

"It is actions that count, sir. Deeds, not words. Now, Mr. Robert has been kind enough to give us the eloquent facts, because he will be followed from the suburbs and his whereabouts watched most carefully."

"Dear me! I hadn't thought of that," said Hilton Fenley slowly. Two ideas were probably warring in his brain at that moment. One classed Furneaux as a garrulous idiot; the other suggested that there might be method in such folly.

"That's a clever simile of Pope's about dense leaves betokening scarcity of fruit," went on Furneaux. "Of course, it might be pushed too far. Think what a poisonous Dead Sea apple the Quarry Wood contained. Your father's murder might not have been possible today but for the cover given by the trees."

Fenley selected a dark overcoat and derby hat. He wore a black tie, but had made no other change in his costume.

"You are quite a literary detective, Mr. Furneaux," he commented.

"More literal than literary, sir. I have little leisure for reading, but I own an excellent memory. Nothing to boast of in that. It's indispensable in my profession."

"Obviously. Well, I must hurry away now. See you later."

He hastened out. His manner seemed to hint an annoyance; it conveyed indefinitely but subtly a suggestion that his father's death was far too serious a thing to be treated with such levity.

Furneaux sauntered slowly to the front door. By that time the Fenley car was speeding rapidly down the avenue.

"With luck," he said to Winter, who had joined him, "with any sort of luck both brothers should pass their father's body on the way to the mortuary. Sometimes, O worthy chief, I find myself regretting the ways and means of the days of old, when men believed in the Judicium Dei.

"Neither of those sons went near his dead father. If one of them had dared I wonder whether the blood would have liquefied. Do you remember, in the 'Nibelungenlied,' that Hagen is forced to prove his innocence by touching Siegfried's corpse—and fails? That is the point—he fails. Our own Shakespeare knew the dodge. When Henry VI was being borne to Chertsey in an open coffin, the Lady Anne made Gloster squirm by her cry:

"O gentlemen, see, see! Dead Henry's wounds
Open their congeal'd mouths, and bleed afresh.

"Why then did those sons fight shy of touching their father's body? Had it been your father or mine who was beaten down by a murderer's spite, we would surely have given him one fare-well clasp of the hand."

Winter recognized the symptoms. His diminutive friend was examining the embryo of a theory already established in his mind. It was a mere shadow, something vague and dark and uncertain in outline. But it existed, and would assume recognizable shape when an active imagination had fitted some shreds of proof to that which was yet without form and void. At that crisis, contradiction was a tonic.

"I think you're in error in one respect," said Winter quietly. "Hilton Fenley went to his father's assistance, and we don't know whether or not Robert did not approach the body."

"You're wrong, most sapient one. Before telephoning Brondesbury I asked Harris to tell me exactly what happened after the banker dropped at his feet. Harris shouted and knelt over him. Miss Manning ran and lifted his head. Tomlinson, Harris and Brodie carried him to the settee. Hilton Fenley never touched him."

"What of Robert? We cleared out, leaving him there alone."

"I watched him until the undertaker's men were called back. Up to that time he hadn't moved. Bet you a new hat the men will tell you he never went nearer."

"You buy your own new hats," said Winter. "Do you want me to stand you two a day? I'm off to the Yard. I'll look up two lines in town. 'Phone through if you want help and I'll come. You sleep here tonight if you care to. Tomlinson will provide. How about the wood?"

"Leave it."

"You'll see that artist, Trenholme?"

"Yes."

"And the bedrooms?"

"Going there now."

"So long! Sorry I must quit, but I'm keen to clear up that telephone call."

"If you're in the office about six I'll tell you the whole story."

"Charles," said Winter earnestly, placing a hand on his colleague's shoulder, "we gain nothing by rushing our fences. This is the toughest job we've handled this year; there's a hard road to travel before we sit down and prepare a brief for counsel."

"Of course, I meant the story up to the six o'clock instalment."

Winter smiled. He sprang into the car, the chauffeur having already started the engine in obedience to a word from the Superintendent.

"Stop at the Brondesbury police station," was the order, and Furneaux was left alone. He reëntered the house and crooked a finger at the butler, who had not summoned up courage to retire to his own sanctum, though a midday meal was awaiting him.

"Take me upstairs," said the detective. "I shall not detain you many minutes. Then you and I will have a snack together and you'll borrow a bicycle for me, and I sha'n't trouble you any more till a late hour."

"No trouble at all, sir," Tomlinson assured him. "If I could advance your inquiry in the least degree I'd fast cheerfully all day."

"What I like about you, Tomlinson, is your restraint," said Furneaux. "Many a man would have offered to fast a week, not meaning to deny himself a toothful five minutes longer than was avoidable. Now you really mean what you say——Ah, this is Mr. Robert's den. And that is his bedroom, with dressing-room adjoining. Very cozy, to be sure. Of course, the rooms have been dusted regularly since he disappeared on Saturday?"

"Every day, sir."

"Well, I hate prying into people's rooms. Beastly liberty, I call it. Now for Mr. Hilton's."

"Is that all, sir?" inquired the butler, manifestly surprised by the cursory glance which the detective had given around the suite of apartments.

"All at present, thank you. Like the Danites' messengers, I'm only spying out the lie of the land. Ah, each brother occupied a corner of the east wing. Robert, north, Hilton, south—a most equitable arrangement. Now these rooms show signs of tenancy, eh?"

They were standing in Hilton Fenley's sitting-room, having traversed the whole of the gallery around the hall to reach it. The remains of a fire in the grate caught Furneaux's eye, and the butler coughed apologetically.

"Mr. Hilton won't have his rooms touched, sir, until he leaves home of a morning," he said. "He likes to find his papers, et cetera, where he put them overnight. As a rule the housemaid comes here soon after breakfast, but this morning—naturally——"

"Of course, of course," assented the other promptly. "Everything is at sixes and sevens. Would you mind sending the girl here? I'd like to have a word with her."

Tomlinson moved ponderously towards an electric bell.

"No," said Furneaux. "Don't ring. Just ask her to come. Then she can bring me to your place and we'll nibble something. Meanwhile I'll enjoy this view."

"Certainly, sir. That will suit me admirably."

Tomlinson walked out with stately tread. His broad back was scarcely turned before the detective's nimble feet had carried him into the bedroom, which stood in the southeast angle. He seemed to fly around the room like one possessed of a fiend of unrest. Picking up a glass tumbler, he sniffed it and put it in a pocket. He peered at the bed, the dressing-table, the carpet; opened drawers and wardrobe doors, examined towels in the bathroom, and stuffed one beneath his waistcoat.

Running back to the sitting-room, he found a torn envelope, and began picking up some specks of grit from the carpet, each of which went into a corner of the envelope, which he folded and stowed away. Then he bent over the fireplace and rummaged among the cinders. Three calcined lumps, not wholly consumed, appeared to interest him. A newspaper was handy; he wrapped the grimy treasure trove in a sheet, and that small parcel also went into a pocket.

When a swish of skirts on the stairs announced the housemaid he retreated to the bedroom, and the girl found him standing at a south window, gazing out over the fair vista of the Italian terraces and the rolling parkland.

"Yes, sir," said the girl timidly.

He turned, as if he had not heard her approach. She was pale, and her eyes were red, for the feminine portion of the household was in a state of collapse.

"I only wanted to ask why a fire is laid in the sitting-room in such fine weather," he said.

"Mr. Hilton sits up late, sir, and if the evening is at all chilly, he puts a match to the grate himself."

"Ah, a silly question. Don't tell anybody I spoke of it or they'll think me a funny detective, won't they?"

He smiled genially, and the girl's face brightened.

"I don't see that, sir," she said. "I don't know why Mr. Hilton wanted a fire last night. It was quite hot. I slept with my window wide open."

"A very healthy habit, too. Do you attend to Mr. Robert's suite?"

"Yes, sir."

"Does *he* have a fire?"

"Never in the summer, sir."

"He's a warmer-blooded creature than Mr. Hilton, I fancy."

"I expect so, sir."

"Well, now, there's nothing here. But we detectives have to nose around everywhere. I'm sure you are terribly upset by your master's death. Everybody gives him a good word."

"Indeed, he deserved it, sir. We all liked him. He was strict but very generous."

Furneaux chatted with her while they descended the stairs and traversed devious passages till the butler's room was gained. By that time the housemaid was convinced that Mr. Furneaux was "a very nice man." When she "did" Hilton Fenley's rooms she missed the glass, but gave no heed to its absence. Who would bother about a glass in a house where murder had been done? She simply replaced it by another of the same pattern.

"May I inquire, sir," said Tomlinson, when Furneaux had washed face and hands and was seated at a table laid for two, "may I inquire if you have any preference as to a luncheon wine?"

"I think," said Furneaux with due solemnity, "that a still wine——"

"I agree with you, sir. At this time of the day a Sauterne or a Johannisberger——"

"To my taste, a Château Yquem, with that delicate flavor which leaves the palate fresh—Frenchmen call it the *sève*——"

"Sir, I perceive that you have a taste. Singularly enough, I have a bottle of Château Yquem in my sideboard."

So the meal was a success.

An under gardener lent Furneaux a bicycle. After a chat with Farrow, to whom he conveyed some sandwiches and a bottle of beer, the detective rode to Easton. He sent a rather long telegram to his own quarters, called at a chemist's, and reached the White Horse at Roxton about two o'clock.

Now the imp of mischance had contrived that John Trenholme should hear no word of the murder until he came downstairs for luncheon after a morning's steady work.

The stout Eliza, fearful lest Mary should forestall her with the news, bounced out from the kitchen when his step sounded on the stairs.

"There was fine goin's on in the park this morning, Mr. Trenholme," she began breathlessly.

He reddened at once, and avoided her fiery eye. Of course, it had been discovered that he had watched that girl bathing. Dash it all, his action was unintentional! What a bore!

"Mr. Fenley was shot dead on his own doorstep," continued Eliza. She gave proper emphasis to the concluding words. That a man should be murdered "on his own doorstep" was a feature of the crime that enhanced the tragedy in the public mind. The shooting was bad enough in itself, for rural England is happily free from such horrors; but swift and brutal death dealt out on one's own doorstep was a thing at once monstrous and awe-compelling. Eliza, perhaps, wondered why Mr. Trenholme flushed, but she fully understood the sudden blanching of his face at her tidings, for all

Roxton was shaken to its foundations when the facts slowly percolated in that direction.

"Good Lord!" cried he. "Could that be the shot I heard?"

"He was killed at half past nine, sir."

"Then it was! A keeper heard it, too—and a policeman—our Roxton policeman."

"That would be Farrow," said Eliza. "What was *he* doin', the lazy-bones, that he couldn't catch the villain?"

"What villain?"

"The man who killed poor Mr. Fenley."

"They know who did it, then?"

"Well, no. There's all sorts o' tales flyin' about, but you can't believe any of 'em."

"But why are you blaming Farrow? He's a good fellow. He sings. No real scoundrel can sing. Read any novel, any newspaper report. 'The prisoner's voice was harsh and unmusical.' You've seen those words scores of times."

In his relief at learning that his own escapade was not published broadcast, Trenholme had momentarily forgotten the dreadful nature of Eliza's statement. She followed him into the dining-room.

"You'll be a witness, I suppose," she said, anxious to secure details of the shot-firing.

"A witness!" he repeated blankly.

"Yes, sir. There can't be a deal o' folk who heard the gun go off."

"By Jove, Eliza, I believe you're right," he said, gazing at her in dismay. "Now that I come to think of it, I am probably the only person in existence who can say where that shot came from. It was a rifle, too. I spoke of it to the keeper and Farrow."

"I was sure something would happen when I dreamed of suffrigettes this mornin'. An' that comes of playin' pranks, Mr. Trenholme. If it wasn't for that alarm clock——"

"Oh, come, Eliza," he broke in. "An alarm clock isn't a Gatling gun. Your association of ideas is faulty. There is much in common between the clatter of an alarm clock and the suffragist cause, but all the ladies promised not to endanger life, you know."

"Anyhow, Mr. Fenley is dead as a doornail," said Eliza firmly.

"Too bad. I take back all the hard things I said about him, and I'm sure you do the same."

"Me!"

"Yes. Didn't you say all the Fenleys were rubbish? One of them, at any rate, was wrongly classified."

"Which one?"

Trenholme bethought himself in time.

"This unfortunate banker, of course," he said.

"I'd a notion you meant Miss Sylvia. She's pretty as a picter—prettier than some picters I've seen—and folk speak well of her. But she's not a Fenley."

At any other time the artist would have received that thrust *en tierce* with a *riposte*; at present, Eliza's facts were more interesting than her wit.

"Who is the lady you are speaking of?" he asked guardedly.

"Mr. Fenley's ward, Miss Sylvia Manning. They say she's rich. Pore young thing! Some schemin' man will turn her head, I'll go bail, an' all for the sake of her brass."

"Most likely a one-legged gunner, name of Jim."

"Well, it won't be a two-legged painter, name of Jack!" And Eliza bounced out.

Now, Mary of the curl papers, having occasion to go upstairs while Trenholme was eating, peeped through the open door of the room which he had converted into a studio. She saw a picture on the easel, and the insatiable curiosity of her class led her to examine it. Even a country kitchen maid came under its spell instantly. After a pause of mingled admiration and shocked prudery, she sped to the kitchen.

"Seein' is believin'," quoted Eliza, mounting the stairs in her turn. She gazed at the drawing brazenly, with hands resting on hips and head cocked sidewise like an inquisitive hen's.

"Well, I never did!" was her verdict.

Back in the kitchen again, she announced firmly to Mary—

"*I'll* take in the cheese."

She put the Stilton on the table with a determined air.

"You don't know anything about Miss Sylvia Manning, don't you?" she said, with calm guile.

"Never heard the lady's name before you mentioned it," said Trenholme.

"Mebbe not, but it strikes me you've *seen* more of her than most folk."

"Eliza," he cried, without any pretense at smiling good humor, "you've been sneaking!"

"Sneakin', you call it? I 'appened to pass your room, an' who could help lookin' in? I was never so taken aback in me life. You could ha' knocked me down with a feather."

"An ostrich feather with an ostrich's leg behind it," was the angry retort.

Eliza's eyes glinted with the fire of battle.

"The shameless ways of girls nowadays!" she breathed. "To let any young man gaze at her in them sort of clothes, if you can call 'em clothes!"

"It was an accident. She didn't know I was there. Anyhow, you dare utter another word about that picture, even hint at its existence, and I'll paint you without any clothes at all. I mean that, so beware!"

"Sorry to interrupt," said a high-pitched voice from the doorway. "You are Mr. John Trenholme, I take it? May I come in? My name's Furneaux."

"Jim, of the Royal Artillery?" demanded Trenholme angrily.

"No. Charles François, of Scotland Yard."

Eliza fled, completely cowed. She began to weep, in noisy gulps.

"I've dud-dud-done it!" she explained to agitated curl papers. "That pup-pup-pore Mr. Trenholme. They've cuc-cuc-come for him. He'll be lul-lul-locked up, an' all along o' my wu-wu-wicked tongue!"

CHAPTER VII
SOME SIDE ISSUES

Trenholme, rather interested than otherwise, did not blanch at mention of Scotland Yard.

"Walk right in, Mr. Furneaux," he said; he had picked up a few tricks of speech from Transatlantic brethren of the brush met at Julien's. "Have you lunched?"

"Excellently," was the reply.

"Not in Roxton. I defy you to produce a cook in this village that shall compare with our Eliza of the White Horse."

"Sir, my thoughts do not dwell on viands. True, I ate with a butler, but I drank wine with a connoisseur. It was a Château Yquem of the eighties."

"Then you should be in expansive mood. Before you demand with a scowl why I shot Mr. Fenley you might tell me why the headquarters of the London Police is named Scotland Yard."

"Because it was first housed in a street of that name near Trafalgar Square. Scotland Yard was a palace at one time, built in a spirit of mistaken hospitality for the reception of prominent Scots visiting London. We entertained so many and so lavishly that 'Gang Sooth' has become a proverb beyond the Tweed."

"There is virtue, I perceive, in a bottle of Château Yquem—or was it two?"

"In one there is light, but two might produce fireworks. Now, sir, if you have finished luncheon, kindly take me to your room and show me the sketches you made this morning."

The artist raised an inquiring eyebrow.

"I have the highest respect for your profession in the abstract, but it is new to find it dabbling in art criticism," he said.

"I assure you, Mr. Trenholme, that any drawings of yours made in the neighborhood of The Towers before half past nine o'clock today will be most valuable pieces of evidence—if nothing more."

Though Furneaux's manner was grave as an owl's, a certain gleam in his eye gave the requisite sting to the concluding words. Trenholme, at any other time, would have delighted in him, but dropped his bantering air forthwith.

"I don't mind exhibiting my work," he said. "It will not be a novel experience. Come this way."

Watched by two awe-stricken women from the passage leading to the kitchen, the artist and his visitor ascended the stairs. Trenholme walked straight to the easel, took off the drawing of Sylvia Manning and the Aphrodite, placed it on the floor face to the wall, and staged the sketch of the Elizabethan house. Furneaux screwed his eyelids to secure a half light; then, making a cylinder of his right hand, peered through it with one eye.

"Admirable!" he said. "Corot, with some of the breadth of Constable. Forgive the comparisons, Mr. Trenholme. Of course, the style is your own, but one uses the names of accepted masters largely as adjectives to explain one's meaning. You are a true impressionist. You paint Nature as you see her, not as she is, yet your technique is superb and your observation just. For instance, every shadow in this lovely drawing shows that the hour was about eight o'clock. But, in painting figures, I have no doubt you sink the impressionist in the realist.... The other sketch, please."

"The other sketch is a mere color note for future guidance," said Trenholme offhandedly.

"It happens also to be a recognizable portrait of Miss Sylvia Manning. I'm sorry, but I must see it."

"Suppose I refuse?"

"It will be obtained by other methods than a polite request."

"I'm afraid I shall have to run the risk."

"No, you won't." And the detective's tone became eminently friendly. "You'll just produce it within the next half minute. You are not the sort of man who would care to drag a lady's name into a police-court wrangle, which can be the only outcome of present stubbornness on your part. I know you were hidden among those cedars between, say, eight o'clock and half past nine. I know that Miss Manning bathed in a lake well within your view. I know, too, that you sketched her, because I saw the canvas a moment ago—an oil, not a water color. These things may or may not be relevant to an inquiry into a crime, but they will certainly loom large in the public mind if the police have to explain why they needed a warrant to search your apartments."

Furneaux had gauged the artistic temperament accurately. Without another word of protest Trenholme placed the disputed canvas on the easel.

"Do you smoke?" inquired the detective suddenly.

"Yes. What the deuce has my smoking got to do with it?"

"I fancied that, perhaps, you might like to have a pipe while I examine this gem at leisure. One does not gabble the common-places of life when in the presence of the supreme in art. I find that a really fine picture induces a feeling of reverence, an emotion akin to the influence of a mountain range, or a dim cathedral. Pray burn incense. I am almost tempted to regret being a non-smoker."

Trenholme had heard no man talk in that strain since last he sat outside the Café Margery and watched the stream of life flowing along the Grand Boulevard. Almost unconsciously he yielded to the spell of a familiar jargon, well knowing he had been inspired in every touch while striving frenziedly to give permanence to a fleeting vision. He filled his pipe, and surveyed the detective with a quickened interest.

Furneaux gazed long and earnestly.

"Perfect!" he murmured, after that rapt pause. "Such a portrait, too, without any apparent effort! Just compare the cold sunlight on the statue with the same light falling on wet skin. Of course, Mr. Trenholme, you'll send this to the Salon. Burlington House finds satiety in Mayors and Masters of Fox Hounds."

"Good, isn't it?" agreed Trenholme. "What a cursed spite that it must be consumed in flame!"

"But why?" cried Furneaux, unfeignedly horrified.

"Dash it all, man, I can never copy it. And you wouldn't have me blazon that girl's face in a gallery after today's tragedy!"

The detective snapped his fingers.

"Poof!" he said. "I shall have Mr. Fenley's murderer hanged long before your picture is hung. London provides one front-rank tragedy a week, but not another such masterpiece in ten years. Burn it because of a sentiment! Perish the thought."

"If I had guessed you were coming here so promptly it would have been in ashes an hour ago," said Trenholme, grimly insistent on sacrifice.

With a disconcerting change of manner the detective promptly assumed a dryly official attitude.

"A mighty good job for you that nothing of the sort occurred," he said. "Your picture is your excuse, Mr. Trenholme. What plea could you have urged for spying on a lady in an open-air bath if deprived of the only valid one?"

"Look here!" came the angry retort. "You seem to be a pretty fair judge of a drawing, but you choose your words rather carelessly. Just now you described me as 'hidden' behind that clump of trees, and again you accuse me of 'spying.' I won't stand that sort of thing from Scotland Yard, nor from Buckingham Palace, if it comes to that."

Furneaux instantly reverted to his French vein. His shrug was eminently Parisian.

"You misunderstand me. I allege neither hiding nor spying on your part. Name of a good little gray man! The President of the Royal Academy would hide and spy for a month if he could palliate his conduct by that picture. But, given no picture, what is the answer? Reflect calmly, Mr. Trenholme, and you'll see that mine are words of wisdom. Burn that canvas, and you cut a sorry figure in the witness box. Moreover, suppose you treat the law with disdain, how do you propose explaining your actions to Miss Sylvia Manning?"

"In all probability, I shall never meet the lady."

"Oh, won't you, indeed! I have the honor to request you to meet her tomorrow morning by the shore of that sylvan lake at nine fifteen, sharp. And kindly bring both sketches with you. Only, for goodness' sake, keep this one covered with a water-proof wrap if the weather breaks, which it doesn't look like doing at this moment. Now, Mr. Trenholme, take the advice of a dried-up chip of experience like me, and be sensible. One word as to actualities. I'm told you didn't see anything in the park which led you to believe that a crime had been committed?"

"Not a thing. I heard the gunshot, and noted where it came from, but so far as I could ascertain, the only creatures it disturbed were some rabbits, rooks and pheasants."

"Ah! Where did the pheasants show up?"

"Out of the wood, close to the spot where the rifle was fired."

"How many?"

"How many what?"

"Pheasants."

"A brace. They flew right across the south front of the house to a covert on the west side. Is that an important detail?"

"When you hear the evidence you may find it so," commented Furneaux. "Why do you say 'rifle'? Why not plain 'gun'?"

"Because any one who has handled both a rifle and a shotgun can recognize the difference in sound. The explosive force of the one is many times greater than that of the other."

"Are you, too, an expert marksman?"

"I can shoot a bit. Hardly an expert, perhaps, seeing that I haven't used a gun during the past five years. If you know France, Mr. Furneaux, you'll agree that British ideas of sport——"

"I do know France," broke in the detective. "There isn't a cock robin or a jenny wren left in the country.... As a mere formality, what magazine are you working for?"

Trenholme told him, and Furneaux hurried away, halting for an instant in the doorway to raise a warning finger.

"Tomorrow, at the cedars, nine fifteen," he said. "And, mind you, no holocausts, or you're up a gum tree. You were either painting a pretty girl or gloating over her. Prove the one and people won't think the other, which they will be only too ready to do, this being a cynical and suspicious world."

He left a bewildered artist glaring after him. Trenholme's acquaintance with the police, either of England or France, was of the slightest. Sometimes, when overexcited by the discovery of some new and entrancing upland in the domain of art, he had bought or borrowed a volume of light fiction in order to read himself to sleep, and a detective figured occasionally in such pages. Usually, the official was a pig-headed idiot, whose blunders and narrow-mindedness served as admirable whetstones for the preternaturally sharp intelligence of an amateur investigator of crime.

Trenholme, like the average reader, did not know that such self-appointed sleuths are snubbed and despised by Scotland Yard, that they seldom or never base their fantastic theories on facts, or that, in fiction, they act in a way which would entail their own speedy appearance in the dock if practiced in real life. Furneaux came as a positive revelation. A small, wiry individual who looked like a comedian and spouted the truisms of the studio, a wizened little whippersnapper who put hardly one direct question to a prospective witness, but whose caustic comments had placed a new and vastly disagreeable aspect on the morning's adventure—such a man to be the representative of staid and heavy-footed Scotland Yard! Well, wonders would never cease. It was not for a bewildered artist yet to know that Furneaux's genius alone excused his eccentricities.

And he, Trenholme, was to meet the girl! He turned to the easel and looked at the picture. A few hours ago he had reviled the fate that seemed to forbid their meeting. Now he was to be brought to her, though somewhat after the fashion of a felon with gyves on his wrists, since Furneaux's request for the morrow's rendezvous rang ominously like a command. Indeed, indeed, it was a mad world!

At any rate, he did not, as he had intended, tear the canvas from its stretcher and apply a match to it in the grate. Thus far, then, had Furneaux's queer method been justified. He had hit on the one certain means of restraint on an act of vandalism. The picture now stood between Trenholme and the scoffing multitude. It was his buckler against the shafts of innuendo. Rather than lose it before his actions were vindicated he would suffer the depletion to the last penny of a not altogether meager bank account.

Of course, this open-souled youngster never dreamed that the detective had read his style and attributes in one lightning-swift glance of intuition. Before ever Trenholme was aware of a stranger standing in the open doorway of the dining-room Furneaux had taken his measure.

"English, a gentleman, art-trained in Paris. Thinks the loss of La Giaconde a far more serious event than a revolution, and regards the Futurist school pretty much as the Home Secretary regards the militant suffragists. Knows as much about the murder as I do about the rings of Saturn. But he ought to provide a touch of humor in an affair that promises little else than heavy tragedy. And it will do Miss Sylvia Manning some good if she is made to see that there are others than Fenleys in the world. So, have at him!"

While going downstairs, the detective became aware of some sniffing in the back passage. Eliza red-eyed now from distress, stood there, dabbing her cheeks with a corner of her apron.

"Pup-pup-please, sir," she began, but quailed under a sudden and penetrating look from those beady eyes.

"Well, what is it?" inquired Furneaux.

A violent nudge from curl papers stirred the cook's wits.

"I do hope you dud-dud-didn't pay any heed to anythink I was a-sayin' of," she stammered. "Mr. Trenholme wouldn't hurt a fuf-fuf-fly. I sus-sus-saw the picter, an' was on'y a-teasin' of 'im, like a sus-sus-silly woman."

"Exactly. Yet he heaps coals of fire on your head by declaring that you are the best cook in Hertfordshire! Is that true?"

Furneaux's impish grin was a tonic in itself. Eliza dropped the apron and squared her elbows.

"I don't know about bein' the best in Hertfordshire," she cried, "but I can hold me own no matter where the other one comes from, provided we start fair."

"Take warning, then, that if I bring a man here tomorrow evening—a big man, with a round head and bulging blue eyes—a man who looks as though he can use a carving-knife with discretion—you prepare a dinner worthy of the reputation of the White Horse! In that way, and in none other, can you rehabilitate your character."

Furneaux was gone before Eliza recovered her breath. Then she turned on the kitchen maid.

"Wot was it he said about my char-ac-ter?" she demanded warmly. "An' wot are *you* grinnin' at? If it wasn't for *your* peepin' an' pryin' I'd never ha' set eyes on that blessed picter. You go an' put on a black dress, an' do yer hair respectable, an' mind yer don't spend half an hour perkin' an' preenin' in front of a lookin'-glass."

Mary fled, and Eliza bustled into the kitchen.

"A big man, with a round head an' bulgin' blue eyes!" she muttered wrathfully. "Does he think I'm afraid of that sort of brewer's drayman, or of a little man with eyes like a ferret, either? If he does, he's very much mistaken. I don't believe he's a real 'tec. I wouldn't be a bit surprised if he wasn't a reporter. They've cheek enough for ten, as a rule. Talkin' about my char-ac-ter, an' before that hussy of a girl, too! Wait till I see him tomorrow, that's all."

Meanwhile, Furneaux had not held the second glass of Château Yquem to the light in Tomlinson's sanctum before Winter's car was halting outside Brondesbury police station. An Inspector assured the Superintendent that a constable was on the track of Robert Fenley, and had instructions to report direct to Scotland Yard. Then Winter reëntered the car, and was driven to Headquarters.

He was lunching in his own room, frugally but well, on bread and cheese and beer, when the Assistant Commissioner came in.

"Ah, Mr. Winter," he said. "I was told you had returned. That telephone call came from a call office in Shaftesbury Avenue. A lady, name unknown, but the youth in charge knows her well by sight, and thinks she lives in a set of flats near by. I thought the information sufficient for your purpose, so suspended inquiries till I heard from you."

"Just what I wanted, sir," said Winter. "There may be nothing in it, but I was curious to know why Hilton Fenley took the trouble to fib about such a trivial matter. His brother, too, is behaving in a way that invites criticism.

I don't imagine that either of the sons shot his father—most certainly, Hilton Fenley could not have done it, and Robert, I think, was in London at the time——"

"Dear me!" broke in the other, a man of quiet, self-contained manner, on whose lips that mild exclamation betokened the maximum of surprise. "Is there any reason whatsoever for believing that one of these young men may be a parricide?"

"So many reasons, sir, and so convincing in some respects, that the local police would be seriously considering the arrest of Robert Fenley if they had the ascertained facts in their possession."

The Assistant Commissioner sat down.

"I hear you keep a sound brand of cigars here, Mr. Winter," he said. "I've just lunched in the St. Stephen's Club, so, if you can spare the time——"

At the end of the Superintendent's recital the Chief offered no comment. He arose, went to the window, and seemed to seek inspiration from busy Westminster Bridge and a river dancing in sunshine. After a long pause he turned, and threw the unconsumed half of a cigar into the fireplace.

"It's a pity to waste such a perfect Havana," he said mournfully, "but I make it a rule not to smoke while passing along the corridors. And—you'll be busy. Keep me posted."

Winter smiled. When the door had closed on his visitor he even laughed.

"By Jove!" he said to himself. "A heart to heart talk with the guv'nor is always most illuminative. Now many another boss would have said he was puzzled, or bothered, or have given me some silly advice such as that I must be discreet, look into affairs closely, and not act precipitately. Not so our excellent A. C. He's clean bowled, and admits it, without speaking a word. He's a tonic; he really is!"

He touched an electric bell. When the policeman attendant, Johnston, appeared, he asked if Detective Sergeant Sheldon was in the building, and Sheldon came. The Superintendent had met him in a Yorkshire town during a protracted and difficult inquiry into the death of a wealthy recluse; although the man was merely an ordinary constable he had shown such resourcefulness, such ability of a rare order, that he was invited to join the staff of the Criminal Investigation Department, and had warranted Winter's judgment by earning rapid promotion.

Though tall, and of athletic build, he had none of the distinctive traits of the average policeman. He dressed quietly and in good taste, and carried himself easily; a peculiarity of his thoughtful, somewhat lawyer-like face was that the left eye was noticeably smaller than the right. Among other qualifications, he ranked as the best amateur photographer in the "Yard," and was famous as a rock climber in the Lake District.

Winter plunged at once into the business in hand.

"Sheldon," he said, "I'm going out, and may be absent an hour or longer. If a telephone message comes through from Mr. Furneaux tell him I have located the doubtful call made to The Towers this morning. Have you read the report of the Fenley murder in the evening papers?"

"Yes, sir. *Is* it a murder?"

"What else could it be?"

"An extraordinary accident."

Winter weighed the point, which had not occurred to him previously.

"No," he said. "It was no accident. I incline to the belief that it was the best-planned crime I've tackled during the past few years. That is my present opinion, at any rate. Now, a man from the Brondesbury police station is following one of the dead man's sons, a Mr. Robert Fenley, who bolted back to London on a motor cycle as soon as I threatened to question him.

"Robert Fenley is twenty-four, fresh-complexioned, clean-shaven, about five feet nine inches in height, stoutish, and of sporty appearance. He had his hair cut yesterday or the day before. His hands and feet are rather small. He talks aggressively, and looks what he is, a pampered youth, very much spoiled by his parents. His clothes—all that I have seen—are a motorist's overalls. If the Brondesbury man reports here during my absence act as you think fit. I want Robert Fenley located, followed, and watched unobtrusively, especially in such matters as the houses he visits and the people he meets. If you need help get it."

"Till what time, sir?" was the laconic question.

"That depends. Try and 'phone me here about five o'clock. But if you are otherwise engaged let the telephone go. Should Fenley seem to leave London by the Edgware Road, which leads to Roxton, have him checked on the way. Here is the number of his cycle," and Winter jotted a memorandum on the back of an envelope.

"What about Mr. Furneaux if I am called out almost immediately?"

"Give the message to Johnston."

Then Winter hurried away, and, repressing the inclination to hail a taxi, walked up Whitehall and crossed Trafalgar Square *en route* to the Shaftesbury Avenue address supplied by the Assistant Commissioner.

He found a sharp-featured youth in charge of the telephone, which was lodged in an estate agent's office. The boy grinned when the Superintendent explained his errand.

"Excuse *me*," he said, with the pert assurance of the born Cockney, "but we aren't allowed to give information about customers."

"You've broken your rules already, young man," said Winter. "You answered a similar inquiry made by Scotland Yard some hours since."

"Oh, was *that* it? Gerrard rang me up, and I thought there was something funny going on. Are you from Scotland Yard, sir?"

Winter proffered a card, and the boy's eyes opened wide.

"Crikey!" he said. "I've read about you, sir. Well, I've been doing a bit of detective work of my own. At lunch time I strolled past the set of flats where I thought the lady lived, and had the luck to see her getting out of a cab at the door. I followed her upstairs, pretending I had business somewhere, and saw her go into No. Eleven. Her name is Miss Eileen Garth—at least, that's the name opposite No. Eleven in the list in the hall."

"When you're a bit older you'll make a detective," said Winter. "You've learned the first trick of the job, and that is to keep your eyes open. Now, to encourage you, I'll tell you the second. Keep your mouth shut. If this lady is Miss Garth she is not the person we want, but it would annoy her if she heard the police were inquiring about her; so here is half a crown for your trouble."

"Can I do anything else for you, sir?" came the eager demand.

"Nothing. I'm on the wrong scent, evidently, but you have saved me from wasting time. This Miss Eileen Garth is English, of course?"

"Yes, sir; very good-looking, but rather snappy."

Winter sighed.

"That just shows how easy it is to blunder," he said. "I'm looking for a Polish Jewess, whose chief feature is her nose, and who wears big gold earrings."

"Oh, Miss Garth is quite different," said the disappointed youth. "She's tall and slim—a regular dasher, big black hat, swell togs, black and white, and smart boots with white spats. She wore pearls in her ears, too, because I noticed 'em."

Winter sighed again.

"Another half day lost," he murmured, and went out.

Knowing well that the boy would note the direction he took, he turned away from the block of flats and made for Soho, where he smoked a thin, raffish Italian cigar with an Anarchist of his acquaintance who kept a restaurant famous for its *risotto*. Then, by other streets, he approached Gloucester Mansions, and soon was pressing the electric bell of No. Eleven.

"Miss Garth in?" he said to an elderly, hatchet-faced woman who opened the door.

"Why do you want Miss Garth?" was the non-committal reply, given in the tone of one who meant the stranger to understand that he was not addressing a servant.

"I shall explain my errand to the lady herself," said Winter civilly. "Kindly tell her that Superintendent Winter, of the Criminal Investigation Department, Scotland Yard, wishes to see her."

To him it was no new thing that his name and description should bring dismay, even terror, to the cheeks of one to whom he made himself known professionally, but unless he was addressing some desperate criminal, he did not expect to be assaulted. For once, therefore, he was thoroughly surprised when a bony hand shot out and pushed him backward; the door was slammed in his face; the latch clicked, and he was left staring at a small brass plate bearing the legend: "Ring. Do not knock."

Naturally, this bold maneuver could not have succeeded had he a right of entry. A woman's physical strength was unequal to the task of disturbing his burly frame, and a foot thrust between door and jamb would have done the rest. As matters stood, however, he was obliged to abandon any present hope of an interview with the mysterious Miss Eileen Garth.

He remained stock still for some seconds, listening to the retreating footsteps of the strong-minded person who had beaten him. It was his habit to visualize for future reference the features and demeanor of people in whom he was interested, and of whom circumstances permitted only the merest glimpse. This woman's face had revealed annoyance rather than fear. "Scotland Yard" was not an ogre but a nuisance. She held, or, at any rate, she had exercised, a definite power of rejecting visitors whom she considered undesirable. Therefore, she was a relative, probably Eileen Garth's mother or aunt.

Eileen Garth was "tall and slim," "good-looking, but rather snappy." Well, twenty years ago, the description would have applied to the woman he had just seen. Her voice, heard under admittedly adverse conditions, was correct in accent and fairly cultured. Before the world had hardened it its tones might have been soft and dulcet. But above all, there was the presumable discovery that Eileen Garth was as decidedly opposed as Robert Fenley to full and free discussion of that morning's crime.

"Furneaux will jeer at me when he hears of this little episode," thought Winter, smiling as he turned to descend the stairs. Furneaux did jeer, but it was at his colleague's phenomenal luck.

The door of No. Twelve, the only other flat on the same landing, opened, and a man appeared. Recognition was prompt on Winter's side.

"Hello, Drake!" he said genially. "Are *you* Signor Maselli? Well met, anyhow! Can you give me a friendly word?"

The occupant of flat No. Twelve, an undersized, slightly built man of middle age, seemed to have received the shock of his life. His sallow-complexioned face assumed a greenish-yellow tint, and his deep-set eyes glistened like those of a hunted animal.

"Friendly?" he contrived to gasp, giving a ghastly look over his shoulder to ascertain whether any one in the interior of the flat had heard that name "Drake."

"Yes. I mean it. Strictly on the q. t.," said Winter, sinking his voice to a confidential pitch. Signor Giovanni Maselli, since that was the name modestly displayed on No. Twelve's card in the hall beneath, closed the door carefully. He appeared to trust Winter, up to a point, but evidently found it hard to regain self-control.

"Not here!" he whispered. "In five minutes—at the Regency Café, Piccadilly. Let me go alone."

Winter nodded, and the other darted downstairs. The detective followed slowly. Crossing the street at an angle, he looked up at the smoke-stained elevation of Gloucester Mansions.

"A well-filled nest," he communed, "and a nice lot of prize birds in it, upon my word!"

The last time he had set eyes on a certain notably expert forger and counterfeiter a judge was passing sentence of five years' penal servitude and three years' police supervision on a felon; and the judge had not addressed the prisoner as Giovanni Maselli, but as John Christopher Drake!

CHAPTER VIII
COINCIDENCES

Winter was blessed with an unfailing memory for dates and faces. Before he had emerged from the main exit of Gloucester Mansions he had fixed Drake as committed from the Old Bailey during the Summer assizes four years earlier, released from Portland on ticket of leave at the beginning of the current year, and marked in the "failure to report" list.

"Poor devil!" he said to himself. "The very man for my purpose!"

Therefore, seeing his way clearly, his glance was not so encouraging nor his voice so pleasant when he found the ex-convict awaiting him in the Regency Café. Nevertheless, obeying the curious code which links the police and noted criminals in a sort of *camaraderie*, he asked the man what he would drink, and ordered cigarettes as well.

"Now, Maselli," he said, when they were seated at a marble-topped table in a corner of a well-filled room, "since we know each other so well we can converse plainly, eh?"

"Yes, sir, but I'm done for now. I've been trying to earn an honest living, and have succeeded, but now——"

The man spoke brokenly. His spirit was crushed. He saw in his mind's eye the frowning portals of a convict settlement, and heard the boom of a giant knocker reverberating through gaunt aisles of despair.

"If you reflect that I am calling you Maselli, you'll drink that whisky and soda, and listen to what I have to say," broke in Winter severely.

The other looked up at him, and a gleam of hope illumined the pallid cheeks. He drank eagerly, and lighted a cigarette with trembling fingers.

"If only I am given a chance——" he began, but the detective interfered again.

"If only you would shut up!" he said emphatically. "I want your help, and I'm not in the habit of rewarding my assistants by sending them back to prison."

Maselli (as he may remain in this record) was so excited that he literally could not obey.

"I've cut completely adrift from the old crowd, sir," he pleaded wistfully. "I'm an engraver now, and in good work. Heaven help me, I'm married, too. She doesn't know. She thinks I was stranded in America, and that I changed my name because Italians are thought more of than Englishmen in my line."

"Giovanni Maselli, may I ask what you are talking about?" said Winter, stiffening visibly.

At last the hunted and haunted wretch persuaded himself that "the Yard" meant to be merciful. Tears glistened in his eyes, but he finished the whisky and soda and remained silent.

"Good!" said Winter more cheerfully. "I sha'n't call you Maselli again if you don't behave. Now, how long have you lived in Gloucester Mansions?"

"Four months, sir. Ever since my marriage."

Winter smiled. The man had gone straight from the gates of Portland to some woman who was waiting for him! He was an old offender, but had proved slippery as an eel—hence a stiff sentence when caught; but penal servitude had conquered him.

"Has Miss Eileen Garth lived in No. Eleven during those four months?" was the next question.

"Yes, sir—two years or more, I believe. Her mother mentioned something of it to my wife one day."

"Her mother? Same name?"

"Yes, Mrs. Garth."

"How do they live?"

"The daughter was learning to be a stage dancer; but they've come into a settled income, and that idea is given up."

"Any male relations?"

"None that I know of, sir. Eileen is engaged to be married. I haven't heard the gentleman's name, but I've seen him scores of times."

"Scores of times—in four months?"

"Yes, sir, every second or third day. That is, I either meet him or know he is there because Mrs. Maselli and Mrs. Garth are friendly, and there is constant coming and going across the landing."

"Is he a man of about thirty, middle height, lanky black hair, smooth dark face, sunken eyes, high cheek bones—rather, shall I say, Italian in appearance?"

Maselli was surprised, and showed it.

"Why, sir, you've described him to a nicety," he said.

"Very well. Next time he is there to your absolute knowledge, slip out and telephone the fact to me at Scotland Yard. If I'm not in, ask for Mr. Furneaux. You remember Mr. Furneaux?"

A sickly smile admitted the acquaintance. Furneaux had recognized the same artist's hand in each of many realistic forgeries, and it was this fact which led to the man's capture and conviction.

"If neither of us is at home, inquire for Mr. Sheldon," went on Winter. "Note him. He's a stranger to you. If you fail to get hold of any of us, say simply that Signor Maselli would like to have a word at our convenience. It will be understood. We sha'n't bother you. Give another call next time the visitor is in Mrs. Garth's flat, and keep on doing this until you find one of the three on the line. Don't use the telephone in Shaftesbury Avenue near the Mansions, because the boy in charge there might be suspicious, and blab. That is all. You are not doing Mrs. Garth or her daughter an ill turn, so far as I can judge. Keep a still tongue. Silence on your part will meet with silence on mine.... Oh, dash it, have another drink! Where's your nerve?"

Signor Giovanni Maselli was crying. A phantom had brushed close, but was passing; nevertheless, its shadow had chilled him to the bone.

Winter walked back to Scotland Yard, and found that Sheldon had gone, leaving a note which read: "Mr. Robert Fenley is at 104, Hendon Road, Battersea Park." He was tempted to have a word with Furneaux, but forbore, and tackled some other departmental business. It was a day fated, however, to evolve the unexpected. About a quarter to four the telephone bell rang, and Maselli informed him that Miss Garth's fiancé had just arrived at Gloucester Mansions.

"Excellent," said Winter. "In future, devote your energies to legitimate engraving. Good-by!"

He rushed out and leaped into a taxi; within five minutes he was at the door of No. Eleven once more. Let it not be imagined that he had not weighed the possible consequences of thrusting himself in this fashion into Hilton Fenley's private affairs. Although the man had summoned the assistance of Scotland Yard to elucidate the mystery of his father's death, that fact alone could not secure him immunity from the law's all-embracing glance. Winter agreed with Furneaux that the profession of a private banker combined with company promotion is too often a cloak for roguery in the City of London, and the little he knew of the Fenley history did not tend to dissipate a certain nebulous suspicion that their record might not be wholly clean.

The theft of the bonds had been hushed up in a way that savored of unwillingness on Mortimer Fenley's part to permit the police to take action. The man's tragic death might well be a sequel to the robbery, and, granted the impossibility of his elder son having committed the murder, there was nothing fantastic in the notion that he might be a party to it.

Again, Hilton Fenley had deliberately misled Scotland Yard in regard to the seemingly trivial incident of the telephone call. Had he told the truth, and grumbled at the lack of discretion on some woman's part in breaking in on a period of acute distress in the household, Winter's subsequent discovery would have lost its point. As matters stood, however, it was one of a large number of minor circumstances which demanded full examination, and the Superintendent decided that the person really responsible for any seeming excess of zeal on his part should be given an opportunity to clear the air in the place best fitted for the purpose; namely, the address from which the call emanated.

Therefore, when the door was opened again by Mrs. Garth, she found that the Napoleonic tactics of an earlier hour were no longer practicable, for the enemy instantly occupied the terrain by leaning inward.

"I want to see Mr. Hilton Fenley," he said suavely. "You know my name already, Mrs. Garth, so I need not repeat it."

The sharp-featured woman was evidently sharp-witted also. Finding that the door might not be closed, she threw it wide.

"I have no objection to your seeing Mr. Fenley," she said. "I am at a loss to understand why you follow him here, but that does not concern me in the least. Come this way."

Latching the door, she led him to a room on the right of the entrance hall, which formed the central artery of the flat. The place had no direct daylight. At night, when an electric lamp was switched on, its contents would be far more distinct than at this hour, when the only light came from a transverse passage at the end, or was borrowed through any door that happened to remain open. Still, Winter could use his eyes, even in the momentary gloom, and he used them so well on this occasion that he noted two trunks, one on top of the other, and standing close to the wall.

They were well plastered with hotel and railway labels, and when a flood of light poured in from the room to which Mrs. Garth ushered him, he deciphered two of the freshest, and presumably the most recent. They were "Hotel d'Italie, Rue Caumartin, Paris," and a baggage number, "517." Not much, perhaps, in the way of information, but something; and Winter could trust his memory.

He found himself in a well-furnished room, and hoped that Mrs. Garth might leave him there, even for a few seconds, when he would be free to examine the apartment without her supervision. But she treated him as if he might steal the spoons. Remaining in the doorway, she called loudly:

"Mr. Fenley! The person I told you of is here again. Will you kindly come? He is in the dining-room."

A door opened, a hurried step sounded on a linoleum floor-covering, and Hilton Fenley appeared.

"Mr.—Mr. Winter, isn't it?" he said, with a fine air of surprise.

"Yes," said the Superintendent composedly. "You hardly expected to meet me here, I suppose?"

"Well, Mrs. Garth mentioned your earlier visit, but I am at a loss to understand——"

"Oh, it is easily explained. We of the Yard take nothing for granted, Mr. Fenley. I learned by chance that a young lady who lives here rang you up at Roxton this morning, and knowing that you took the trouble to conceal the fact, I thought it advisable——"

Mrs. Garth was a woman of discretion. She closed the door on the two men. Fenley did not wait for Winter to conclude.

"That was foolish of me, I admit," he said, readily enough. "One does not wish all one's private affairs to be canvassed, even by the police. The moment Mrs. Garth mentioned your name I saw my error. You checked the telephone calls to The Towers, I suppose, and thus learned I had misled you."

"Something of the sort. Miss Garth is a lady not difficult of recognition."

"She and her mother are very dear friends. It was natural they should be shocked by the paragraphs in the newspapers and wish to ascertain the truth."

"Quite so. I'm sorry if my pertinacity has annoyed them, or you."

"I think they will rather be pleased by such proof of your thoroughness. Certainly I, for my part, do not resent it."

"Very well, sir. Since I am here, I may inquire if you know any one living at 104, Hendon Road, Battersea Park?"

"Now that you mention the address, I recall it as the residence of the lady in whom my brother is interested. This morning I had forgotten it, but you have refreshed my memory."

"You're a tolerably self-possessed person," was the detective's unspoken thought, for Fenley was a different man now from the nervous, distrait son who had clamored for vengeance on his father's murderer. "You own up to the facts candidly when it is useless to do anything else, and you never fail to hammer a nail into Robert's coffin when the opportunity offers."

But aloud he said—

"You really don't know the lady's name, I suppose?"

Fenley hesitated a fraction of a second.

"Yes, I do know it, though I withheld the information this morning," he replied. "But, I ask you, is it quite fair to make me a witness against my brother?"

"Some one must explain Mr. Robert's movements, and, since he declines the task, I look to you," was the straightforward answer.

"She is a Mrs. Lisle," said Fenley, after another pause—a calculated pause this time.

"Have you visited your City office today?"

"I went straight there from The Towers. I told you I was going there. What object could I have in deceiving you?"

"None that I can see, Mr. Fenley. But I have been wondering if any new light has been shed on the motive which might have led to the crime. Have you examined Mr. Mortimer Fenley's papers, for instance? There may be documents, letters, memoranda secreted in some private drawer or dispatch case."

The other shook his head. He appeared not to resent the detective's tone. It seemed as if regret for the morning's lack of confidence had rendered him apologetic.

"No," he said. "I have not had time yet to go through my father's papers. This afternoon I was taken up wholly with business. You see, Mr. Winter, I can not allow my personal suffering to cost other men thousands of pounds, and that must be the outcome if certain undertakings now in hand are not completed. But my father was most methodical, and his affairs are sure to be thoroughly in order. Within the next few days, when I have time to make a proper search, I'll do it. Meanwhile, I can practically assure you that he had no reason to anticipate anything in the nature of a personal attack from any quarter whatsoever."

"Do you care to discuss your brother's extraordinary behavior?"

"In what respect?"

"Well, he virtually bolted from Roxton today, though I had warned him that his presence was imperative."

"My brother is self-willed and impetuous, and he was dreadfully shocked at finding his father dead."

"Did he tell you he meant returning to London at once?"

"No. When I came downstairs, after the distressing scene with Mrs. Fenley, he had gone."

The Superintendent was aware already that he was dealing with a man cast in no ordinary mold, but he did not expect this continued meekness. Ninety-nine people out of a hundred would have grown restive under such cross-examination, and betrayed their annoyance by word or look; not so Hilton Fenley, who behaved as if it were the most natural thing in the world that he should be tracked to his friends' residence and made to explain his comings and goings during the day. Swayed by a subconscious desire to nettle his victim into protest, Winter tried a new tack.

"I suppose, Mr. Fenley, you have seen your father's solicitors today?" he said suddenly.

"If you mean that question in the ordinary sense, I must tell you that my father employed no firm of solicitors for family purposes. Of course, at one time or another, he has availed himself of the services of nearly every leading firm of lawyers in the City, but each transaction was complete in itself. For instance, his will is a holograph will, if that is what you are hinting at. He told me its provisions at the time it was signed and witnessed, and I shall surely find it in his private safe at the office."

"You have not looked for it today?"

"No. Why should I?"

Feeling distinctly nonplussed, for there was no denying that Fenley had chosen the best possible way of carrying off a delicate situation, Winter turned, walked slowly to a window and gazed down into the street. He was perturbed, almost irritated, by a novel sense of failure not often associated with the day's work. He had to confess now that he had made no material stride in an inquiry the solution of which did not seem, at the outset, to offer any abnormal difficulty.

True, there were circumstances which might serve to incriminate Robert Fenley; but if that young man were really responsible for the crime, he was what "the Yard" classes privately as a monumental idiot, since his subsequent conduct was well calculated to arouse the suspicion which the instinct of self-preservation would try to avert. A long experience of the methods of criminals warned Winter of the folly of jumping at conclusions, but he would be slow to admit and hard to be convinced that Robert Fenley took any active part in his father's murder.

Of course, it was not with a view toward indulging in a reverie that he approached the window. He was setting a simple trap, into which many a man and woman had fallen. Any one of moderately strong character can control face and eyes when the need of such discipline is urgent, but howsoever impregnable the mask, the strain of wearing it is felt, and relief shows itself in an unguarded moment. At the farther end of the room there was a mirror above the fireplace, and as he turned his back on Fenley, by a hardly perceptible inclination of his head he could catch the reflection of his companion's face.

The maneuver succeeded, but its result was negative. Hilton Fenley's eyes were downcast. He had lifted a hand to his chin in one of those nervous gestures which had been so noticeable during the morning's tumult. His face wore an expression of deep thought. Indeed, he might be weighing each word he had heard and uttered, and calculating its effect on his own fortunes.

Still obeying that unworthy instinct which bade him sting Fenley into defiance, Winter tossed a question over his shoulder.

"May I have a word with Miss Garth?" he said suddenly.

"Why?" was the calm answer.

"Just to settle that telephone incident once and for all."

"But if you imagine it might not have been Miss Garth who made the call, why are you here?"

Then the detective laughed. His wonted air of cheerful good humor smoothed the wrinkles from his forehead. He was beaten, completely discomfited, and he might as well confess it and betake himself to some quarter where a likelier trail could be followed.

"True," he said affably. "I need not bother the young lady. Perhaps you will make my excuses and tell her that I ran you to earth in Gloucester Mansions merely to save time. By the way, I led the youth at the call office to believe that I was searching for an undersized Polish Jewess, all nose and gold earrings, a description which hardly applies to Miss Garth. And one last question—do you return to Roxton tonight?"

"Within the hour."

So Winter descended the stone stairs a second time, a prey to a feeling of failure. What had he gained by his impetuous actions? He had ascertained that Hilton Fenley was on terms of close intimacy with a pretty girl and her mother. Nothing very remarkable in that. He had secured a Paris address and the number of a baggage registration label. But similar information might be gleaned from a hundred thousand boxes and portmanteaux in London that day. He had been told that Mortimer Fenley had made a holograph will. Such procedure was by no means rare. Millions sterling have been disposed of on half sheets of note paper. Even his Majesty's judges have written similar wills, and blundered, with the result that a brother learned in the law has had to decide what the testator really meant. He wondered whether or not Mortimer Fenley had committed some technical error, such as the common one of creating a trust without appointing trustees. That would be seen in due course, when the will was probated.

At any rate, he grinned at his own expense.

"The only individual who has scored today," he said to himself, "is John Christopher Drake, alias Giovanni Maselli. I must keep mum about him. By gad, I believe I've compounded a felony!"

But because he had not scored inside Gloucester Mansions there was no valid reason why he should not accomplish something in their immediate neighborhood. For instance, who and what were the Garths, mother and daughter? He looked in on a well-known dramatic agent, and raised the point. Reference to a ledger showed that Eileen Garth, age eighteen, tall, good-looking, no previous experience, had been a candidate for musical comedy, London engagement alone accepted; the almost certain sequel being that she had kept her name six months on the books without an offer to secure her valuable services.

"I remember the girl well," said the agent. "She had the makings of a coryphée, but lacked training. She could sing a little, so I advised her to take dancing lessons. I believe she began them, with a teacher I recommended, but I've seen nothing of her for a year or more."

"Again has Giovanni filled the bill," mused Winter as he made for his office. "I wish now I had curbed my impulsiveness and kept away from Gloucester Mansions—the second time, anyhow."

Though chastened in spirit, the fact that no news of any sort awaited him at Scotland Yard, did not help to restore his customary poise.

"Dash it all!" he growled. "I'm losing grip. The next thing I'll hear is that Sheldon is enjoying himself at Earl's Court and that Furneaux has gone fishing."

Restless and ill at ease, he decided to ring up The Towers, Roxton. A footman answered the telephone, and announced that Mr. Furneaux had "just come in."

"Hello, Charles," said Winter, when a thin voice squeaked along the line. "Any luck?"

"Superb!"

"Good! I've drawn blanks, regular round O's, except three probably useless addresses."

"Addresses are never useless, friend. The mere knowing of a number in a street picks out that street from all the other streets where one knows no numbers."

"Tell me things, you rat, if conditions permit."

"Well, I've hit on two facts of profound importance. First, Roxton contains an artist of rare genius, and, second, it holds a cook of admitted excellence."

"Look here——"

"I'm listening here, which is all that science can achieve at present."

"I'm in no mood for ill timed pleasantries."

"But I'm not joking, 'pon me honor. The cook, name of Eliza, does really exist, and is sworn to surprise even your jaded appetite. The artist is John Trenholme. In years to come you'll boast of having met him before he was famous."

"So you, like me, have done nothing?"

"Ah, I note the bitterness of defeat in your tone. It has warped your judgment, too, as you will agree when a certain dinner I have arranged for tomorrow night touches the spot."

"Can't you put matters more plainly?"

"I'm guessing and planning and contriving. Like Galileo, I am convinced that the world moves." Then Furneaux broke into French. "Regarding those addresses you speak of, what are they?"

Using the same language, Winter told him, substituting "the Eurasian" and "the motorcyclist" for names, and adding that he was writing Jacques Faure, the Paris detective, with reference to the hotel and the label, the figures on the latter being of the long, thin, French variety.

"Are you coming here tonight?" went on Furneaux.

"Do you want me?"

"I'm only a little chap, and I'd like to have you near when it is dark."

Winter sighed, but it was with relief. He knew now that Furneaux had not failed.

"Very well," he said. "I'll arrive by the next convenient train."

"The point is," continued Furneaux, who delighted in keeping his chief on tenterhooks when some new development in the chase was imminent, "that the position here requires handling by a man of your weight and authority. The motor cyclist came back an hour ago, and is now walking in the garden with the girl."

"The deuce! Why hasn't Sheldon reported?" blurted out Winter.

"Because, in all likelihood, he is watching the other girl. Isn't that what you were doing? Isn't half the battle won when we find the woman?"

"I haven't set eyes on *my* woman."

"You surprise me. That kind of modest self-effacement isn't your usual style, at all, at all, as they say in Cork."

"Probably you're right about Sheldon. He is a worker, not a talker like some people I know," retorted Winter.

"What very dull acquaintances you must possess! Workers are the small fry who put spouters into Parliament, and pay them £400 a year, and make them Cabinet Ministers."

"Evidently things have happened at Roxton, or you wouldn't be so chirpy. Well, so long! See you later."

Having ascertained that an express train was timed to leave St. Pancras for Roxton at six P. M., he was packing a suitcase when a telegram arrived. It had been handed in at Folkestone at four thirty, and read:

Decided to follow lady instead of motor cyclist. Will explain reasons verbally. Reaching London seven o'clock.

SHELDON.

"I'm the only one of the three who has accomplished nothing," was Winter's rueful comment. Nor could any critic have gainsaid him, for he seemed to have been wasting precious hours while his subordinates were making history in the Fenley case.

He left instructions with Johnston that Mr. Sheldon was to write fully, care of the Roxton police station, and took a cab for St. Pancras. He was passing along the platform when he caught sight of Hilton Fenley seated on the far side of a first-class carriage, which was otherwise untenanted. An open dispatch box lay beside him, and he was so engrossed in the perusal of some document that he gave no heed to externals. Winter threw wide the door, and entered.

"We are fated to meet today, Mr. Fenley," he said pleasantly. "First, you send for me; then I hunt you, and now we come together by chance. I don't think coincidence can arrange any fourth way of bringing us in touch today."

But he was mistaken. Coincidence had already done far more than he imagined in providing unseen clues to the ultimate clearing up of a ghastly crime, and the same subtle law of chance was fated to assist the authorities once more before the sun rose again over the trees from whose cover Mortimer Fenley's murderer had fired the fatal shot.

CHAPTER IX
WHEREIN AN ARTIST BECOMES A MAN OF ACTION

Furneaux's visit left Trenholme in no happy frame of mind. The man who that morning had not a care in the world was now a prey to disquieting thought. The knowledge that he had been close to the scene of a dastardly murder at the moment it was committed, that he was in a sense a witness of the crime, was depressing in itself, for his was a kindly nature; and the mere fact that circumstances had rendered him impotent when his presence might have acted as a deterrent was saddening.

Then, again, he was worried by the reflection that, no matter how discriminating the police might prove with regard to his sketch of Sylvia Manning, he would undoubtedly be called as a witness, both at the inquest and at the trial of any person arrested for the crime. It was asking too much of editorial human nature to expect that the magazine which had commissioned the illustrated article on Roxton would not make capital of the fact that its special artist was actually sketching the house while Mr. Fenley's murderer was skulking among the trees surrounding it. Thus there was no escape for John Trenholme. He was doomed to become notorious. At any hour the evening newspapers might be publishing his portrait and biography!

On going downstairs he was cheered a little by meeting an apologetic Eliza.

"I hope I didn't do any reel 'arm, sir," she said, dropping an aspirate in sheer emphasis.

"Any harm to whom, or what?" he asked.

"By talkin' as I did afore that 'tec, sir."

"All depends on what you said to him. If you told him, for instance, that I carry Browning pistols in each pocket, and that my easel is a portable Maxim gun, of course——"

"Oh, sir, I never try to be funny. I mean about the picter."

"Good Heavens! You, too!"

Eliza failed to understand this, but she was too subdued to inquire his meaning.

"You see, sir, he must ha' heerd what I said about it, an' him skulkin' there in the passage. Do you reelly think a hop-o'-me-thumb like that can be a Scotland Yard man? It's my belief he's a himpostor."

It had not dawned on Trenholme that Furneaux's complete fund of information regarding the sketches had been obtained so recently. He imagined that Police Constable Farrow and Gamekeeper Bates had supplied details, so his reply cheered Eliza.

"Don't worry about unnecessary trifles," he said. "Mr. Furneaux is not only a genuine detective, but a remarkably clever one. You ought to have heard him praising the picture you despised."

"I never did," came the vehement protest. "The picter is fine. It was the young lady's clothes, or the want of 'em, that I was condemnin'."

"I've seen four thousand ladies walking about the sands at Trouville in far scantier attire."

"That's in France, isn't it?" inquired Eliza.

"Yes, but France is a more civilized country than England."

Eliza sniffed, sure sign of battle.

"Not it," she vowed. "I've read things about the carryin' on there as made me blood boil. Horse-racin' on Sundays, an' folks goin' to theaters instead of church. France more civilized than England, indeed! What'll you be sayin' next?"

"I'll be saying that if our little friend behaves himself I shall ask him to dine here tomorrow."

"He's axed himself, Mr. Trenholme, an' he's bringing another one, a big fellow, who knows how to use a carvin'-knife, he says. What would you like for dinner?"

Trenholme fled. That question was becoming a daily torment. The appearance of Furneaux had alone saved him from being put on the culinary rack after luncheon; having partaken of one good meal, he never had the remotest notion as to his requirements for the next.

He wandered through the village, calling at a tobacconist's, and looking in on his friend the barber. All tongues were agog with wonder. The Fenley family, known to that district of Hertfordshire during the greater part of a generation, was subjected to merciless criticism. He heard gossip of Mr. Robert, of Mr. Hilton, even of the recluse wife, now a widow; but every one had a good word for "Miss Sylvia."

"We don't see enough of her, an' that's a fact," said the barber. "She must find life rather dull, cooped up there as she is, for all that it's a grand house an' a fine park. They never had company like the other big houses. A few bald-headed City men an' their wives for an occasional week end in the summer or when the coverts were shot in October—never any nice young people. Miss Sylvia wept when the rector's daughter got married last year, an' well I knew why—she was losin' her only chum."

"Surely there are scores of good families in this neighborhood?"

"Plenty, sir, but nearly all county. The toffs never did take on the Fenleys, an', to be fair, I don't believe the poor man who's dead ever bothered his head about them."

"But Miss Manning can not have lived here all her life? She must have been abroad, at school, for instance?"

"Well, yes, sir. I remember her comin' home from Brussels two years ago. But school ain't society. The likes of her, with all her money, should mix with her own sort."

"Is she so wealthy, then?"

"She's Mr. Fenley's ward, an' the servants at The Towers say she'll come in for a heap when she's twenty-one, which will be next year."

Somehow, this item of gossip, confirming Eliza's statement, was displeasing. Sylvia Manning, nymph of the lake, receded to some dim altitude where the high and mighty are enthroned. Biting his pipe viciously, Trenholme sought the solitude of a woodland footpath, and tried to find distraction in studying the effects of diffused light.

Returning to the inn about tea time, he was angered anew by a telegram from the magazine editor. It read:

News in Pictures wants sketches and photographs of Fenley case and surroundings. Have suggested you for commission. Why not pick up a tenner? Rush drawings by train.

"That's the last straw," growled Trenholme fiercely. He raced out, bought a set of picture postcards showing the village and the Tudor mansion, and dispatched them to the editor of *News in Pictures* with his compliments. Coming back from the station, he passed the Easton lodge of The Towers. A daring notion seized him, and he proceeded to put it into practice forthwith. He presented himself at the gate, and was faced by Mrs. Bates and a policeman. Taught by experience to beware of strangers that day, the keeper's wife gazed at him through an insurmountable iron palisade. The constable merely surveyed him with a professional air, as one who would interfere if needful.

"I am calling on Miss Sylvia Manning," announced Trenholme promptly.

"By appointment, sir?"

"No, but I have reason to believe that she would wish to see me."

"My orders are that nobody is to be admitted to the house without written instructions, sir."

"How can Miss Manning give written instructions unless she knows I am here?"

"Them's my orders," said Mrs. Bates firmly.

"But," he persisted, "it really amounts to this—that you decide whether or not Miss Manning wishes to receive me, or any other visitor."

Mrs. Bates found the point of view novel. Moreover, she liked this young man's smile. She hesitated, and temporized.

"If you don't mind waitin' a minute till I telephone——" she said.

"Certainly. Say that Mr. John Trenholme, who was sketching in the park this morning, asks the favor of a few words."

The guardian of the gate disappeared; soon she came out again, and unlocked the gate.

"Miss Manning is just leavin' the house," she said. "If you walk up the avenue you'll meet her, sir."

Now, it happened that Trenholme's request for an interview reached Sylvia Manning at a peculiar moment. She had been shocked and distressed beyond measure by the morning's tragedy. Mortimer Fenley was one of those men whom riches render morose, but his manner had always been kind to his ward. A pleasant fiction enabled the girl to regard Mr. and Mrs. Fenley as her "uncle" and "aunt," and the tacit relationship thus established served to place the financier and his "niece" on a footing of affectionate intimacy. Of late, however, Sylvia had been aware of a splitting up of the family into armed camps, and the discovery, or intuition, that she was the cause of the rupture had proved irksome and even annoying.

Mortimer Fenley had made no secret of his desire that she should marry his younger son. When both young people, excellent friends though they were, seemed to shirk the suggestion, though by no means actively opposing it, Fenley was angered, and did not scruple to throw out hints of coercion. Again, the girl knew that Hilton Fenley was a rival suitor, and meant to defy his father's intent with regard to Robert. Oddly enough, neither of the young men had indulged in overt love-making. According to their reckoning, Sylvia's personal choice counted for little in the matter. Robert seemed to assume that his "cousin" was merely waiting to be asked, while Hilton's attitude was that of a man biding his time to snatch a prize when opportunity served.

Sylvia herself hated the very thought of matrimony. The only married couples of her acquaintance were either hopelessly detached, like Fenley and his wife, or uninteresting people of the type which the village barber had etched so clearly for Trenholme's benefit. Whatsoever quickening of romance might have crept into such lives had long yielded to atrophy. Marriage, to the girl's imaginative mind, was synonymous with a dull and prosy middle age. Most certainly the vague day-dreams evoked by her reading of books and converted into alluring vistas by an ever-widening horizon were not sated by the prospect of becoming the wife of either of the only two young men she knew.

There was a big world beyond the confines of Roxton Park. There were interests in life that called with increasing insistence. In her heart of hearts she had decided, quite unmistakably, to decline any matrimonial project for several years, and while shrinking from a downright avowal of her intentions, which her "uncle" would have resented very strongly, the fact that father and sons were at daggers drawn concerning her was the cause of no slight feeling of dismay, even of occasional moments of unhappiness.

She had no one to confide in. For reasons beyond her ken Mortimer Fenley had set his face against any of her school friends being invited to the house, while Mrs. Fenley, by reason of an unfortunate failing, was a wretched automaton that ate and drank and slept, and alternated between brief fits of delirium and prolonged periods of stupor induced by drugs.

Still, until a murderous gunshot had torn away the veil of unreality which enshrouded the household, Sylvia had contrived to avoid a crisis. All day, during six days of the week, she was free in her own realm. She had books and music, the woods, the park, and the gardens to occupy busy hours. Unknown to any, her favorite amusement was the planning of extensive foreign tours by such simple means as an atlas and a set of guide books. She had a talent for sketching in water color, and her own sanctum contained a dozen or more copious records of imaginary journeys illustrated with singular accuracy of detail.

She was athletic in her tastes, too. She had fitted up a small gymnasium, which she used daily. At her request, Mortimer Fenley had laid out a nine-hole links in the park, and in her second golfing year (the current one) Sylvia had gone around in bogey. She would have excelled in tennis, but

Robert Fenley was so much away from home that she seldom got a game, while Hilton professed to be too tired for strenuous exercise after long days in the City. She could ride and drive, though forbidden to follow any of the local packs of fox-hounds, and it has been seen that she was a first-rate swimmer. Brodie, too, had taught her to drive a motor car, and she could discourse learnedly on silencers and the Otto cycle.

On the whole, then, she was content, and hugged the conceit that when she came of age she would be her own mistress and order her life as she chose. The solitary defect of any real importance in the scheme of things was Mortimer Fenley's growing insistence on her marriage to Robert.

It was astounding, therefore, and quite bewildering, that Robert Fenley should have hit on the day of his father's death to declare his prosaic passion. He had motored back from London about four o'clock. Hurrying to change his clothing for the attire demanded by convention in hours of mourning, he sent a message to Sylvia asking her to meet him at tea. Afterwards he took her into the garden, on the pretext that she was looking pale and needed fresh air. There, without the least preamble, he informed her that the day's occurrences had caused him to fall in unreservedly with his father's wishes. He urged her to agree to a quiet wedding at the earliest possible date, and pointed out that a prompt announcement of their pact would stifle any opposition on Hilton's part.

Evidently he took it for granted that if Barkis was willing, Peggotty had no option in the matter. He forgot to mention such a trivial element as love. Their marriage had been planned by the arbiter of their destinies, and who were they that they should gainsay that august decision? Why, his father's death had made it a duty that they owed to a sacred memory!

Though Sylvia's experience of the world was slight, and knowledge of her fellow creatures rather less, Cousin Robert's eagerness, as compared with his deficiencies as a wooer, warned her that some hidden but powerful motive was egging him on now. She tried to temporize, but the more she eluded him the more insistent he became.

At last, she spoke plainly, and with some heat.

"If you press for my answer today it is 'No,'" she said, and a wave of color flooded her pale cheeks. "I think you can hardly have considered your actions. It is monstrous to talk of marriage when my uncle has only been dead a few hours. I refuse to listen to another word."

Perforce, Robert had left it at that. He had the sense to bottle up his anger, at any rate in her hearing; perhaps he reflected that the breaking of the ice would facilitate the subsequent plunge.

Far more disturbed in spirit than her dignified repulse of Fenley had shown, Sylvia reëntered the house, passing the odd-looking little detective as she crossed the hall. She took refuge in her own suite, but determined forthwith to go out of doors again and seek shelter among her beloved trees. Through a window, as her rooms faced south, she saw Robert Fenley pacing moodily in the garden, where he was presently joined by the detective.

Apparently, Fenley was as ungracious and surly of manner as he knew how to be, but Furneaux continued to chat with careless affability; soon the two walked off in the direction of the lake. That was Sylvia's chance. She ran downstairs and was at the door when a footman came and said that Mrs. Bates wanted her on the telephone.

At first she was astounded by Trenholme's message. Then sheer irritation at the crassness of things, and perhaps some spice of feminine curiosity, led her to give the order which opened the gates of Roxton Park to a man she had never seen.

The two met a few hundred yards down the avenue. Police Constable Farrow, who had been replaced by another constable while he went home for a meal, was on guard in the Quarry Wood again until the night men came on duty, and noticed Miss Manning leaving the house. He descended from his rock and strolled toward the avenue, with no other motive than a desire to stretch his legs; his perplexity was unbounded when he discovered Mortimer Fenley's ward deep in conversation with the artist.

"Well, I'm jiggered!" he said, dodging behind a giant rhododendron. Whipping out a notebook and consulting his watch, he solemnly noted time and names in a laboriously accurate round hand. Then he nibbled his chin strap and dug both thumbs into his belt. His luck was in that day. He knew something now that was withheld from the Scotland Yard swells. Sylvia Manning and John Trenholme were acquaintances. Nay, more; they must be old friends; under his very eyes they went off together into the park.

Back to his rock went Police Constable Farrow, puzzled but elated. Was he not a repository of secrets? And that funny little detective had betaken himself in the opposite direction! Fate was kind indeed.

He would have been still more surprised had Fate permitted him to be also an eavesdropper, if listeners ever do drop from eaves.

Sylvia was by no means flurried when she came face to face with Trenholme. The female of the species invariably shows her superiority on such occasions. Trenholme knew he was blushing and rather breathless. Sylvia was cool and distant.

"You are Mr. Trenholme, I suppose?" she said, her blue eyes meeting his brown ones in calm scrutiny.

"Yes," he said, trying desperately to collect his wits. The well-balanced phrases conned while walking up the avenue had vanished in a hopeless blur at the instant they were needed. His mind was in a whirl.

"I am Miss Manning," she continued. "It is hardly possible to receive visitors at the house this afternoon, and as I happened to be coming out when Mrs. Bates telephoned from the lodge, I thought you would have no objection to telling me here why you wish to see me."

"I have come to apologize for my action this morning," he said.

"What action?"

"I sketched you without your knowledge, and, of course, without your permission."

"You sketched me? Where?"

"When you were swimming in the lake."

"You didn't dare!"

"I did. I'm sorry now, though you inspired the best picture I have ever painted, or shall ever paint."

For an instant Sylvia forgot her personal troubles in sheer wonderment, and a ghost of a smile brightened her white cheeks. John Trenholme was a person who inspired confidence at sight, and her first definite emotion was one of surprise that he should look so disconsolate.

"I really don't understand," she said. "The quality of your picture has no special interest for me. What I fail to grasp is your motive in trespassing in a private park and watching me, or any lady, bathing."

"Put that way, my conduct needs correcting with a horsewhip; but happily there are other points of view. That is—I mean——Really, Miss Manning, I am absurdly tongue-tied, but I do beg of you to hear my explanation."

"Have you one?"

"Yes. It might convince any one but you. You will be a severe judge, and I hardly know how to find words to seek your forgiveness, but I—I was the victim of circumstances."

"Please don't regard me as a judge. At present, I am trying to guess what happened."

Then John squared his shoulders and tackled the greatest difficulty he had grappled with for years.

"The simple truth should at least sound convincing," he said. "I came to Roxton three days ago on a commission to sketch the village and its environment. This house and grounds are historical, and I applied for permission to visit them, but was refused. By chance, I heard of a public footpath which crosses the park close to the lake——"

Sylvia nodded. She, too, had heard much of that footpath. Its existence had annoyed Mortimer Fenley as long as she could remember anything. That friendly little nod encouraged Trenholme. His voice came under better control, and he contrived to smile.

"I was told it was a bone of contention," he said, "but that didn't trouble me a bit, since the right of way opened the forbidden area. I meant no disturbance or intrusion. I rose early this morning, and would have made my sketches and got away without seeing you if it were not for a delightful pair of wrought iron gates passed *en route*. They detained me three quarters of an hour. Instead of reaching the clump of cedars at a quarter to seven or thereabouts, I arrived at half past seven.

"I sketched the house and lawns and then turned to the lake. When you appeared I imagined at first you were coming to pitch into me for entering your domain. But, as I was partly hidden by some briers beneath the cedars, you never saw me, and, before I realized what was taking place, you threw off your wraps and were in the water."

"Oh!" gasped Sylvia.

"Now, I ask you to regard the situation impersonally," said Trenholme, sinking his eyes humbly to the ground and keeping them there. "I had either to reveal my presence and startle you greatly, or remain where I was and wait until you went off again.

"Whether it was wise or not, I elected for the easier course. I think I would act similarly if placed in the like predicament tomorrow or next day. After all, there is nothing so very remarkable in a lady taking a morning swim that an involuntary onlooker should be shocked or scandalized by it. You and I were strangers to each other. Were we friends, we might have been swimming in company."

Sylvia uttered some incoherent sound, but Trenholme, once launched in his recital, meant to persevere with it to the bitter end.

"I still hold that I chose the more judicious way out of a difficult situation," he said. "Had I left it at that, all would have been well. But the woman tempted me, and I did eat."

"Indeed, the woman did nothing of the sort," came the vehement protest.

"I speak in the artistic sense. You can not imagine, you will never know, what an exquisite picture you and the statue of Aphrodite made when mirrored in that shining water. I forgot every consideration but the call of art, which, when it is genuine, is irresistible, overwhelming. Fearing only that you might take one plunge and go, I grabbed my palette and a canvas and began to work.

"I used pure color, and painted as one reads of the fierce labor of genius. For once in my life I was inspired. I had caught an effect which I might have sought in vain during the remainder of my life. I painted real flesh, real water. Even the reeds and shrubs by the side of the lake were veritable glimpses of actuality. Then, when I had given some species of immortality to a fleeting moment, you returned to the house, and I was left alone with a dream made permanent, a memory transfixed on canvas, a picture which would have created a sensation in the Salon——"

"Oh, surely, you would not exhibit me—it——" breathed the girl.

"No," he said grimly. "That conceit is dead and buried. But I want you to realize that during those few minutes I was not John Trenholme, an artist struggling for foothold on the steep crags of the painter's rock of endeavor, but a master of the craft gazing from some high pinnacle at a territory he had won. If you know anything of painting, Miss Manning, you will go with me so far as to admit that my indiscretion was impersonal. I, a poet who expressed his emotions in terms of color, was alone with Aphrodite and a nymph, on a June morning, in a leafy English park. I don't think I should be blamed, but envied. I should not be confessing a fault, but claiming recognition as one favored of the gods."

Trenholme was speaking in earnest now, and Sylvia thrilled to the music of his voice. But if her heart throbbed and a strange fluttering made itself felt in her heart, her utterance, by force of repression, was so cold and unmoved that Trenholme became more downcast than ever.

"I do paint a little," she said, "and I can understand that the—er—statue and the lake offer a charming subject; but I am still at a loss to know why you have thought fit to come here and tell me these things."

"It is my wretched task to make that clear, at least," he cried contritely, forcing himself to turn and look through the trees at a landscape now glowing in the mellow light of a declining sun. "When you had gone I sat there, working hard for a time, but finally yielding to the spell of an unexpected and, therefore, a most delightful romance. A vision of rare beauty had come into my life and gone from it, all in the course of a magic hour. Is it strange that I should linger in the shrine?

"I was aroused by a gunshot, but little dreamed that grim Death was stalking through Fairyland. Still, I came to my everyday senses, packed up my sketches and color box, and tramped off to Roxton, singing as I went. Hours afterward, I learned of the tragedy which had taken place so near the place where I had snatched a glimpse of the Hesperides. It was known that I had been in the park at the time. I had met and spoken to Bates, your head keeper, and the local policeman, Farrow.

"A detective came, a man named Furneaux; a jolly clever chap, too, but a most disturbing reasoner. He showed me that my drawings—the one sketch, at any rate, which I held sacred—would prove my sheet anchor when I was brought into the stormy waters of inquest and law courts. It is obvious that every person who was in that locality at half past nine this morning must explain his or her presence beyond all doubt or questioning. I shall be obliged to say, of course, that I was in the park fully two hours, from seven thirty A. M. onward. What was I doing? Painting. Very well; where is the result? Is it such that any artist will testify that I was busily engaged? Don't you see, Miss Manning? I must either produce that sketch or stand convicted of the mean offense you yourself imputed to me instantly when you heard of my whereabouts."

"Oh, I didn't really imply that," said Sylvia, and a new note of sympathy crept into her voice. "It would be horrid if—if you couldn't explain; and—it seems to me that the sketches—you made more than one, didn't you?—should be shown to the authorities."

Trenholme's face lit with gratitude because of her ready tact. He was sorely impelled to leave matters on their present footing, but whipped himself to the final stage.

"There is worse to come," he said miserably.

"Goodness me! What else *can* there be?"

"Mr Furneaux has asked me—ordered me, in fact—to meet you by the side of the lake tomorrow morning at a quarter past nine and bring the drawings. Now you know why I have ventured to call this afternoon. I simply could not wait till I was brought before you like a collared thief with the loot in his possession. I *had* to meet you without the intervention of a grinning policeman. When you heard my plea I thought, I hoped, that you might incline to a less severe view than would be possible if the matter came to your notice without warning."

He stopped abruptly. A curiously introspective look had come into the girl's eyes, for he had summoned up courage to glance at her again, and snatch one last impression of her winsome loveliness before she bade him be gone.

"Where are you staying in Roxton, Mr. Trenholme?" she asked. The unexpected nature of the question almost took his breath away.

"At the White Horse Inn," he said.

She pointed across the park.

"That farm there, Mr. Jackson's, lies nearly opposite the inn. I suppose the detective has not impounded your sketch?"

"No," he murmured, quite at a loss to follow her intent.

"Well, Mr. Jackson will let you go and come through his farmyard to oblige me. It will be a short cut for you, too. If you have no objection, I'll walk with you to the boundary wall, which you can climb easily.

"Then you might bring this debatable picture, and let me see it—the others as well, if you wish. Wouldn't that be a good idea? I mightn't get quite such a shock in the morning, when the detective man parades you before me. It is not very late. I have plenty of time to stroll that far before dinner."

Hardly believing his ears, Trenholme walked off by her side. No wonder Police Constable Farrow was surprised. And still less room was there for wonder that Hilton Fenley, driving with Winter from the station, should shout an imperative order to Brodie to stop the car when he saw the couple in the distance.

"Isn't that Miss Sylvia?" he said harshly, well knowing there could be only one answer.

"Yes, sir," said the chauffeur.

"Who is the man with her?"

"Mr. Trenholme, the artist, from the White Horse, sir."

"Are you sure?"

"Yes, sir. I've seen him several times hereabouts."

Fenley was in a rare temper already, for Winter had told him Brother Robert was at home, a development on which he had by no means counted. Now his sallow face darkened with anger.

"Drive on!" he said. "I gave orders, at your request, Mr Winter, that no strangers were to be admitted. I must see to it that I am obeyed in future. It is surprising, too, that the police are so remiss in such an important matter."

For once, Winter was perforce silent. In his heart of hearts he blamed Detective Inspector Furneaux.

CHAPTER X
FURNEAUX STATES SOME FACTS AND CERTAIN FANCIES

This record of a day remarkable beyond any other in the history of secluded Roxton might strike a more cheerful note if it followed the two young people across the park. It is doubtful whether or not Sylvia Manning's unpremeditated action in accompanying Trenholme was inspired by a sudden interest in art or by revolt against the tribulations which had befallen her. Of course there is some probability that a full and true account of the conversation between man and maid as they walked the half mile to Jackson's farm might throw a flood of light on this minor problem. Be that as it may, stern necessity demands that the chronicle should revert for a time to the sayings and doings of the Fenleys and the detectives.

Despite a roundabout route, Furneaux had merely led Robert Fenley through the gardens to the Quarry Wood. Somewhat to the detective's surprise, the rock was unguarded. The two were standing there, discussing the crime, when Police Constable Farrow returned to his post. Furneaux said nothing—for some reason he did not emphasize the fact to his companion that a sentry should have been found stationed there—but a sharp glance at the policeman warned the latter that he ran considerable risk of a subsequent reprimand.

Conscious of rectitude, Farrow saluted, and produced his notebook.

"I've just made a memo of this, sir," he said, pointing to an entry.

Furneaux read:

Miss Sylvia Manning left home 6.45 P. M. Met Mr. John Trenholme, artist, White Horse Inn, in avenue 6.47 P. M. The two held close conversation, and went off together across park in direction of Roxton 6.54 P. M. Lady wore no hat. Regarded incident as unusual, so observed exact times.

"I note what the Inspector says, and will discuss the point later," said Furneaux, returning the book. The policeman grinned. As between Scotland Yard and himself a complete understanding was established.

"Have the local police discovered anything of importance?" inquired Fenley, who, now that his own affairs called for no immediate attention, seemed to give more heed to the manner of his father's death. At first, his manner to Furneaux had been churlish in the extreme. Evidently he thought he could treat the representative of the Criminal Investigation Department just as he pleased. At this moment he elected to be gruffly civil in tone.

"They are making full inquiries, of course," replied the detective, "but I think the investigation will be conducted in the main by my Department——As I was saying, Mr. Fenley, undoubtedly the shot was fired from this locality. Dr. Stern, who is an authority on bullet wounds, is convinced of that, even if there was no other evidence, such as the chauffeur's and the artist's I told you of, together with the impressions formed by Bates and others."

"Were there no footprints?" was the next question, and Fenley eyed the ground critically. He deemed those Scotland Yard Johnnies thickheaded chaps, at the best.

"None of any value. Since ten o'clock, however, dozens of new ones have been made. That is why the policeman is keeping an eye on the place—chiefly to warn off intruders. Shall we return to the house?"

"It's a strange business," said Fenley, striding down the slope by Furneaux's side. "Why in the world should any one want to shoot my poor old guv'nor? He was straight as a die, and I don't know a soul who had any real grievance against him."

Furneaux did not appear to be listening. The two were approaching the patch of moist earth which bore the impress of Robert Fenley's boots. "By the way," he said suddenly, "are you aware that there is a sort of a theory that your father was shot by a rifle belonging to you?"

"What?" roared the other, and it was hard to say whether rage or astonishment predominated in his voice. "Is that one of Hilton's dodges to get me into trouble?"

"But you do own an Express rifle, which you keep in your sitting-room. Where is it now?"

"In the place where it always is. Standing in a corner behind the bookcase."

"When did you see it last, Mr. Fenley?"

"How the deuce do I know? I give it a run through with an oiled rag about once a month. It must be nearly a month since I cleaned it."

"It has gone."

"Gone where?"

"I wish I knew."

"But who the devil could have taken it?"

If ever a man was floundering in a morass of wrath and amazement it was this loud-voiced youngster. He was a slow-witted lout, but the veriest dullard must have perceived that the disappearance of the weapon which presumably killed his father was a serious matter for its owner.

In order to grasp this new phase of the tragedy in its proper bearings he stood stock still, and gazed blankly into the serious face of the detective. Furneaux knew he would do that. It was a mannerism. Some men can not think and move at the same moment, and Robert Fenley was one.

Naturally, young Fenley did not know that he was leaving a new set of footprints by the side of the others already attributed to him. Having done that, he was no longer wanted.

"We'll solve every part of the puzzle in time," said Furneaux slowly, moistening his thin lips with his tongue as if he were about to taste another glass of rare old-vintage wine.

"I mentioned the fact of the gun being missing to show you how unwise you were this morning. You shouldn't have bolted off as you did when Mr. Winter requested you to remain. I haven't the least doubt, Mr. Fenley, that you can prove you were in London at the time the murder was committed, and during some days prior to it, but the police like these matters to be cleared up; if I may give you a hint, you'll tell the Superintendent that you regret your behavior, and show you mean what you say by giving him all the information he asks for. Here he is now. I hear Mr. Hilton's car, and Mr. Winter is coming with him from town."

"Mr. Hilton's car? It's no more his car than mine. You mark my words, there will be trouble in the family if my brother starts bossing things. He hates me, and would do me an ill turn if he could. Was it Hilton who spread this story about my gun?"

"No. Rather the reverse. He kept your name studiously out of it."

"Who was it, then? I have a right to know."

"I fail to recollect just how the matter cropped up. It was the direct outcome of the common observation of several persons who heard the report, and who were able to discriminate between one class of gun and another. Anyhow, there is no occasion for you to squeal before you are hurt. You acted like a fool this morning. Try and behave yourself more reputably now."

The prophet Balaam was not more taken aback when rebuked by his ass than Robert Fenley when Furneaux turned and rent him in this fashion.

Hitherto the detective's manner had been mildness itself, so this change of front was all the more staggering.

"Oh, I say!" came the blustering protest. "I don't allow any of you fellows to talk to me like that. I——"

"You'll hear worse in another second if you really annoy me," said Furneaux. "Heretofore no one seems to have troubled to inform you what a special sort of idiot you are. Though your last words to your father were a threat that you were inclined to shoot him and your precious self, when you saw him lying dead you thought of nothing but your own wretched follies, and bolted off to Hendon Road, Battersea, instead of remaining here and trying to help the police.

"When I tell you your gun is missing you yelp about your brother's animosity. Before your father is laid in his grave you threaten to upset the household because your brother acts as its master. Why shouldn't he? Are you fitted to take the reins or share his responsibility? If you were at your right job, Robert Fenley, you'd be carrying bricks and mortar in a hod; for you haven't brains enough to lay a brick or use a trowel."

The victim of this outburst thought that the little detective had gone mad, though the reference to Hendon Road had startled him, and a scared expression had come into his eyes.

"Look here——" he began, but Furneaux checked him again instantly.

"I've looked at you long enough to sum you up as a sulky puppy," he said. "If you had any sort of gumption you would realize that you occupy a singularly precarious position. Were it not for the lucky accident that my colleague and I were on the spot this morning it is more than likely that the county police would have arrested you at sight. Don't give us any more trouble, or you'll be left to stew in your own juice. I have warned you, once and for all. If you care to swallow your spleen and amend your manners, I shall try to believe you are more idiot than knave. At present I am doubtful which way the balance tips."

Furneaux stalked off rapidly, leaving the other to fume with indignation as he followed. With his almost uncanny gift of imaginative reasoning, the Jersey man had guessed the purport of Fenley's talk with Sylvia in the garden. He had watched the two from a window of the dining-room, and had read correctly the girl's ill-concealed scorn, not quite devoid of dread, as revealed by face and gesture. To make sure, he waylaid her in the hall while she was hurrying to her own apartments. Then he sauntered after Robert Fenley, and only bided his time to empty upon him the vials of his wrath.

He had taken the oaf's measure with a nice exactitude. To trounce him without frightening him also was only inviting a complaint to the Commissioner, but Furneaux was well aware that the longer Robert Fenley's dull brain dwelt on the significance of that address in Battersea being known to the police, the less ready would he be to stir a hornets' nest into activity by showing his resentment. Obviously, Furneaux's methods were not those advocated in the Police Manual. Any other man who practiced them would risk dismissal, but the "Little 'Un" of the Yard was a law unto himself.

Meanwhile, he was hurrying after the "Big 'Un," (such, it will be recalled, were the respective nicknames Furneaux and Winter had received in the Department) who had alighted from the car, and was listening to Hilton Fenley berating a servant for having permitted Trenholme to make known his presence to Miss Manning. The man, however, protested that he had done nothing of the sort. Miss Sylvia had been called to the lodge telephone, and the footman's acquaintance with the facts went no farther. Smothering his annoyance as best he could, Fenley rang up Mrs. Bates and asked for particulars. When the woman explained what had happened, he rejoined Winter in the hall, paying no heed to Furneaux, who was entering at the moment.

"That artist fellow who was trespassing in the park this morning—if nothing worse is proved against him—must have a superb cheek," he said angrily. "He actually had the impertinence to ask Miss Manning to meet him, no doubt offering some plausible yarn as an excuse. I hope you'll test his story thoroughly, Mr. Winter. At the least, he should be forced to say what he was doing in these grounds at such an unusual hour."

"He is putting himself right with Miss Manning now," broke in Furneaux.

"Putting himself right with Miss Manning? What the deuce do you mean, sir?" Fenley could snarl effectively when in the mood, and none might deny his present state of irritation, be the cause what it might.

"That young lady is the only person to whom he owes an explanation. He is giving it to her now."

"Will you kindly be more explicit?"

Furneaux glanced from his infuriated questioner to Winter, his face one note of mild interrogation and non-comprehension.

"Really, Mr. Fenley, I have said the same thing in two different ways," he cried. "As a rule I contrive to be tolerably lucid in my remarks—don't I, Mr. Robert?" for the younger Fenley had just come in.

"What's up now?" was Robert's non-committal answer.

For some reason his brother did not reply, but Furneaux suddenly grew voluble.

"Of course, you haven't heard that an artist named Trenholme was painting near the lake this morning when your father was killed," he said. "Fortunately, he was there before and after the shot was fired. He can prove, almost to a yard, the locality where the murderer was concealed. In fact, he is coming here tomorrow, at my request, to go over the ground with me.

"An interesting feature of the affair is that Mr. Trenholme is a genius. I have never seen better work. One of his drawings, a water color, has all the brilliancy and light of a David Cox, but another, in oil, is a positive masterpiece. It must have been done in a few minutes, because Miss Manning did not know he was sitting beneath the cedars, and it is unreasonable to suppose that she would preserve the same pose for any length of time—sufficiently long, that is——"

"Did the bounder paint a picture of Sylvia bathing?" broke in Robert, his red face purple with rage.

"Allow me to remind you that you are speaking of a painter of transcendent merit," said Furneaux suavely.

"When *I* meet him I'll give him a damned good hiding."

"He's rather tall and strongly built."

"I don't care how big he is, I'll down him."

"Oh, stop this pothouse talk," put in Hilton, giving the blusterer a contemptuous glance. "Mr. Furneaux, you seem primed with information. Why should Mr. Trenholme, if that is his name, have the audacity to call on Miss Manning? He might have the impudence to skulk among the shrubs and watch a lady bathing, but I fail to see any motive for his visit to The Towers this evening."

Furneaux shook his head. Evidently the point did not appeal to him.

"There is no set formula that expresses the artistic temperament," he said. "The man who passes whole years in studying the nude is often endowed with a very high moral sense. Mr. Trenholme, though carried away by enthusiasm this morning, may be consumed with remorse tonight if he imagines that the lady who formed the subject of his sketch is likely to be distressed because of it.

"I fear I am to blame. I stopped Mr. Trenholme from destroying the picture today. He meant burning it, since he had the sense to realize that he would be summoned as a witness, not only at tomorrow's inquest, but when the affair comes before the courts. I was bound to point out that the drawings supplied his solitary excuse for being in the locality at all. He saw that—unwillingly, it is true, but with painful clearness—so I assume that his visit to Miss Manning was expiatory, a sort of humble obeisance to a goddess whom he had offended unwittingly. I assume, too, that his plea for mercy has not proved wholly unsuccessful or Miss Manning would not now be walking with him across the park."

"What!" roared Robert. He turned to the gaping footman, for the whole conversation had taken place in the hall. "Which way did Miss Sylvia go?" he cried.

"Down the avenue, sir," said the man. "I saw Miss Sylvia meet the gentleman, and after some talk they went through the trees to the right."

Robert raced off. Winter, who had not interfered hitherto, because Furneaux always had a valid excuse for his indiscretions, made as if he would follow and restrain the younger Fenley; but Furneaux caught his eye and winked. That sufficed. The Superintendent contented himself with gazing after Robert Fenley, who ran along the avenue until clear of the Quarry Wood, when he, too, plunged through the line of elms and was lost to sight.

Hilton watched his impetuous brother with a brooding underlook. He still held in his hand a leather portfolio bulging with papers, some of which he had placed there when Winter opened the door of the railway coach in St. Pancras station. The footman offered to relieve him of it, but was swept aside with a gesture.

"I have never known Robert so excited and erratic in his movements as he has been today," he said at last. "I hope he will not engage in a vulgar quarrel with this Mr. Trenholme, especially in Miss Manning's presence."

Apparently he could not quite control his voice, in which a sense of unctuous amusement revealed itself. Furneaux could not resist such an opportunity. He had pierced Robert's thick skin; now he undertook a more delicate operation.

"That would be doubly unfortunate," he said, chuckling quietly. "If I am any judge of men, Mr. Robert Fenley would meet more than his match in our artist friend, while he would certainly undo all the good effect of an earlier and most serious and convincing conversation with the young lady."

Hilton swung around on him.

"When did my brother return from London?" he asked.

"Shortly before five o'clock. He and Miss Manning had tea together, and afterward strolled in the gardens. I don't wonder at any artist wishing to sketch Miss Manning? Do you? If I may be allowed to say it, I have never seen a more graceful and charming girl."

"May I inquire if you have made any progress in the particular inquiry for which I brought you here?"

Hilton Fenley spoke savagely. He meant to be offensive, since the innuendo was unmistakable. Apparently Furneaux's remarks had achieved some hypodermic effect.

"Oh, yes," was the offhand answer. "I have every reason to believe that Mr. Winter and I will make an arrest without undue loss of time."

"I am glad to hear it. Thus far your methods have not inspired the confidence I, as a member of the public, was inclined to repose in Scotland Yard. I am going to my rooms now, and dine at a quarter to eight. About nine o'clock I wish to go into matters thoroughly with Mr. Winter and you. At present, I think it only fair to say that I am not satisfied with the measures, whatever they may be, you have seen fit to adopt."

He seemed to await a retort, but none came, so he strode across the hall and hurried up the stairs. Furneaux continued to gaze blankly down the long, straight avenue, nor did he utter a word till a door opened and closed on the first floor in the southeast corner.

Then he spoke.

"Some people are very hard to please," he said plaintively.

Winter beckoned to the footman.

"Do you mind asking Mr. Tomlinson if he can come here for a moment?" he said. When the man disappeared he muttered—

"Why are you stroking everybody's fur the wrong way, Charles?"

"A useful simile, James. If they resemble cats we may see sparks, and each of those young men has something of the tiger in him."

"But things have gone horribly wrong all day—after a highly promising start, too. I don't see that we are any nearer laying hands on a murderer because we have unearthed various little scandals in the lives of Mortimer Fenley's sons. And what game are you playing with this artist, Trenholme?"

"The supremely interesting problem just now is the game which he is playing with Robert Fenley. If that young ass attacks him he'll get the licking he wants, and if you're in any doubt about my pronouns———"

"Oh, dash you and your pronouns! Here's Tomlinson. Quick! Have you a plan of any sort?"

"Three! Three separate lines of attack, each deadly. But there are folk whose mental equipment renders them incapable of understanding plain English. Now, my friend Tomlinson will show you what I mean. I'll ask him a simple question, and he will give you a perfect example of a direct answer. Tomlinson, can you tell me what the extrados of a voussoir is?"

"No, Mr. Furneaux, I can not," said the butler, smiling at what he regarded as the little man's humor.

"There!" cried Furneaux delightedly. "Ain't I a prophet? No evasions about Tomlinson, are there?"

"I think you're cracked," growled Winter, picking up his suitcase. "If I'm to stay here tonight, I shall want a room of some sort. Mr. Tomlinson, can you——"

"Share mine," broke in Furneaux. "I'm the quietest sleeper living. Our friend here is sure to have at disposal a room with two beds in it."

"The principal guest room is unoccupied," said the butler.

"Where is it?"

"On the first floor, sir, facing south."

"Couldn't be better. The very thing. Ah! Here comes my baggage." And the others saw a policeman bicycling up the avenue, with a small portmanteau balanced precariously between the handlebars and the front buttons of his tunic.

"You gentlemen will dine in my room, I hope?" said Tomlinson, when he had escorted them upstairs.

"We are not invited to the family circle, at any rate," said Winter.

"Well, you will not suffer on that account," announced Tomlinson genially. "Of course, I shall not have the pleasure of sharing the meal with you, but dinner will be served at a quarter to eight. Mr. Furneaux knows his way about the house, so, with your permission, I'll leave you at present. If you're disengaged at nine thirty I'll be glad to see you in my sanctum."

"Isn't he a gem?" cried Furneaux, when the door had closed, and he and Winter were alone.

Winter sat down on the side of a bed. He was worried, and did not strive to hide it. For the first time in his life he felt distrustful of himself, and he suspected, too, that Furneaux was only covering abject failure by a display of high spirits.

"Why so pensive an attitude, James?" inquired the other softly. "Are you still wondering what the extrados of a voussoir is?"

"I don't care a tuppenny damn what it is."

"But that's where you're wrong. That's where you're crass and pig-headed. The extrados of a voussoir——"

"Oh, kill it, and let it die happy——"

"——is the outer curve of a wedge-shaped stone used for building an arch. Now, mark you, those are words of merit. Wedge, arch—wedges of fact which shall construct the arch of evidence. We'll have our man in the dock across that bridge before we are much older."

"Confound it, how? He couldn't be in his bedroom and in the Quarry Wood, four hundred yards away, at one and the same moment."

Furneaux gazed fixedly at his friend's forehead, presumably the seat of reason.

"Sometimes, James, you make me gasp with an amazed admiration," he cooed. "You do, really. You arrive at the same conclusion as I, a thinker, without any semblance of thought process on your part. How do you manage it! Is it through association with me? You know, there's such a thing as inductive electricity. A current passing through a highly charged wire can excite another wire, even a common iron one, without actual contact."

"I've had a rotten afternoon, and don't feel up to your far-fetched jokes just now; so if you have nothing to report, shut up," said the Superintendent crossly.

"Then I'll cheer your melancholy with a bit of real news brightened by imagination," answered Furneaux promptly. "Hilton Fenley couldn't have fired the rifle himself, except by certain bizarre means which I shall lay before the court later; but he planned and contrived the murder, down to the smallest detail. He wore Brother Robert's boots when available; from appearances Brother Robert is now wearing the identical pair which made those footprints we saw, but I shall know in the morning, for that fiery young sprig obligingly left another well-marked set of prints in the same place twenty minutes ago. When circumstances compelled Hilton to walk that way in his own boots, he slipped on two roughly made moccasins, which he burned last night, having no further use for them. Therefore, he knew the murder would take place this morning.

"I've secured shreds of the sacking out of which he made the pads to cover his feet; and an under gardener remembers seeing Mr. Hilton making off with an empty potato sack one day last week, and wondering why he wanted it. During some mornings recently Hilton Fenley breakfasted early and went out, but invariably had an excuse for not accompanying his father to the City. He was then studying the details of the crime, making sure that an expert, armed with a modern rifle, could not possibly miss such a target as a man standing outside a doorway, and elevated above the ground level by some five feet or more.

"No servant could possibly observe that Mr. Hilton was wearing Mr. Robert's boots, because they do not differ greatly in size; but luckily for us, a criminal always commits an error of some sort, and Hilton blundered badly when he made those careful imprints of his brother's feet, as the weather has been fine recently, and the only mud in this locality lies in that hollow of the Quarry Wood. It happens that some particles of that identical mud were imbedded in the carpet of Hilton Fenley's sitting-room. I'm sorry to have to say it, because the housemaid is a nice girl."

"Never mind the housemaid. Go on."

"Exactly what the housemaid would remark if she heard me; only she would giggle, and you look infernally serious. Next item: Hilton Fenley, like most high-class scoundrels, has the nerves of a cat, with all a cat's fiendish brutality. He could plan and carry out a callous crime and lay a subtle trail which must lead to that cry baby, Robert, but he was unable to control his emotions when he saw his father's corpse. That is where the murderer nearly always fails. He can never picture in death that which he hated and doomed in life. There is an element in death——"

"Chuck it!" said Winter unfeelingly.

Furneaux winced, and affected to be deeply hurt.

"The worst feature of service in Scotland Yard is its demoralizing effect on the finer sentiments," he said sadly. "Men lose all human instincts when they become detectives or newspaper reporters. Now the ordinary policeman ofttimes remains quite soft-hearted. For instance, Police Constable Farrow, though preening himself on being the pivot on which this case revolves, was much affected by Hilton Fenley's first heart-broken words to him. 'Poor young gentleman,' said Farrow, when we were discussing the affair this afternoon, 'he was cut up somethink orful. I didn't think he had it in him, s'elp me, I didn't. Tole me to act for the best. Said some one had fired a bullet which nearly tore his father to pieces.'

"There was more of the same sort of thing, and I got Farrow to jot down the very words in his notebook. Of course, he doesn't guess why.... Now, I wonder how Hilton Fenley knew the effect of that bullet on his father's body. The doctor had not arrived. There had been only a superficial examination by Tomlinson of the orifice of the wound. What other mind in Roxton would picture to itself the havoc caused by an expanding bullet? The man who uttered those words *knew* what sort of bullet had been used. He *knew* it would tear his father's body to pieces. A neurotic imagination was at work, and that cry of horror was the soul's unconscious protest against the very fiendishness of its own deed....

"Oh, yes. Let these Fenleys quarrel about that girl, and we'll see Hilton marching steadily toward the Old Bailey. Of course, we'll assist him. We'll make certain he doesn't deviate or falter on the road. But he'll follow it, and of his own accord; and the first long stride will be taken when he goes to the Quarry Wood to retrieve the rifle which lies hidden there."

Winter whistled softly. Then he looked at his watch.

"By Jove! Turned half past seven," he said.

"Ha!" cackled Furneaux. "James is himself again. We have hardly a scrap of evidence, but that doesn't trouble our worthy Superintendent a little bit, and he'll enjoy his dinner far better than he thought possible ten minutes ago. *Sacré nom d'une pipe!* By the time you've tasted a bottle from Tomlinson's favorite bin you'll be preparing a brief for the Treasury solicitor!"

CHAPTER XI
SOME PRELIMINARY SKIRMISHING

Now, perhaps, taking advantage of an interval while the representatives of Scotland Yard sought the aid of soap and water as a preliminary to a meal, it is permissible to wander in the gloaming with Sylvia Manning and her escort. To speak of the gloaming is a poetic license, it is true. Seven o'clock on a fine summer evening in England is still broad daylight, but daylight of a quality that lends itself admirably to the exigencies of romance. There is a species of dreaminess in the air. The landscape assumes soft tints unknown to a fiery sun. Tender shadows steal from undiscovered realms. It is permissible to believe that every night on Parnassus is a night in June.

At first these two young people were at a loss to know what to talk about. By tacit consent they ignored the morning's tragedy, yet they might not indulge in the irresponsible chatter which would have provided a ready resource under normal conditions. Luckily Trenholme remembered that the girl said she painted.

"It is a relief to find that you also are of the elect," he said. "An artist will look at my pictures with the artist's eye. There are other sorts of eyes—Eliza's, for instance. Do you know Eliza, of the White Horse?"

Sylvia collected her wits, which were wool-gathering.

"I think I have met her at village bazaars and tea fights," she said. "Is she a stout, red-faced woman?"

"Both, to excess; but her chief attribute is her tongue, which has solved the secret of perpetual motion. Had it kept silent even for a few seconds at lunch time today, that sharp-eyed and rabbit-eared detective would never have known of the second picture—your picture—because I can eke out my exhibits by a half finished sketch of the lake and a pencil note of the gates. But putting the bits of the puzzle together afterwards, I came to the conclusion that Mary, our kitchen maid, passed my room, saw the picture on the easel and was scandalized. She of course told Eliza, who went to be shocked on her own account, and then came downstairs and pitched into me. At that moment the Scotland Yard man turned up."

"Is it so very—dreadful, then?"

"Dreadful! It may fall far short of the standard set by my own vanity; but given any sort of skill in the painter, how can a charming study of a girl in a bathing costume, standing by the side of a statue of Aphrodite, be dreadful?

Of course, Miss Manning, you can hardly understand the way in which a certain section of the public regards art. In studio jargon we call it the 'Oh, ma!' crowd, that being the favorite exclamation of the young ladies who peep and condemn. These people are the hopeless Philistines who argue about the sex of angels, and demand that nude statues shall be draped. But my picture must speak for itself. Tell me something about your own work. Are you taking up painting seriously?"

Now, to be candid, Sylvia herself was not wholly emancipated from the state of Philistinism which Trenholme was railing at. Had he been less eager to secure a favorable verdict, or even less agitated by the unlooked-for condescension she was showing, he would have seen the absurdity of classing a girl of twenty with the lovers of art for art's sake, those earnest-eyed enthusiasts who regard a perfect curve or an inimitable flesh tint as of vastly greater importance than the squeamishness of the young person. Painters have their limitations as well as Mrs. Grundy, and John Trenholme did not suffer a fool gladly.

Sylvia, however, had the good sense to realize that she was listening to a man whose finer instincts had never been trammeled by conventions which might be wholesome in an academy for young ladies. Certainly she wondered what sort of figure she cut in this much debated picture, but that interesting point would be determined shortly. Meanwhile she answered demurely enough:

"I'm afraid you have taken me too seriously. I have hardly progressed beyond the stage where one discovers, with a sort of gasp, that trees may be blue or red, and skies green. Though I am going to look at your pictures, Mr. Trenholme, it by no means follows that I shall ever dare to show you any of mine."

"Still, I think you must have the artistic soul," he said thoughtfully.

"Why?"

"There was more than mere physical delight in your swimming this morning. You reveled in the sunlight, in the golden air, in the scents of trees and shrubs and flowering grass. First-rate swimmer as you are, you would not have enjoyed that dip half as much if it were taken in a covered bath, where your eyes dwelt only on white tiles and dressing-booths."

The girl, subtly aware of a new element in life, was alarmed by its piercing sweetness, and with ruthless logic brought their talk back to a commonplace level.

"Roxton seems to be a rather quaint place to find you in, Mr. Trenholme," she said. "How did you happen on our tiny village? Though so far from London, we are quite a byway. Why did you pay us a visit?"

So Trenholme dropped to earth again, and they spoke of matters of slight import till the boundary wall was reached.

Sylvia hailed a man attending cattle in the farmyard, and the artist vaulted the wall, which was breast high. The girl wondered if she could do that. When opportunity served she would try. Resting her elbows on the coping-stones, she watched Trenholme as he hurried away among the buildings and made for the village. She had never before met such a man or any one even remotely like him. He differed essentially from the Fenleys, greatly as the brothers themselves differed. Without conscious effort to please, he had qualities that appealed strongly to women, and Sylvia knew now that no consideration would induce her to marry either of her "cousins."

If asked to put her thought into words, she would have boggled at the task, for intuition is not to be defined in set speech. In her own way, she had summed up the characteristics of the two men with one of whom marriage had been at least a possibility. Hilton she feared and Robert she despised, so if either was to become her husband, it would be Hilton. But five minutes of John Trenholme's companionship had given her a standard by which to measure her suitors, and both fell wofully short of its demands. She saw with startling clearness of vision that Hilton, the schemer, and Robert, the wastrel, led selfish lives. Souls they must possess, but souls starved by lack of spirituality, souls pent in dun prisons of their own contriving.

She was so lost in thought, thought that strayed from crystal-bright imageries to nebulous shapes at once dark and terrifying, that the first intimation she received of Robert Fenley's approach was his stertorous breathing. From a rapid walk he had broken into a jog trot when he saw Trenholme vanish over the wall. Of late he seldom walked or rode a horse, and he was slightly out of condition, so his heavy face was flushed and perspiring, and his utterance somewhat labored when the girl turned at his cry:

"I say, Sylvia—you've given me such a chase! Who the deuce is that fellow, an' what are you doing here?"

Robert had appeared at an inauspicious moment. Sylvia eyed him with a new disfavor. He was decidedly gross, both in manner and language. She was sure he could not have vaulted the wall.

"I'm not aware that I called for any chasing on your part," she said, with an aloofness perilously akin to disdain.

He halted, panting, and eyed her sulkily.

"No, but dash it all! You can't go walking around with any rotten outsider who forces himself into your company," was the most amiable reply he could frame on the spur of the moment.

"You are short of breath," she said, smiling in a curiously impersonal way. "Run back to the house. It will do you good."

"All right. You run with me. The first gong will go any minute, and we've got to eat, you know, even though the pater *is* dead."

It was an unhappy allusion. Sylvia stiffened.

"My poor uncle's death did not seem to trouble you greatly this morning," she said. "Kindly leave me now. I'll follow soon. I am waiting for Mr. Trenholme, who wants to show me some sketches."

"A nice time to look at sketches, upon my word! And who's Trenholme, I'd like to know?"

Sylvia bethought herself. Certainly an explanation was needful, and her feminine wit supplied one instantly.

"Mr. Trenholme was sent here by the Scotland Yard people," she said, a trifle less frigidly. "I suppose we shall all be mixed up in the inquiry the detectives are holding, and it seems that Mr. Trenholme was at work in the park this morning when that awful affair took place. Unknown to me, I was near the spot where he was sketching before breakfast, and one of the detectives, the little one, says it is important that—that the fact should be proved. Mr. Trenholme called to tell me just what happened. So you see there is nothing in his action that should annoy any one—you least of any, since you were away from home at the time."

"But why has he mizzled over the wall?"

"He is staying at the White Horse Inn, and has gone to fetch the drawings."

"Oh, I didn't understand. If that's it, I'll wait till he turns up. You'll soon get rid of him."

Sylvia had no valid reason to urge against this decision, but she did not desire Robert's company, and chose a feminine method of resenting it.

"I don't think Mr. Trenholme will be anxious to meet you," she said coolly.

"Why not?"

"You are such a transparent person in your likes and dislikes. You have never even seen him, in the ordinary sense of the word, yet you speak of him in a way so unwarranted, so ridiculously untrue, that your manner might annoy him."

"My manner, indeed! Is he so precious then? By gad, it'll be interesting to look this rare bird over."

She turned her back on him and leaned on the wall again. Her slight, lissome figure acquired a new elegance from her black dress. Robert had never set eyes on Sylvia in such a costume before that day. Hitherto she had been a schoolgirl, a flapper, a straight-limbed, boyish young person in long frocks; but today she seemed to have put on a new air of womanliness, and he found it strangely attractive.

"There's no sense in our quarreling about the chap anyhow," he said with a gruff attempt to smooth away difficulties. "Of course, I sh'an't let on I followed you. Just spotted you in the distance and joined you by chance, don't you know."

Sylvia did not answer. She was comparing Robert Fenley's conversational style with John Trenholme's, and the comparison was unflattering to Robert.

So he, too, came and leaned on the wall.

"I'm sorry if I annoyed you just now, Syl," he said. "That dashed little detective is to blame. He does put things in such a beastly unpleasant way."

"What things?"

"Why, about you and me and all of us. Gave me a regular lecture because I went back to town this morning. I couldn't help it, old girl. I really couldn't. I had to settle some urgent business, but that's all ended now. The pater's death has steadied me. No more gallivanting off to London for me. Settle down in Roxton, Board of Guardians on Saturdays, church on Sunday, tea and tennis at the vicarage, and 'you-come-to-our-place-tomorrow.' You know the sort of thing—old-fashioned, respectable and comfy. I'll sell my motor bike and start a car. Motor bikes make a fellow a bit of a vagabond—eh, what? They *will* go the pace. You can't stop 'em. Fifty per, and be hanged to the police, that's their motto."

"It sounds idyllic," the girl forced herself to say lightly, but her teeth met with a snap, and her fingers gripped the rough surface of the stones, for she remembered how Trenholme had said of her that she "reveled in the sunlight, in the golden air, in the scents of trees and shrubs and flowering grasses."

There was a musical cadence in her voice that restored Robert's surly good humor; he was of that peculiar type of spoiled youth whose laugh is a guffaw and whose mirth ever holds a snarl.

"Here comes your paint slinger," he said. "Wonder if he really can stage a decent picture. If so, when the present fuss is ended we'll get him to do a group. You and me and the keepers and dogs in front of the Warren Covert, next October, after a big drive. How would that be?"

"I'm sure Mr. Trenholme will feel flattered."

When Trenholme approached he was not too well pleased to find Miss Manning in charge of a new cavalier.

From items gathered earlier in the village he guessed the newcomer's identity. Perhaps he expected that the girl would offer an introduction, but she only smiled pleasantly and said:

"You must have hurried. I do hope I haven't put you to any inconvenience?"

"Eliza informed me that she had just popped my chicken in the oven, so there is plenty of time," he said. "I suppose it makes one hot to be constantly popping things into ovens. In the course of years one should become a sort of salamander. Have you ever read the autobiography of that great artist and very complete rascal, Benvenuto Cellini? He is the last person reputed to have seen a real salamander in the fire, and he only remembered the fact because his father beat him lest he should forget it."

"Ben who?" broke in Robert cheerfully.

"Benvenuto Cellini."

"Never heard of him.... Well, let's have a peep-o. Miss Manning and I dine at a quarter to eight. You've been taking some snapshots in the park, I'm told. If they've got any ginger in them———"

"Probably you will describe them as hot stuff," said Trenholme, laying a portfolio on the wall in front of Sylvia and opening it.

"This is a pencil drawing of the great gates," he went on, ignoring Fenley. "Of course, they're Wren's, and therefore beautiful. Roxton Park holds a real treasure in those gates, Miss Manning. Here is a water-color sketch of the house and grounds. Do you like it?"

"Oh, it is exquisite! Why, you have caught the very glint of sunshine on the walls and roofs, and it is shimmering in the leaves of that copper beech. Ah me! It looks so easy."

Robert peered over her shoulder. Sylvia's gasp of admiration annoyed him; but he looked and said nothing.

"This," continued Trenholme, "is an unfinished study of the lake. I was so busily occupied that I was not aware of your presence until you were quite near at hand. Then when you dived into the water I grabbed a canvas and some tubes of paint. Here is the result—completed, to a large extent, in my room at the inn."

He took a picture out of a compartment of the portfolio specially constructed to protect an undried surface, and placed it at an angle that suited the light. His tone was unconcerned, for he had steeled himself against this crucial moment. Would she be angered? Would those limpid blue eyes, violet now in shadow, be raised to his in protest and vexed dismay? During the brief walk to and from the inn he had recollected the girl's age, her surroundings, the cramping influences of existence in a society of middle-class City folk. He felt like a prisoner awaiting a verdict when the issue was doubtful, and a wave of impulse might sway the jury one way or the other.

But he held his head high, and his face flushed slightly, for there could be no gainsaying the message glowing from that cunning brush work. There were two goddesses, one in marble and one palpitating with life. The likeness, too, was undeniable. If one was a replica of Greek art at its zenith, the other was unmistakably Sylvia Manning.

The girl gazed long and earnestly. Her pale cheeks had reddened for an instant, but the flood of surprise and emotion ebbed as quickly as it flowed, and left her wan, with parted lips.

At last she looked at Trenholme and spoke.

"Thank you!" she said, and their eyes met.

The artist understood; and he in turn, blanched somewhat. Rather hastily he replaced the picture in its receptacle.

Robert Fenley coughed and grinned, and the spell was broken.

"You said I'd call it hot stuff," he said. "Well, you sized my opinion up to a T. Of course, it's jolly clever—any fellow can see that——"

"Good night, Mr. Trenholme," said Sylvia, and she made off at a rapid pace. Robert grinned again.

"No young lady would stand that sort of thing," he chuckled. "You didn't really think she would—eh, what? But look here, I'll buy it. Send me a line later."

He hurried after Sylvia, running to overtake her. Trenholme stood there a long time; in fact, until the two were hidden by the distant line of trees. Then he smiled.

"So you are Robert Fenley," he communed, packing the portfolio leisurely. "Well, if Sylvia Manning marries you, I'll be a bachelor all my days, for I'll never dare imagine I know anything about a woman's soul; though I'm prepared at this hour of grace to stake my career that that girl's soul is worthy of her very perfect body."

Puffing a good deal, Fenley contrived to overhaul his "cousin."

"By jing, Sylvia, you can step out a bit," he said. "And you change your mind mighty quick. Five minutes ago you were ready to wait any length of time till that Johnny turned up, and now you're doing more than five per. What's the rush? It's only half past seven, and we don't dress tonight."

"I'm not dining downstairs," she answered.

"Oh, I say, I can't stand Hilton all alone."

"Nor can I stand either of you," she was tempted to retort, but contented herself by saying that she had arranged for a meal to be served in her aunt's room. Grumble and growl as he might, Robert could not shake her resolve; he was in a vile temper when he reached the dining-room.

His brother had not arrived, so he braced himself for an ordeal by drinking a stiff whisky and soda. When Hilton came in the pair nodded to each other but ate in silence. At last Robert glanced up at Tomlinson.

"Just shove the stuff on the table and clear out," he said. "We'll help ourselves. Mr. Hilton and I want to have a quiet talk."

Hilton gave him a quick underlook but did not interfere. Perhaps purposely, when the servants had left the room he opened the battle with a sneer.

"I hope you didn't make a fool of yourself this evening," he said.

"As how?" queried Robert, wondrously subdued to all appearance, though aching to give the other what he called "a bit of his mind."

"I understand you made after Sylvia and the artist, meaning to chastise somebody."

"You were wrong," said Robert slowly. "You nearly always are. I make mistakes myself, but I own up handsomely. You don't. That's where we differ, see?"

"I see differences," and Hilton helped himself to a glass of claret.

"Trenholme, the artist Johnny, is a clever chap—slightly cracked, as they all are, but dashed clever. By gad, you ought to see the picture he's painted of Sylvia. Anyhow, you *will* see it. I've bought it."

"Really?"

"I said I'd buy it—same thing. He'll jump at the offer. It'll hang in my dressing-room. I don't suppose Sylvia will kick about a trifle like that when we're married."

Hilton was holding the glass of wine to his lips. His hand shook, and he spilled a little, but he drank the remainder.

"When did you decide to marry Sylvia?" he inquired, after a pause which might have been needed to gain control of his voice.

"It's been decided for a long time," said Robert doggedly, himself showing some signs of enforced restraint. "It was the pater's wish, as you know. I'm sorry now I didn't fix matters before he died; but 'better late than never.' I asked Sylvia today, and we've arranged to get married quite soon."

"Are you by any chance telling the truth?"

"What the blazes do you mean?" and Robert's fist pounded the table heavily.

"Exactly what I say. You say that you and Sylvia have arranged to get married quite soon. Those were your words. Is that true?"

"Confound you, of course it is."

"Sylvia has actually agreed to that?"

"I asked her. What more do you want?"

"I am merely inquiring civilly what she said."

"Dash it, you know what girls are like. You ought to. Isn't Eileen Garth a bit coy at times?"

"One might remark that Mrs. Lisle also was coy."

"Look here——" began the other furiously, but the other checked him.

"Let us stop bickering like a couple of counter jumpers," he said, and a shrewder man than Robert might have been warned by the slow, incisive utterance. "You make an astonishing announcement on an occasion when it might least be expected, yet resent any doubt being thrown on its accuracy. Did or did not Sylvia accept you?"

"Well, she said something about not wishing to talk of marriage so soon after the old man's death, but that was just her way of putting it. I mean to marry her; and when a fellow has made up his mind on a thing like that it's best to say so and have done with it. Sylvia's a jolly nice girl, and has plenty of tin. I'm first in the field, so I'm warning off any other candidates. See?"

"Yes, I see," said Hilton, pouring out another glass of wine. This time his hand was quite steady, and he drank without mishap.

"Ain't you going to wish me luck?" said Robert, eying him viciously.

"I agree with Sylvia. The day we have lost our father is hardly a fitting time for such a discussion; or shall I say ceremony?"

"You can say what the devil you like. And you can do what you like. Only keep off my corns and I won't tread on yours."

Having, as he fancied, struck a decisive blow in the struggle for that rare prize, Sylvia, Robert Fenley pushed back his chair, arose, waited a second for an answer which came not, and strode out, muttering something about being "fed up."

Hilton's face was lowered, and one nervous hand shaded his brows. Robert thought he had scored, but he could not see the inhuman rage blazing in those hidden eyes. The discovery, had he made it, might not have distressed him, but he would surely have been puzzled by the strange smile which wrinkled Hilton's sallow cheeks when the door closed and the Eurasian was left alone in the dining-room.

CHAPTER XII
WHEREIN SCOTLAND YARD IS DINED AND WINED

Three dinners for two were in progress in The Towers at one and the same hour. One feast had been shortened by the ill-concealed hatred of each brother for the other. At the second, brooding care found unwonted lodging in the charming personality of Sylvia Manning—care, almost foreboding, heightened by the demented mutterings of her "aunt." At the third, with the detectives, sat responsibility; but light-heartedly withal, since these seasoned man-hunters could cast off their day's work like a garment.

The first and second meals were of the high quality associated with English country houses of a superior class; the third was a spread for epicures. Tomlinson saw to that. He was catering for a gourmet in Furneaux, and rose to the requisite height.

The little man sighed as he tasted the soup.

"What is it now?" inquired Winter, whose glance was dwelling appreciatively on a dusty bottle labeled "Clos Vosgeot, 1879."

"I hate eating the food of a man whom I mean to produce as a star turn at the Old Bailey," was the despondent answer.

"So do I, if it comes to that," said Winter briskly. "But this appetizing menu comes out of another larder. I shall be vastly mistaken if we're not actually the guests of a certain pretty young lady. Finance of the Fenley order is not in good odor in the City.

"Have no scruples, my boy. We may be vultures at the feast; but before we see the end of the Fenley case there'll be a smash in Bishopsgate Street, and Miss Sylvia Manning will be lucky if some sharp lawyer is able to grab some part of the wreckage for her benefit."

"Clear logic, at any rate." And Furneaux brightened visibly.

"I'll tell you what it's based on. Our swarthy friend was examining lists of securities in the train. He didn't lift his head quickly enough—took me for a ticket puncher, I expect—so I had time to twig what he was doing. I'd like to run my eye over the papers in that leather portfolio."

"You may manage it. You're the luckiest fellow breathing. Such opportunities come your way. *I* have to make them."

After an interlude played by sole Colbert, Winter shot an amused question at his companion.

"What's at the back of your head with regard to the artist and Miss Sylvia?" he said.

"It's high time she spoke to a real man. These Fenleys are animals, all of 'em. John Trenholme is a genius, and a good-looking one."

"I met the girl in a corridor a while ago, and she was rather disconsolate, I thought."

"And with good reason. You've noticed how each brother eyes her. They'll fight like jackals before this night is out. I hope Sylvia will indulge in what women call a good cry. That will be Trenholme's golden hour. Some Frenchman—of course he was clever, being French—says that a man should beware when a woman smiles but he may dare all when she weeps."

"Are we marriage brokers, then?"

"We must set the Fenleys at each other's throats."

"Yes," mused Winter aloud, when a *ris de veau bonne maman* had passed like a dream, "this affair is becoming decidedly interesting. But every why hath a wherefore, according to Shakespeare. Tell me"—and his voice sank to a whisper—"tell me why you believe Hilton Fenley killed his father."

"You nosed your way into that problem this afternoon. Between his mother and that girl, Eileen Garth, he was in a tight place. He stole those bonds. I fancied it at the time, but I know it now. They were negotiated in Paris by a woman who occupied a room in the Hotel d'Italie, Rue Caumartin, Paris, and one of her registered boxes bore the rail number, 517."

"You little devil!" blazed out Winter. "And you never said a word when I told you!"

"Astonishment has rendered you incoherent. You mean, of course, when you told me you had seen in Gloucester Mansions a box labeled in accordance with the facts I have just retailed. But I yield that minor point. It is a purist's, at the best. I have supplied a motive, one motive, for the crime; the plotter feared discovery. But there are dozens of others. He was impatient of the old man's rigid control. Hilton is sharp and shrewd, and he guessed things were going wrong financially. He knew that his father's methods were out of date, and believed he could straighten the tangle if the reins of power were not withheld too long.

"He saw that Sylvia Manning's gold was in the melting-pot, and appreciated precisely the cause of the elder Fenley's anxiety that she should marry

Robert. Once in the family, you know, her fortunes were bound up with theirs; while any 'cute lawyer could dish her in the marriage settlements if sufficiently well paid for a nasty job. When Sylvia was Mrs. Robert Fenley, and perhaps mother of a squalling Fenley, the head of the business could face the future if not with confidence, at least with safety. But where would Hilton be then? The girl lost, the money in jeopardy, and he himself steadily elbowed out. *'Cré nom!* I've known men murdered for less convincing reasons."

"Men, yes; not fathers."

"Some sons are the offspring of Beelzebub. Consider the parentage in this instance. Fenley, a groom and horse coper on the one hand, and the dark daughter of a Calcutta merchant on the other. If the progeny of such a union escaped a hereditary taint it would be a miracle. Cremate Hilton Fenley and his very dust will contain evil germs."

"You're strong in theory but weak in proof."

That style of argument invariably nettled Furneaux.

"You must butt into a few more mysterious suites of apartments in London and elsewhere, and you'll supply proof in bucketfuls," he snapped.

"But was there an accomplice? Squirm as you like, you can't get over the fact that Hilton was in his room when the bullet that killed his father came from the wood."

"He is not the sort of person likely to trust his liberty, his life even, to the keeping of any other human being. I start from the hypothesis that he alone planned and carried out the crime, so I do not lift my hand and cry 'Impossible,' but I ask myself, 'How was it done?' Well, there are several methods worthy of consideration—clockwork, electricity, even a time fuse attached to the proper mechanism. I haven't really bothered myself yet to determine the means, because when that knowledge becomes indispensable we must have our man under lock and key."

"Of course, the rifle is securely fixed in that——"

The door opened. Tomlinson came in, smiling blandly.

"I hope you are enjoying your dinner, gentlemen both?" he said.

"You have made your cook an artist," said Furneaux.

"I suppose you are happier here than in a big London restaurant," said Winter.

The butler appreciated such subtle compliments, and beamed on them.

"With a little encouragement and advice, our chef can prepare a very eatable dinner," he said. "As for my own ambitions, I have had them, like every man worth his salt; but I fill a comfortable chair here—no worry, no grumbling, not a soul to say *nem* or *con*, so long as things go smoothly."

"It must have been *nem* all the time," giggled Furneaux, and Winter was so afflicted by a desire to sneeze that he buried his face in a napkin.

"And how was the wine?" went on Tomlinson, with an eye on the little man. Furneaux's features were crinkled in a Japanese smile. He wanted to kick Winter, who was quivering with suppressed laughter.

"I never expected to find such vintages in a house of the *mauvais riches*," he said. "Perhaps you don't speak French, Mr. Tomlinson, so allow me to explain that I am alluding to men of wealth not born in the purple."

"Precisely—self-made. Well sir, poor Mr. Fenley left the stocking of his cellar entirely to me. I gave the matter much thought. When my knowledge was at fault I consulted experts, and the result——"

"That is the result," cried Furneaux, seizing the empty claret bottle, and planting it so firmly on the table that the cutlery danced.

A shoulder of lamb, served *à la Soubise*, appeared; and Tomlinson, announcing that his presence in the dining-room had been dispensed with, thought he would join them in a snack. Being a hospitable creature, he opened another bottle of the Clos Vosgeot, but his guests were not to be tempted.

"Well, then," he said, "in a few minutes you must try our port. It is not Alto Douro, Mr. Furneaux, but it has body and bowket."

Winter was better prepared this time. Moreover he was carving, and aware of a master's criticism, and there are occult problems connected with even such a simple joint as a shoulder of lamb. Furneaux, too, was momentarily subdued. He seemed to be reflecting sadly that statues of gold, silver and bronze may have feet of clay.

"I have often thought, gentlemen," said the butler, "that yours must be a most interesting profession. You meet all sorts and conditions of men and women."

"We consort with the noblest malefactors," agreed Furneaux.

"Dear me, sir, you do use the queerest words. Now, I should never dream of describing a criminal as noble."

"Not in the generally accepted sense, perhaps. But you, I take it, have not had the opportunity of attending a really remarkable trial, when, say, some intellectual giant among murderers is fighting for his life. Believe me, no drama of the stage can rival that tragedy.

"The chief actor, remote, solitary, fenced away from the world he is hoping to reënter, sits there in state. Every eye is on him, yet he faces judge, jury, counsel, witnesses and audience with a calm dignity worthy of an emperor. He listens imperturbably to facts which may hang him, to lies which may lend color to the facts, to well-meaning guesses which are wide of the mark. Truthful and false evidence is equally prone to err when guilt or innocence must be determined by circumstances alone.

"But the prisoner *knows*. He is the one man able to discriminate between truth and falsity, yet he must not reveal the cruel stab of fact or the harmless buffet of fiction by so much as a flicker of an eyelid. He surveys the honest blunderer and the perjured ruffian—I mean the counsel for the defense and the prosecution respectively—with impartial scrutiny. If he is a sublime villain, he will call on Heaven to testify that he is innocent with a solemnity not surpassed by the judge who sentences him to death.... Yes, please, a bit off the knuckle end."

The concluding words were addressed to Winter, and Tomlinson started, for he was wrapped up in the scene Furneaux was depicting.

"That point of view had not occurred to me," he admitted.

"You'll appreciate it fully when you see Mr. Fenley's murderer in the dock," said Furneaux.

"Ah, sir. That brings your illustration home, indeed. But shall we ever know who killed him?"

"Certainly. Look at that high dome of intelligence glistening at you across the table. But that it is forbid to tell the secrets of the prison house, it could a tale unfold whose slightest word would harrow up thy soul——"

Harris, the footman, entered, carrying a decanter.

"Mr. Hilton Fenley's compliments, gentlemen, and will you try this port? He says Mr. Tomlinson will recommend it, because Mr. Fenley himself seldom takes wine. Mr. Fenley will not trouble you to meet him again this evening. Mr. Tomlinson, Mr. Fenley wants you for a moment."

The butler rose.

"That is the very wine I spoke of," he said. "If Mr. Hilton did not touch it, Mr. Robert evidently appreciated it."

He glanced at Harris, but the footman did not even suspect that his character was at stake. The decanter was nearly full when placed on the sideboard; now it was half empty.

Singularly enough, both Winter and Furneaux had intercepted that questioning glance, and had acquitted Harris simultaneously.

"Are the gentlemen still in the dining-room?" inquired Winter.

"Mr. Hilton is there, sir, but Mr. Robert went out some time since."

"Please convey our thanks to Mr. Hilton. I'm sure we shall enjoy the wine."

When Tomlinson and Harris had gone, the eyes of the two detectives met. They said nothing at first, and it may be remembered that they were reputedly most dangerous to a pursued criminal when working together silently. Winter took the decanter, poured out a small quantity into two glasses, and gave Furneaux one. Then they smelled, and tasted, and examined the wine critically. The rich red liquid might have been a poisonous decoction for the care they devoted to its analysis.

Furneaux began.

"I have so many sleepless nights that I recognize bromide, no matter how it is disguised," he murmured.

"Comparatively harmless, though a strong dose," said Winter.

"If one has to swallow twenty grains or so of potassium bromide I can not conceive any pleasanter way of taking them than mixed with a sound port."

Winter filled one of the glasses four times, pouring each amount into a tumbler. Furneaux looked into a cupboard, and found an empty beer bottle, which he rinsed with water. Meanwhile Winter was fashioning a funnel out of a torn envelope, and in a few seconds the tumblerful of wine was in the bottle, and the bottle in Winter's pocket. This done, the big man lit a cigar and the little one sniffed the smoke, which was his peculiar way of enjoying the weed.

"It was most thoughtful of Mr. Hilton Fenley to try and secure us a long night's uninterrupted sleep," said Winter between puffs.

"But what a vitiated taste in wine he must attribute to Scotland Yard," said Furneaux bitterly.

"Still, we should be grateful to him for supplying a gill of real evidence."

"I may forgive him later. At present, I want to dilate his eyes with atropine, so that he may see weird shapes and be tortured of ghouls."

"Poor devil! He won't need atropine for that."

"Don't believe it, James. In some respects he's cold-blooded as a fish. Besides, he carries bromide tablets for his own use. He simply couldn't have arranged beforehand to dope us."

"He's getting scared."

"I should think so, indeed—in the Fenley sense, that is. His plot against Robert has miscarried in one essential. The rifle has not been found in the wood. Now, I'm in chastened mood, because the hour for action approaches; so I'll own up. I've been keeping something up my sleeve, just for the joy of watching you floundering 'midst deep waters. Of course, you chose the right channel. I knew you would, but it's a treat to see your elephantine struggles. For all that, it's a sheer impossibility that you should guess who put a sprag in the wheel of Hilton's chariot. Give you three tries, for a new hat."

"You're desperately keen today on touching me for a new hat."

"Well, this time you have an outside chance. The others were certs—for me."

Winter smoked in silence for a space.

"I'll take you," he said. "The artist?"

"No." The Jerseyman shook his head.

"Police Constable Farrow?" ventured Winter again.

Furneaux's dismay was so comical that his colleague shook with mirth.

"I wanted a new silk topper," wheezed Winter.

"Silk topper be hanged. I meant a straw, and that's what you'll get. But how the deuce did you manage to hit upon Farrow?"

"He closed the Quarry Wood at the psychological moment."

"You're sucking my brains, that's what you're doing," grumbled Furneaux. "Anyhow, you're right. Hilton had the scheme perfected to the last detail, but he didn't count on Farrow. After a proper display of agitation—not all assumed, either, because he was more shaken than he expected to be—he 'phoned the Yard and the doctor. We couldn't arrive for nearly an hour, and the doctor starts on his rounds at nine o'clock sharp. What so easy, therefore, as to wander out in a welter of grief and anger, and search the wood for the murderer on his own account? One solitary minute would enable him to put the rifle in a hiding-place where it would surely be discovered.

"But Farrow stopped him. I wormed the whole thing out of our sentry this afternoon. Fenley tried hard to send Farrow and Bates off on a wild-goose chase, but Farrow, quite mistakenly, saw the chance of his life and clung on to it. Had Farrow budged we could never have hanged Hilton. Don't you see how the scheme works? He had some reason for believing that Robert will refuse to give a full account of his whereabouts this morning. Therefore, he must contrive that the rifle shall be found. Put the two damning facts together, and Robert is tied in a knot. Of course, he would be forced to prove an alibi, but by that time all England would be yelping, 'Thou art the man.' In any event, Hilton's trail would be hopelessly lost."

"The true bowket of our port and bromide begins to tickle my nostrils."

A good-looking maid brought coffee, and Furneaux grinned at her.

"How do you think he'd look in a nice straw hat?" he asked, jerking his head toward Winter. The girl smiled. The little man's reputation had reached the kitchen. She glanced demurely at the Superintendent's bullet head.

"Not an ordinary straw. You mean a Panama," she said.

"Certainly," laughed Winter.

"Nothing of the sort," howled Furneaux. "Just run your eye over him. He isn't an isthmus—he's a continent."

"A common straw wouldn't suit him," persisted the girl. "He's too big a gentleman."

"How little you know him!" said Furneaux.

The girl blushed and giggled.

"Go on!" she said, and bounced out.

"This inquiry will cost you a bit, my boy, if you're not careful," sniggered Winter. "I'll compound on a straw; but take my advice, and curb your sporting propensities. Now, if this coffee isn't doctored, let's drink it, and interview Robert before the bromide begins to act."

Robert Fenley received them in his own room. He strove to appear at ease and business-like, but, as Furneaux had surmised, was emphatic in his refusal to give any clear statement as to his proceedings in London. He admitted the visit to Hendon Road, which, he said, was necessitated by a promise to a friend who was going abroad, but he failed to see why the police should inquire into his private affairs.

Winter did not press him. There was no need. A scapegrace's record could always be laid bare when occasion served. But one question he was bound to put.

"Have you any theory, however remote or far-fetched, that will account for your father's death in such a way?" he inquired.

The younger Fenley was smoking a cigarette. A half consumed whisky and soda stood on a table; a bottle of whisky and a siphon promised refreshers. He was not quite sober, but could speak lucidly.

"Naturally, I've been thinking a lot about that," he said, wrinkling his forehead in the effort to concentrate his mind and express himself with due solemnity. "It's funny, isn't it, that my rifle should be missing?"

"Well, yes."

Some sarcastic inflection in Winter's voice seemed to reach a rather torpid brain. Fenley looked up sharply.

"Of course, funny isn't the right word," he said. "I mean it's odd, a bit of a mystery. Why should anybody take my gun if they wanted to shoot my poor old guv'nor? That beats me. It's a licker—eh, what?"

"It is more important to know why any one should want to shoot your father."

"That's it. Who benefits? Well, I suppose Hilton and I will be better off—no one else. And I didn't do it. It's silly even to say so."

"But there is only your brother left in your summary."

"By Jove, yes. That's been runnin' in my head. It's nonsense, anyhow, because Hilton was in the house. I wouldn't believe a word he said, but Sylvia, and Tomlinson, and Brodie, and Harris all tell the same yarn. No; Hilton couldn't have done it. He's ripe for any mischief, is Hilton, but he can't be in this hole; now, can he?"

They could extract nothing of value out of Robert, and left him after a brief visit.

In the interim, Hilton Fenley had kept Tomlinson talking about the crime. The dining-room door was ajar, and he knew when the detectives had gone to Robert's room. Then he glanced around the table, and affected to remember the decanter of port.

"By the way," he said, "I feel as if a glass of that wine would be a good notion tonight. I don't suppose the Scotland Yard men have finished the lot. Just send for it, will you?"

Harris brought the decanter, and Tomlinson was gratified by seeing that his favorite beverage had been duly appraised.

"Sorry if I've detained you," said Fenley, and the butler went out. Rising, Fenley strolled to the door and closed it. Instantly he became energetic, and his actions bore a curious similitude to those of Winter a little while earlier. Pouring the wine into a tumbler, he rinsed the decanter with water, and partly refilled it with the contents of another tumbler previously secreted in the sideboard, stopping rather short of the amount of wine returned from the butler's room. He drank the remainder, washed the glass, and put a few drops of whisky into it.

Carrying the other tumbler to an open window, he threw the medicated wine into a drain under a water spout, and making assurance doubly sure, douched the same locality with water; also, he rinsed this second glass. He seemed to be rather pleased at his own thoroughness.

As Furneaux had said, Hilton Fenley was cold-blooded as a fish.

CHAPTER XIII
CLOSE QUARTERS

Human affairs are peculiarly dependent on the weather. It is not easy to lay down a law governing this postulate, which, indeed, may be scoffed at by the superficial reasoner, and the progression from cause to effect is often obscured by contradictory facts. For instance, a fine summer means a good harvest, much traveling, the prolongation of holiday periods, a free circulation of money, and the consequent enhanced prosperity and happiness of millions of men and women. But there are more suicides in June and July than in December and January. On the one hand, fine weather improves humanity's lot; on the other, it depresses the individual.

Let the logician explain these curiously divergent issues as he may; there can be no question that the quality of the night which closed a day eventful beyond any other in the annals of Roxton exercised a remarkable influence on the lives of five people. It was a perfect night in June. There was no moon; the stars shone dimly through a slight haze; but the sun had set late and would rise early, and his complete disappearance followed so small a chord of the diurnal circle that his light was never wholly absent. A gentle westerly breeze was so zephyr-like that it hardly stirred the leaves of the trees, but it wafted the scent of flowers and meadow land into open windows, and was grateful alike to the just and the unjust.

Thus to romantic minds it was redolent of romance; and as Sylvia Manning's room faced south and John Trenholme's faced north, and lay nearly opposite each other, though separated by a rolling mile of park, woodland, tillage and pasture, it is not altogether incredible that those two, gazing out at the same hour, should bridge the void with the eyes of the soul.

It was a night, too, that invited to the open.

In some favored lands, where the almanac is an infallible Clerk of the Weather, fine nights succeed each other with the monotonous regularity of kings in an Amurath dynasty. But the British climate, a slave to no such ordered sequence, scatters or withholds these magic hours almost impartially throughout the seasons, so that June may demand overcoats and umbrellas, and October invite Summer raiment.

Hence this superb Summer's night found certain folk in Roxton disinclined to forego its enchantments. Trenholme, trying to persuade himself that his brooding gaze rested on the Elizabethan roofs and gables rising above the trees because of some rarely spiritual quality in the atmosphere, suddenly awoke to the fact that the hour was eleven.

Some men issued from the bar parlor and "snug" beneath, and there were sounds of bolts being shot home and keys turned in recognition of the curfew imposed by the licensing laws. Then the artistic temperament arose in revolt. Chafing already against the narrow confines of the best room the White Horse Inn could provide, it burst all bounds when a tired potman attempted unconsciously to lock it in.

Grabbing a pipe and tobacco pouch, Trenholme ran downstairs, meeting the potman in the passage.

"Get me a key, Bill," he said. "I simply can't endure the notion of bed just yet, so I'm off for a stroll. I don't want to keep any one waiting up, and I suppose I can have a key of sorts."

Now it happened that the proprietor of the inn was absent at a race meeting, and Eliza was in charge. Trenholme's request was passed on to her, and a key was forthcoming.

Hatless, pipe in mouth, and hands in pockets, Trenholme sauntered into the village street. Romance was either a dull jade or growing old and sedate in Roxton. Nearly every house was in darkness, and more than one dog barked because of a passing footstep.

About half past eleven, Sylvia Manning, sitting in melancholy near her window after an hour of musing, heard a light tap on the door.

"Come in," she said, recognizing the reason of this late intrusion. An elderly woman entered. She was an attendant charged with special care of Mrs. Fenley. A trained nurse would have refused to adopt the lenient treatment of the patient enjoined by the late head of the family, so this woman was engaged because she was honest, faithful, rather stupid and obeyed orders.

"She has quieted down now, miss, and is fast asleep," she said in a low tone. "You may feel sure she won't wake before six or seven. She never does."

The "she" of this message was Mrs. Fenley. Rural England does not encourage unnecessary courtesy nor harbor such foreign intruders as "madam." The reiterated pronoun grated on Sylvia; she was disinclined for further talk.

"Thank you, Parker," she said. "I am glad to know that. Good night."

But Parker had something to say, and this was a favorable opportunity.

"She's been awful bad today, miss. It can't go on."

"That is hardly surprising, taking into account the shock Mrs. Fenley received this morning."

"That's what I have in me mind, miss. She's changed."

"How changed? You need not close the door. Never mind the light. It is hardly dark when the eyes become used to the gloom."

Parker drew nearer. Obeying the instincts of her class, she assumed a confidential tone.

"Well, miss, you know why you went out?"

"Yes," said Sylvia rather curtly. She had left the invalid when the use of a hypodermic syringe became essential if an imminent outburst of hysteria was to be prevented. The girl had no power to interfere, and was too young and inexperienced to make an effective protest; but she was convinced that to encourage a vice was not the best method of treating it. More than once she had spoken of the matter to Mortimer Fenley; but he merely said that he had tried every known means to cure his wife, short of immuring her in an asylum, and had failed. "She is happy in a sort of a way," he would add, with a certain softening of voice and manner. "Let her continue so." Thus a minor tragedy was drifting to its close when Fenley himself was so rudely robbed of life.

"As a rule, miss," went on the attendant, "she soon settles after a dose, but this time she seemed to pass into a sort of a trance. Gen'rally her words are broken-like an' wild, an' I pays no heed to 'em; but tonight she talked wonderful clear, all about India at first, an' of a band playin', with sogers marchin' past. Then she spoke about some people called coolies. There was a lot about them, in lines an' tea gardens. An' she seemed to be speakin' to another Mrs. Fenley."

The woman's voice sank to an awe-stricken whisper, and Sylvia shivered somewhat in sympathy. "Another Mrs. Fenley!" It was common knowledge in the household that Fenley had married a second time, but the belief was settled that the first wife was dead; Parker, by an unrehearsed dramatic touch, conveyed the notion that the unhappy creature in a neighboring room had been conversing with a ghost.

Somewhat shaken and perturbed, Sylvia wished more than ever to be alone, so she brought her informant back to the matter in hand.

"I don't see that Mrs. Fenley's rambling utterances give rise to any fear of immediate collapse," she said, striving to speak composedly.

"No, miss. That isn't it at all. I was just tellin' you what happened. There was a lot more. She might ha' been givin' the story of her life. But—please forgive me, miss, for what I'm goin' to say. I think some one ought to know—I do, reelly—an' you're the only one I dare tell it to."

"Oh, what is it?"

The cry was wrung from the girl's heart. She had borne a good deal that day, and feared some sinister revelation now.

"She remembered that poor Mr. Fenley was dead, but didn't appear so greatly upset. She was more puzzled-like—kep' on mutterin': 'Who did it? Who could have the cool darin' to shoot him dead in broad daylight, at his own door, before his servants?' She was sort of forcin' herself to think, to find out, just as if it was a riddle, an' the right answer was on the tip of her tongue. An' then, all at once, she gev a queer little laugh. 'Why, of course, it was Hilton,' she said."

Sylvia, relieved and vastly indignant, rose impetuously.

"Why do you trouble to bring such nonsense to my ears?" she cried.

But Parker was stolid and dogged.

"I had to tell some one," she vowed, determined to put herself straight with one of her own sex. "I know her ways. If that's in her mind she'll be shoutin' it out to every maid who comes near her tomorrow; an' I reelly thought, miss, it was wise to tell you tonight, because such a thing would soon cause a scandal, an' it should be stopped."

"Perhaps you are right, and I ought to be obliged to you for being so considerate. But no one would pay heed to my aunt's ravings. Every person in the house knows that the statement is absurd. Mr. Hilton was in his room. I myself saw him go upstairs after exchanging a few words with his father in the hall, and he came down again instantly when Harris ran to fetch him."

"I understand that, miss, an' I'm not so silly as to think there is any sense in her blamin' Mr. Hilton. But it made my flesh creep to hear all the rest so clear an' straightforward, an' then that she should say: 'Hilton did it, the black beast. He always hated Bob an' me, because we were white, an' the jungle strain has come out at last.' Oh, it was somethink dreadful to hear her laughin' at her cleverness. I——"

"Please, please, don't repeat any more of these horrible things," cried the girl, for the strain was becoming unbearable.

"I agree with you, miss. They aren't fit to be spoke of; an' I say, with all due respec', that they shouldn't be allowed to leak out. You know what young maid servants are like. They're bound to chatter. My idee is that another nurse should be engaged tomorrow, a woman old enough to hold her tongue an' mind her own business; then the two of us can take turns at duty, so as to keep them housemaids out of the way altogether."

"Yes, I'm sure you are right. I'll speak to Mr. Hilton in the morning. Thank you, Parker. I see now that you meant well, and I'm sorry if I spoke sharply."

"I'm not surprised, miss. It was not a pleasant thing to have to say, nor for you to hear, but duty is duty. Good night, miss, I hope you'll sleep well."

Sleep! Parker should not have conjured up a new apparition if Sylvia were to seek the solace of untroubled rest. At present the girl felt that she had never before been so distressfully awake. Splendidly vital in mind and body as she was, she almost yielded now to a morbid horror of her environment. Generations of men and women had lived and died in that ancient house, and tonight dim shapes seemed to throng its chambers and corridors. Physically fearless, she owned to a feminine dread of the unknown. It would be a relief to get away from this abode of grief and mystery. The fantastic dreaming of the unhappy creature crooning memories of a past life and a lost husband had unnerved her. She resolved to seek the fresh air, and wander through gardens and park until the fever in her mind had abated.

Now a rule of the house ordained that all doors should be locked and lower windows latched at midnight. A night watchman made certain rounds each hour, pressing a key into indicating-clocks at various points to show that he had been alert. Mortimer Fenley had been afraid of fire; there was so much old woodwork in the building that it would burn readily, and a short circuit in the electrical installation was always possible, though every device had been adopted to render it not only improbable but harmless. After midnight the door bells and others communicated with a switchboard in the watchman's room; and a burglary alarm, which the man adjusted during his first round, rang there continuously if disturbed.

Sylvia, leaving the door of her bedroom ajar, went to the servants' quarters by a back staircase. There she found MacBain, the watchman, eating his supper.

"I don't feel as though I could sleep," she explained, "so I am going out into the park for a while. I'll unlatch one of the drawing-room windows and disconnect the alarm; and when I come in again I'll tell you."

"Very well, miss," said MacBain. "It's a fine night, and you'll take no harm."

"I'm not afraid of rabbits, if that is what you mean," she said lightly, for the very sound of the man's voice had dispelled vapors.

"Oh, there's more than rabbits in the park tonight, miss. Two policemen are stationed in the Quarry Wood."

"Why?" she said, with some surprise.

"They don't know themselves, miss. The Inspector ordered it. I met them coming on duty at ten o'clock. They'll be relieved at four. They have instructions to allow no one to enter the wood. That's all they know."

"If I go there, then, shall I be locked up?"

"Not so bad as that, miss," smiled MacBain. "But I'd keep away from it if I was you. 'Let sleeping dogs lie' is a good motto."

"But these are not sleeping dogs. They're wide-awake policemen."

"Mebbe, miss. They have a soft job, I'm thinking. Of course——"

The man checked himself, but Sylvia guessed what was passing in his mind.

"You were going to say that the wretch who killed my uncle hid in that wood?" she prompted him.

"Yes, miss, I was."

"He is not there now. He must have run away while we were too terrified to take any steps to capture him. Who in the world could have wished to kill Mr. Fenley?"

"Ah, miss, there's no knowing. Those you'd least suspect are often the worst."

MacBain shook his head over this cryptic remark; he glanced at a clock. It was five minutes to twelve.

"It's rather late, miss," he hinted. Sylvia agreed with him, but she was young enough to be headstrong.

"I sha'n't remain out very long," she said. "I ought to feel tired, but I don't; and I hope the fresh air will make me sleepy."

To reach the drawing-room, she had to cross the hall. Its parquet floor creaked under her rapid tread. A single lamp among a cluster in the ceiling burned there all night, and she could not help giving one quick look at the oaken settle which stood under the cross gallery; she was glad when the drawing-room door closed behind her.

She had no difficulty with the window, but the outer shutters creaked when she opened them. Then she passed on to the first of the Italian terraces, and stood there irresolutely a few minutes, gazing alternately at the sky and the black masses of the trees. At first she was a trifle nervous. The air was so still, the park so solemn in its utter quietude, that the sense of adventure was absent, and the funeral silence that prevailed was almost oppressive.

Half inclined to go back, woman-like she went forward. Then the sweet, clinging scent of a rose bed drew her like a magnet. She descended a flight of steps and gained the second terrace. She thought of Trenholme and the picture, and the impulse to stroll as far as the lake seized her irresistibly. Why not! The grass was short, and the dew would not be heavy. Even if she wetted her feet, what did it matter, as she would undress promptly on returning to her room? Besides, she had never seen the statue on just such a night, though she had often visited it by moonlight.

La Rochefoucauld is responsible for the oft quoted epigram that the woman who hesitates is lost, and Sylvia had certainly hesitated. At any rate, after a brief debate in which the arguments were distinctly one-sided, she resolved that she might as well have an object in view as stroll aimlessly in any other direction; so, gathering her skirts to keep them dry, she set off across the park.

She might have been halfway to the lake when a man emerged from the same window of the drawing-room, ran to the terrace steps, stumbled down them so awkwardly that he nearly fell, and swore at his own clumsiness in so doing. He negotiated the next flight more carefully, but quickened his pace again into a run when he reached the open. The girl's figure was hardly visible, but he knew she was there, and the distance between pursued and pursuer soon lessened.

Sylvia, wholly unaware of being followed, did not hurry; but she was constitutionally incapable of loitering, and moved over the rustling grass with a swiftness that brought her to the edge of the lake while the second inmate of The Towers abroad that night was yet a couple of hundred yards distant.

In the dim light the statue assumed a lifelike semblance that was at once startling and wonderful. Color flies with the sun, and the white marble did not depend now on tint alone to differentiate it from flesh and blood. Seen thus indistinctly, it might almost be a graceful and nearly nude woman standing there, and some display of will power on the girl's part was called for before she approached nearer and stifled the first breath of apprehension. Then, delighted by the vague beauty of the scene, with senses soothed by the soft plash of the cascade, she decided to walk around the lake to the spot where Trenholme must have been hidden when he painted that astonishingly vivid picture. Its bold treatment and simplicity of note rendered it an easy subject to carry in the mind's eye, and Sylvia thought it would be rather nice to conjure up the same effect in the prevailing conditions of semi-darkness and mystery. She need not risk tearing her dress among the briers which clung to the hillside. Knowing every inch of the ground, she could follow the shore of the lake until nearly opposite the statue, and then climb a few feet among the bushes at a point where a zigzag path, seldom used and nearly obliterated by undergrowth, led to the clump of cedars.

She was still speeding along the farther bank when a man's form loomed in sight in the park, and her heart throbbed tumultuously with a new and real terror. Who could it be? Had some one seen her leaving the house? That was the explanation she hoped for at first, but her breath came in sharp gusts and her breast heaved when she remembered how one deadly intruder at least had broken into that quiet haven during the early hours of the past day.

Whoever the oncomer might prove to be, he was losing no time, and he was yet some twenty yards or more away from the statue—itself separated from Sylvia by about the same width of water—when she recognized, with a sigh of relief, the somewhat cumbrous form and grampus-like puffing of Robert Fenley.

Evidently he was rather blear-eyed, since he seemed to mistake the white marble Aphrodite for a girl in a black dress; or perhaps he assumed that Sylvia was there, and thought he would see her at any moment.

"I say, Sylvia!" he cried. "I say, old girl, what the deuce are you doin'—in the park—at this time o' night?"

The words were clear enough, but there was a suspicious thickness in the voice. Robert had been drinking, and Sylvia had learned already to abhor and shun a man under the influence of intoxicants more than anything else in the wide world. She did not fear her "cousin." For years she had tolerated him, and that day she had come to dislike him actively, but she had not the least intention of entering into an explanation of her actions with him at that hour and under existing circumstances. She had recovered from her sudden fright, and was merely annoyed now, and bent her wits to the combined problems of escape and regaining the house unseen.

Remembering that her white face and hands might reveal her whereabouts she turned, bent and crept up the slope until a bush afforded welcome concealment. Some thorns scratched her ankles, but she gave no heed to such trivial mishaps. A rabbit jumped out from under her feet, and it cost something of an effort to repress a slight scream; but—to her credit be it said—she set her lips tightly, and was almost amused by the game of hide and seek thus unexpectedly thrust on her.

Meanwhile Robert had reached the little promontory on which the statue was poised, and no Sylvia was in sight.

"Sylvia!" he cried again. "Where are you? No use hidin', because I know you're here! Dash it all, if you wanted a bit of a stroll why didn't you send for me? You knew I'd come like a shot—eh, what?"

He listened and peered, but might as well have been deaf and blind for aught he could distinguish of the girl he sought.

Then he laughed; and a peculiar quality in that chuckle of mirth struck a new note of anxiety, even of fear, in Sylvia's laboring heart.

"So you won't be good!" he guffawed thickly. "Playin' Puss in the Corner, I suppose? Very well, I give you fair warnin'. I mean to catch you, an' when I do I'll claim forfeit.... *I* don't mind. Fact is, I like it. It's rather fun chasin' one's best girl in the dark.... Dashed if it isn't better'n a bit out of a French farce.... Puss! Puss!... I see you.... Hidin' there among the bushy bushes.... Gad! How's that for a test after a big night? Bushy bushes! I must not forget that. Try it on one of the b-boys.... Now, come out of it!... Naughty puss! I'll get you in a tick, see if I don't!"

He was keeping to the track Sylvia herself had taken, since the lie of the land was familiar to him as to her. Talking to himself, cackling at his own flashes of wit, halting after each few paces to search the immediate neighborhood and detect any guiding sound, he was now on the same side of the lake as the girl, and coming perilously near. At each step, apparently, he found the growing obscurity more tantalizing. He still continued calling aloud: "Sylvia! Sylvia, I say! Chuck it, can't you? You must give in, you know. I'll be grabbin' you in a minute." There were not lacking muttered ejaculations, which showed that he was losing his temper.

Once he swore so emphatically that she thought he was acknowledging himself beaten; but some glimmering notion that she was crouching almost within reach, and would have the laugh of him in the morning, flogged him to fresh endeavor. Now he was within ten yards, eight, five! In another few seconds his hand might touch her, and she quivered at the thought. If concealment could not save her she must seek refuge in flight, since therein lay a sure means of escape. Not daring to delay, she tried to stand upright, but felt a pull on her dress as if a hand were detaining her. It was only a brier, insidiously entangled in a fold of her skirt; but she was rather excited now, and there was little to be gained by excess of caution, for any rapid movement must betray her. Stooping, she caught the thorn-laden branch and tore it out of the soft material.

Fenley heard the ripping sound instantly.

"Ha! There you are, my beauty! Got you this time!" he cried, and plunged forward.

Sylvia sprang from her hiding-place like a frightened fawn and valiantly essayed the steep embankment. Therein she erred. She would have succeeded in evading her pursuer had she leaped down to the open strip of turf close to the water, dodging him before he realized what was happening. As it was, the briers spread a hundred cruel claws against her; with each upward step she encountered greater resistance; desperation only added to her panic, and she struggled frenziedly.

The man, unhampered by garments such as clogged each inch of Sylvia's path, pushed on with renewed ardor. He no longer spoke, for his hearing alone could help him now, the girl's black-robed form being utterly merged in the dense shadow cast by brushwood and cedars. He, however, was silhouetted against the luminous gray of the park, and Sylvia, casting a frantic glance over her shoulder, saw him distinctly. In her distress she fancied she could feel his hot breath on her neck; and when some unusually venomous branch clutched her across the knees, and rendered farther movement impossible until her dress was extricated, she wailed aloud in anger and dismay.

"How dare you!" she cried, and her voice was tremulous and broken. "I warn you that if you persist in following me I shall strike you!"

"Will you, by Jove!" cried Robert elatedly. "I'd risk more than that, my dear! A kiss for every blow! Only fair, you know! Eh, what!"

On he came. He was so near that in one active bound he would be upon her, but he advanced warily, with hands outstretched.

"Oh, what shall I do!" she sobbed. "Go back, you brute! I—I hate you. There are policemen in the wood. I'll scream for help!"

"No need, Miss Manning," said a calm voice which seemed to come from the circumambient air. "Don't cry out or be alarmed, no matter what happens!"

A hand, not Robert Fenley's caught her shoulder in a reassuring grip. A tall figure brushed by, and she heard a curious sound that had a certain smack in it—a hard smack, combined with a thudding effect, as if some one had smitten a pillow with a fist. A fist it was assuredly, and a hard one; but it smote no pillow. With a gurgling cough, Robert Fenley toppled headlong to the edge of the lake, and lay there probably some minutes, for the man who had hit him knew how and where to strike.

Sylvia did not scream. She had recognized Trenholme's voice, but she felt absurdly like fainting. Perhaps she swayed slightly, and her rescuer was aware of it, for he gathered her up in his arms as he might carry a scared child, nor did he set her on her feet when they were clear of the trees and in the open park.

"You are quite safe now," he said soothingly. "You are greatly upset, of course, and you need a minute or two to pull yourself together; but no one will hurt you while I am here. When you feel able to speak, you'll tell me where to take you, and I'll be your escort."

"I can speak now, thank you," said Sylvia, with a composure that was somewhat remarkable. "Please put me down!"

He obeyed, but she imagined he gave her a silent hug before his clasp relaxed. Even then his left hand still rested on her shoulder in a protective way.

CHAPTER XIV
THE SPREADING OF THE NET

That John Trenholme should be in the right place at the right moment, and that the place should happen to be one where his presence was urgently required in Sylvia Manning's behalf, was not such a far-fetched coincidence as it might be deemed, for instance, by a jury. Juries are composed mainly of bald-headed men, men whose shining pates have been denuded of hair by years and experience, and these factors dry the heart as surely as they impoverish the scalp. Consequently, juries (in bulk, be it understood; individual jurors may, perhaps, retain the emotional equipment of a Chatterton) are skeptical when asked to accept the vagaries of the artistic temperament in extenuation of some so-called irrational action.

In the present case counsel for the defense would plead that his clients (Sylvia would undoubtedly figure in the charge) were moved by an overwhelming impulse shared in common. It was a glorious night, he might urge; each had been thinking of the other; each elected to stroll forth under the stars; their sympathies were linked by the strange circumstances which had led to the production of a noteworthy picture—what more likely than that they should visit the scene to which that picture owed its genesis?

Trenholme, it might be held, had not knowingly reached that stage of soul-sickness which brings the passionate cry to *Valentine's* lips:

Except I be by Sylvia in the night,
There is no music in the nightingale;
Unless I look on Sylvia in the day,
There is no day for me to look upon.

"But, gentlemen," the wily one would continue, "that indefinable excitation of the nervous system which is summed up in the one small word 'love' must have a beginning; and whether that beginning springs from spore or germ, it is admittedly capable of amazingly rapid growth. The male defendant may not even have been aware of its existence, but subsequent events establish the diagnosis beyond cavil; and I would remind you that the melodious lines I have just quoted could not have been written by our immortal bard, Shakespeare, if two gentlemen of Verona, and two Veronese ladies as well, had not yielded to influences not altogether unlike those which governed my clients on this memorable occasion."

Juries invariably treat Shakespeare's opinions with profound respect. They know they ought to be well acquainted with his "works," but they are not, and hope to conceal their ignorance by accepting the poet's philosophy without reservation.

If, however, owing to the forensic skill of an advocate, romance might be held accountable for the wanderings of John and Sylvia, what of Robert? He, at least, was not under its magic spell. He, when the fateful hour struck, was merely drinking himself drowsy. To explain *him*, witnesses would be needed, and who more credible than a Superintendent and Detective Inspector of the Criminal Investigation Department?

When Winter had smoked, and Furneaux had contributed some personal reminiscences the whole aim and object of which was the perplexing and mystification of that discreet person, Tomlinson, the two retired to their room at an early hour. The butler pressed them hospitably to try the house's special blend of Scotch whisky, but they had declined resolutely. Both acknowledged to an unwonted lassitude and sleepiness—symptoms which Hilton Fenley might expect and inquire about. When they were gone, the major domo sat down to review the day's doings.

His master's death at the hands of a murderer had shocked and saddened him far more than his manner betrayed. If some fantastic chain of events brought Tomlinson to the scaffold he would still retain the demeanor of an exemplary butler. But beneath the externals of his office he had a heart and a brain; and his heart grieved for a respected employer, and his brain told him that Scotland Yard was no wiser than he when it came to suspecting a likely person of having committed the crime, let alone arresting the suspect and proving his guilt.

Of course, therein Tomlinson was in error. Even butlers of renown have their limitations, and his stopped far short of the peculiar science of felon-hunting in which Winter and Furneaux were geniuses, each in his own line.

Assuredly he would have been vastly astonished could he have seen their movements when the bedroom door closed on them. In fact, his trained ear might have found some new quality in such a commonplace thing as the closing of the door. Every lock and bolt and catch in The Towers was in perfect working order, yet the lock of this door failed to click, for the excellent reason that it was jammed by a tiny wedge. Hence, it could be opened noiselessly if need be; and lest a hinge might squeak each hinge was forthwith drenched with vaseline. Further, a tiny circlet of India rubber, equipped with a small spike, was placed between door and jamb.

Then, murmuring in undertones when they spoke, the detectives unpacked their portmanteaux. Winter produced no article out of the ordinary run, but Furneaux unrolled a knotted contrivance which proved to be a rope ladder.

"One or both of us may have to go out by the window," he said. "At any rate, we have Wellington's authority for the military axiom that a good leader always provides a line of retreat."

"I wonder what became of the rest of that wine?" said Winter, rolling the beer bottle in a shirt and stowing it away.

"I didn't dare ask. Tomlinson can put two and two together rather cleverly. He *almost* interfered when Harris brought the decanter, so I dropped the wine question like a hot potato."

"It had gone, though, when we came back from Robert's room. Hilton sent for it. Bet you another new hat he emptied——"

"You'll get no more new hats out of me," growled Furneaux savagely, giving an extra pressure to a pair of sharp hooks which gripped the window sill, and from which the rope ladder could be dropped to the ground instantly.

"Sorry. Where did you retrieve that dirty towel?" For the little man had taken from a pocket an object which merited the description, and was placing it in his bag.

"It's one of Hilton's. He used it to wipe bark moss off his clothes. Queer thing that such rascals always omit some trivial precaution. He should have burned the towel with the moccasins; but he don't. This towel will help to strangle him."

"You're becoming a bloodthirsty detective," mused Winter aloud. "I've seldom seen you so vindictive. Why is it?"

"I dislike snakes, and this fellow is a poisonous specimen. If there were no snakes in the world, we should all be so happy!"

"Blessed if I see that."

"I have always suspected that your religious education had been neglected. Read the Bible and Milton. Then you'll understand; and incidentally speak and write better English."

"Can you suggest any means whereby I can grasp your jokes without being bored to weariness? They're more soporific than bromide. Anyhow, it's time we undressed."

Though the blind was drawn the window was open; there was no knowing who might be watching from the garden, so they went through all the motions of undressing and placed their boots outside the door.

Then the light was switched off, the blind raised, and they dressed again rapidly, donning other boots. Each pocketed an automatic pistol and an electric torch and, by preconcerted plan, Winter sat by the window and Furneaux by the door. It was then a quarter to eleven, and they hardly looked for any developments until a much later hour, but they neglected no precaution. Unquestionably it would be difficult for any one to move about in that part of the house, or cross the gardens without attracting their attention.

Their room was situated on the south front, two doors from Sylvia's, and two from Hilton Fenley's bedroom. The door lay in shadow beyond the range of the light burning in the hall. Sylvia's room was farther along the corridor. The door of Hilton's bedroom occupied the same plane; the door of his sitting-room faced the end of the corridor.

The walls were massive, as in all Tudor houses, and the doors so deeply recessed that there was space for a small mat in front of each. Ordinarily boots placed there were not visible in the line of the corridor, but the detectives' footgear stood well in view. There were two reasons for this. In the first place, Hilton Fenley might like to see them, so his highly probable if modest desire was gratified; secondly, when Parker visited Sylvia and quitted her, and when Sylvia went downstairs, Furneaux's head, lying between two pairs of boots, could scarcely be distinguished, while his scope of vision was only slightly, if at all, diminished.

Soon the girl's footsteps could be heard crossing the hall, and the raising of the drawing-room window and opening of the shutters were clearly audible. Winter, whose office had been a sinecure hitherto, now came into the scheme.

He saw Sylvia's slight form standing beneath, marked her hesitancy, and watched her slow progress down the terraces and into the park. This nocturnal enterprise on her part was rather perplexing, and he was in two minds whether or not to cross the room and consult with Furneaux, when the latter suddenly withdrew his head, closed the door, and hissed "Snore!"

Winter crept to a bed, and put up an artistic performance, a duet, musical, regular, not too loud. In a little while his colleague's "S-s-t!" stopped him, and a slight crack of a finger against a thumb called him to the door, which was open again.

Explanation was needless. Hilton Fenley, like the other watchers, hearing the creaking of window and shutters, had looked out from his own darkened room. In all likelihood, thanking his stars for the happy chance given thus unexpectedly, he noted the direction the girl was taking, and acted as if prepared for this very development; the truth being, of course, that he was merely adapting his own plans to immediate and more favorable conditions.

Coming out into the corridor, he consulted his watch. Then he glanced in the direction of the room which held the two men he had cause to fear—such ample cause as he little dreamed of at that moment. To make assurance doubly sure, he walked that way, not secretly, but boldly, since it was part of his project now to court observation—by others, at any rate, if not by the drugged emissaries of Scotland Yard. He waited outside the closed door and heard what he expected to hear, the snoring of two men sound asleep.

Returning, he did not reënter his own room, but crossed the head of the staircase to Robert's. He knocked lightly, and his brother's "Hello, there! Come in!" reached Furneaux's ears. Not a word of the remainder of the colloquy that ensued was lost on either of the detectives.

"Sorry to disturb you, Bob," said Hilton, speaking from the doorway, "but I thought you might not be in bed, and I've come to tell you that Sylvia has just gone out by way of the drawing-room and is wandering about the park."

"Sylvia! On her lonesome?" was Robert's astounded cry.

"Yes. It isn't right. I can't understand her behavior. I would have followed her myself; but in view of your statement at dinner tonight, I fancied it would save some annoyance if I entrusted that duty to you."

"Look here, Hilton, old chap, are you really in earnest?"

"About Sylvia? Yes. I actually saw her. At this moment she is heading for the lake. If you hurry you'll see her yourself."

"I say, it's awfully decent of you ... I take back a lot of what I said tonight.... Of course, as matters stand, this is *my* job.... Tell MacBain not to lock us out."

"I'll attend to that, if necessary. But don't mention me to Sylvia. She might resent the notion of being spied on. Say that you, too, were strolling about. You see, I heard the window being opened, and looked out, naturally. Anyhow, drop me, and run this affair on your own."

Robert was slightly obfuscated—the fresh air quickly made him worse—but he was sensible of having grossly misjudged Hilton.

"Right-O," he said, hurrying downstairs. "We'll have a talk in the mornin'. Dash it! It's twelve o'clock. That silly kid! What's she after, I'd like to know?"

Robert gone, Hilton returned to his own room and rang a bell. MacBain came, and was asked if he was aware that Miss Sylvia had quitted the house. MacBain gave his version of the story, and Fenley remarked that he might leave the window unfastened until he made his rounds at one o'clock.

Seemingly as an afterthought, Hilton mentioned his brother's open door, and MacBain discovered that Mr. Robert was missing also.

By that time the detectives, without exchanging a word, had each arrived at the same opinion as to the trend of events. Hilton Fenley was remodeling his projects to suit an unforeseen development. No matter what motive inspired Sylvia Manning's midnight ramble, there could be no disputing the influence which dominated Robert Fenley. He was his brother's catspaw. When his rifle was found next day MacBain's testimony would be a tremendous addition to the weight of evidence against him, since any unprejudiced judgment must decide that the pursuit of his "cousin" was a mere pretense to enable him to go out and search for the weapon he had foolishly left in the wood.

Hilton might or might not admit that he told Robert of the girl's escapade. If he did admit it, he might be trusted to give the incident the requisite kink to turn the scale against Robert. Surveying the facts with cold impartiality afterwards, Scotland Yard decided that while Hilton could not hope that Robert would be convicted of the murder, the latter would assuredly be suspected of it, perhaps arrested and tried; and in any event his marriage with Sylvia Manning would become a sheer impossibility.

Moreover, once the rifle was found by the police, the only reasonable prospect of connecting Hilton himself with the crime would have vanished into thin air. If that weapon were picked up in the Quarry Wood, or for that matter in any other part of the estate, the hounds of the law were beaten. Winter's level-headed shrewdness and Furneaux's almost uncanny intuition might have saddled Hilton with blood guiltiness, but a wide chasm must be bridged before they could provide the requisite proof of their theory.

In fact, thus far they dared not even hint at bringing a charge against him. To succeed, they had to show that the incredible was credible, that a murderer could be in a room within a few feet of his victim and in a wood distant fully four hundred yards. It was a baffling problem, not wholly incapable of solution by circumstantial evidence, but best left to be elucidated by Hilton Fenley himself. They believed now that he was about to oblige them by supplying that corroborative detail which, in the words of Poohbah, "lends artistic verisimilitude to an otherwise bald and unconvincing narrative."

Winter drew Furneaux into the room, and breathed the words into his ear:

"You go. You stand less chance of being seen. I'll search his room."

"If there is a misfire, show a signal after five minutes."

"Right!"

Furneaux, standing back from the window, but in such a position that a light would be visible to any one perched on the rock in the wood, pressed the button of an electric torch three times rapidly. Then he lowered the rope ladder and clambered down with the nimbleness of a sailor. In all probability, Hilton Fenley was still talking to MacBain and creating the illusion that the last thing he would think of was a stroll out of doors at that late hour. But the little man took no chances. Having surveyed the ground carefully during the day, he was not bothered now by doubts as to the most practicable path.

Creeping close to the house till he reached the yew hedge, and then passing through an arch, he remained in the shadow of the hedge till it turned at a right angle in front of the Italian garden. From that point to the edge of the Quarry Wood was not a stone's throw, and clumps of rhododendrons and other flowering shrubs gave shelter in plenty. Arrived at the mouth of the footpath, which he had marked by counting the trees in the avenue, he halted and listened intently. There was no sound of rustling grass or crunched gravel. Hilton was taking matters leisurely. Fifteen minutes would give him ample time for the business he had in hand. Even if Robert and Sylvia reached home before him, which was unlikely—far more unlikely even than he imagined—he could say that he thought it advisable to follow his brother and help in the search for the girl. The same excuse would serve if he met any of those pestilential police prowling about the grounds. Indeed, he could dispatch the alert and intelligent ones on the trail of the wanderers, especially on Robert's. In a word, matters were going well for Hilton, so well that Furneaux laughed as he turned into the wood.

Here the detective had to advance with care. Beneath the trees the darkness was now so complete that it had that peculiar quality of density which everyday speech likens to a wall. Cats, gamekeepers, poachers, and other creatures of predatory and nocturnal habits can find and follow a definite track under such conditions; but detectives are nearly human, and Furneaux was compelled to use the torch more than once. He ran no risk in doing this. Hilton Fenley could not yet be in a position to catch the gleam of light among the trees. The one thing to avoid was delay, and Furneaux had gained rather than lost time, unless Fenley was running at top speed.

After crossing the damp hollow the Jerseyman had no further difficulty; he breasted the hill and kept a hand extended so as to avoid colliding with a tree trunk. Expecting at any instant to have a bull's-eye lantern flashed in his eyes, which he did not want to happen, he said softly:

"Hi! You two! Don't show a light! How near are you?"

"Oh, it's you, sir!" said a voice. "We thought it would be. We saw the signal, and you said you might be the first to arrive."

"Any second signal?"

"No, sir."

Furneaux recognized the pungent scent of the colza oil used in policemen's lamps.

"By gad," he said, "if the average criminal had the nose of the veriest cur dog he'd smell that oil a mile away. Now, where are you? There." He had butted into a constable's solid bulk. "Take me to the rock—quick. We must hide behind it, on the lower side.... Is this the place? Right! Squat down, both of you, and make yourselves comfortable, so that you won't feel your position irksome, and move perhaps at the wrong moment. When you feel me crawling away, follow to the upper foot of the rock—no farther.

"Stand upright then, and try to keep your joints from cracking. There must be no creaking of belts or boots. Absolute silence is the order. Not a word spoken. No matter what you hear, don't move again until you see the light of my electric torch. Then run to me, turning on your own lamps, and help in arresting any one I may be holding. Use your handcuffs if necessary, and don't hesitate to grab hard if there is a struggle. Remember, you are to arrest *any one*, no matter who it may be. Got that?"

"Yes, sir," came two eager voices.

"Don't be excited. It will be an easy thing. If we make a mistake, I bear the responsibility. Now, keep still as mice when they hear a cat."

One of the men giggled. Both constables had met Furneaux in the local police station that afternoon, as he had asked the Inspector to parade the pair who would be on duty during the night. It was then that he had arranged a simple code of flash signals, and warned them to look out for Winter or himself during the night. Any other person who turned up was not to be challenged until he reached the higher ground beyond the rock, but that instruction was to be acted on only in the unavoidable absence of one of the Scotland Yard officers. Privately, the constables hoped Furneaux would be their leader. They deemed him "a funny little josser," and marveled greatly at his manner and appearance. Still, they had heard of his reputation; the Inspector, in an expansive moment, had observed that "Monkey Face was sharper than he looked."

Thinking example better than precept, Furneaux did not reprove the giggler. Lying there, screened even in broad daylight by the bulk of the rock and some hazels growing vigorously in that restricted area owing to the absence of foliage overhead, he listened to the voices of the night, never dumb in a large wood. Birds fluttered uneasily on the upper branches of the trees—indeed, Furneaux was lucky in that the occasional gleam of the torch had not sent a pheasant hurtling off with frantic clamor ere ever the rendezvous was reached—and some winged creature, probably an owl, swept over the rock in stealthy flight. The rabbits were all out in the open, nibbling grass and crops at leisure, but there were other tiny forms rustling among the shrubs and scampering across the soft carpet of fallen leaves.

Twitterings, and subdued squeaks, and sudden rushes of pattering feet, the murmuring of myriad fronds in the placid breeze, the whispering of the neighboring elms, even the steady chant of the distant cascade—all swelled into a soft and continuous chorus, hardly heard by the country policemen, accustomed as they were to the sounds of a woodland at night, but of surprising volume and variety to the man whose forests lay in the paved wilderness of London.

Suddenly a twig cracked sharply and a match was struck. It was of the safety type and made little noise, but it was too much for the nerves of a bird, which flew away noisily. Furneaux pursed his lips and wanted to whistle. He realized now what an escape he had earlier. But the intruder seemed to care less about attracting attention than making rapid progress. He came on swiftly, striking other matches when required, until he stood on the bare ground near the rock. Not daring to lift a head, none of the three watchers could see the newcomer, and in that respect their hiding-place was almost too well chosen. Whoever it was, he needed no more matches to guide his footsteps. They heard him advancing a few paces; then he halted again. After a marked interval, punctuated by a soft, whirring noise hard to interpret, there were irregular scrapings and the creaking of a branch.

Furneaux arose. Keeping a hand on the rock until he was clear of the shrubs, he crept forward on thievish feet. His assistants, moving more clumsily to their allotted station, were audible enough to him, but to a man unconscious of their presence, and actively climbing a tree, they were remote and still as Uranus and Saturn.

The scraping of feet and heavy breathing, to say nothing of the prompt flight of several birds, led the detective unerringly to the trunk of a lofty chestnut which he had already fixed on as the cover whence the shot that killed Mortimer Fenley was fired. He was convinced also that the rifle was yet hidden there, and his thin lips parted in a smile now that his theory was about to be justified.

He could follow the panting efforts of the climber quite easily. He knew when the weapon was unlashed from the limb to which it was bound, and when the descent was begun. He could measure almost the exact distance of his prey from the ground, and was awaiting the final drop before flashing the torch on his prisoner, when something rapped him smartly on the forehead. It was a rope, doubled and twisted, and subsequent investigation showed that it must have been thrown in a coil over the lowermost branch in order to facilitate the only difficult part of the climb offered by ten feet of straight bole.

That trivial incident changed the whole course of events. Taken by surprise, since he did not know what had struck him, Furneaux pressed the governor of the torch a second too soon, and his eyes, raised instantaneously, met those of Hilton Fenley, who was on the point of letting go the branch and swinging himself down.

During a thrilling moment they gazed at each other, the detective cool and seemingly unconcerned, the self-avowed murderer livid with mortal fear. Then Furneaux caught the rope and held it.

"I thought you'd go climbing tonight, Fenley," he said. "Let me assist you. Tricky things, ropes. You're at the wrong end of this one."

Even Homer nods, but Furneaux had erred three times in as many seconds. He had switched on the light prematurely, and his ready banter had warned the parricide that a well-built scheme was crumbling to irretrievable ruin. Moreover, he had underrated the nervous forces of the man thus trapped and outwitted. Fenley knew that when his feet touched the earth he would begin a ghastly pilgrimage to the scaffold. Two yellow orbs of light were already springing up the slight incline from the rock, betokening the presence of captors in overwhelming number. What was to be done? Nothing, in reason, yet Furneaux had likened him to a snake, and he displayed now the primal instinct of the snake to fight when cornered. Thrusting the heavy gun he was carrying straight downward, he delivered a vicious and unerring blow.

The stock caught the detective on the crown of the head, and he fell to his knees, dropping the torch, which of course went out as soon as the thumb relaxed its pressure.

CHAPTER XV
SOME STAGE EFFECTS

Fenley himself dropped almost simultaneously with the rifle, landing with both feet on Furneaux's back, and thus completing the little man's discomfiture. By that time the two policemen were nearly upon him, but he was lithe and fierce as a cobra, and had seized the rifle again before they could close with him. Jabbing the nearer adversary with the muzzle, he smashed a lamp and sent its owner sprawling backward. Then, swinging the weapon, he aimed a murderous blow at the second constable.

The man contrived to avoid it to a certain extent, but it glanced off his left arm and caught the side of his head; and he, too, measured his length. All three, detective and police, were on their feet promptly, for none was seriously injured; but Furneaux was dazed and had to grope for the torch, and the second constable's lamp had gone out owing to a rush of oil from the cistern. Thus, during some precious seconds, they were in total darkness.

Meanwhile Fenley had escaped. Luck, after deserting him, had come to his rescue in the nick of time. He had blundered into the path, and managed to keep to it, and the somewhat strong language in which Furneaux expressed his feelings anent the Hertfordshire Constabulary, and the no less lurid comments of two angry members of the force, helped to conceal the sounds which would otherwise have indicated the direction taken by the fugitive.

At last, having found the torch, Furneaux collected his scattered wits.

"Now don't be scared and run away, you two," he said sarcastically, producing an automatic pistol. "I'm only going to tell Mr. Winter that we've bungled the job."

He fired twice in the air, and two vivid spurts of flame rose high among the branches of the chestnut; but the loud reports of the shooting were as nothing compared with the din that followed. Every rook within a mile flew from its eyrie and cawed strenuously. Pheasants clucked and clattered in all directions, owls hooted, and dogs barked in the kennels, in the stable yard, and in nearly every house of the two neighboring villages.

"I don't see what good that'll do, sir," was the rueful comment of the policeman who had, in his own phrase, "collected a thick ear," and was now feeling the spot tenderly. "He hasn't shinned up the tree again; that's a positive certainty."

"I should have thought that a really clever fellow like you would guess that I wanted to raise a row," said Furneaux. "Have you breath enough left to blow your whistles?"

"But, sir, your orders were———"

"Blow, and be damned to you. Don't I know the fault is mine! Blow, and crack your cheeks! Blow wild peals, my Roberts, else we are copped coppers!"

The mild radiance of the torch showed that the detective's face was white with fury and his eyes gleaming red. To think that a dangling rope's end should have spoiled his finest capture, undone a flawless piece of imaginative reasoning which his own full record had never before equaled! It was humiliating, maddening. No wonder the policemen thought him crazy!

But they whistled with a will. Winter heard them, and was stirred to strange activities. Robert Fenley, recovering from an ague and sickness, heard and marveled at the pandemonium which had broken loose in the park. The household at The Towers was aroused, heads were craned out of windows, women screamed, and men dressed hastily. Keepers, estate hands, and stablemen tumbled into their garments and hurried out, armed with guns and cudgels. An unhappy woman, tossing in the fitful dreams of drug-induced sleep, was awakened by the pistol shots and terrified by the noise of slamming doors and hurrying feet.

She struggled out of bed and screamed for an attendant, but none came. She pressed an electric bell, which rang continuously in the night watchman's room; but he had run to the front of the house and was unlocking the front door, where a squad of willing men soon awaited Winter's instructions. For the Superintendent, after rushing to the telephone, had shouted an order to MacBain before he made off in the direction of the Quarry Wood.

The one tocsin which exercises a dread significance in a peaceful and law-abiding English community at the present day struck a new and awful note in Hilton Fenley's brain. Fool that he was, why had he fought? Why was he flying? Had he brazened it out, the police would not have dared arrest him. His brain was as acute as the best of theirs. He could have evolved a theory of the crime as subtle as any detective's, and who so keen-witted as a son eager to avenge a father's murder? But he had thrown away a gambler's chance by a moment of frenzied struggle. He was doomed now. No plausible explanation would serve his need. He was hunted. The pack was after him. The fox had broken cover, and the hounds were in full cry.

Whither should he go? He knew not. Still clutching the empty gun—for which he had not even one cartridge in his pockets—he made hopelessly for the open park. Already some glimmer of light showed that he was winning free of these accursed trees, which had stretched forth a thousand hands to tear his flesh and trip his uncertain feet. That way, at least, lay the world. In the wood he might have circled blindly until captured.

Now a drawback of such roaring maelstroms of alarm and uncertainty is their knack of submerging earlier and less dramatic passages in the lives of those whom Fate drags into their sweeping currents. Lest, therefore, the strangely contrived meeting between Sylvia and her knight errant should be neglected by the chronicler, it is well to return to those two young people at the moment when Sylvia was declaring her unimpaired power of standing without support.

Trenholme was disposed to take everything for the best in a magic world. "Whatever is, is right" is a doctrine which appeals to the artistic temperament, inasmuch as it blends fatalism and the action of Providence in proportions so admirably adjusted that no philosopher yet born has succeeded in reducing them to a formula. But Eve did not bite the apple in that spirit. It was forbidden: she wanted to know why. Sylvia's first thought was to discover a reasonable reason for Trenholme's presence. Of course, there was one that jumped to the eye, but it was too absurd to suppose that he had come to the tryst in obedience to the foolish vagaries which accounted for her own actions. She blushed to the nape of her neck at the conceit, which called for instant and severe repression, and her voice reflected the passing mood.

"I don't wish to underrate the great service you have rendered me," she said coldly, "and I shall always be your debtor for it; but I can not help asking how you came to be standing under the cedars at this hour of the night?"

"I wonder," he said.

She wriggled her shoulder slightly, as a polite intimation that his hand need not rest there any longer, but he seemed to misinterpret the movement, and drew her an inch or so nearer, whereupon the wriggling ceased.

"But that is no answer at all," she murmured, aware of a species of fear of this big, masterful man: a fear rather fascinating in its tremors, like a novice's cringing to the vibration of electricity in a mildly pleasant form; a fear as opposed to her loathing of Robert Fenley as the song of a thrush to the purr of a tiger.

"I can tell you, in a disconnected sort of way," he said, evidently trying to focus his thoughts on a problem set by the gods, and which, in consequence, was incapable of logical solution by a mere mortal. "It was a fine night. I felt restless. The four walls of a room were prison-like. I strolled out. I was thinking of you. I am here."

She trembled a little. Blushing even more deeply than before, she fancied he must be able to feel her skin hot through silk and linen. For all that, she contrived to laugh.

"It sounds convincing, but there is something missing in the argument," she said.

"Most likely," he admitted. "A woman analyzes emotion far more intimately than a man. Perhaps, if you were to tell me why *you* were drawn to cross the park at midnight, you might supply a clue to my own moon madness."

"But there isn't any moon, and I think I ought to be returning to the house."

He knew quite well that she had evaded his question, and, so readily does the heart respond to the whisperings of hope, he was aware of a sudden tumult in that which doctors call the cardiac region. She, too, had come forth to tell her longings to the stars! That thrice blessed picture had drawn them together by a force as unseen and irresistible as the law of gravitation! Then he became aware of a dreadful qualm. Had he any right to place on her slim shoulders the weight of an avowal from which he had flinched? He dropped that protecting hand as if it had been struck sharply.

"I have annoyed you by my stupid word-fencing," he said contritely.

"No, indeed," she said, and, reveling in a new sense of power, her tone grew very gentle. "Why should we seek far-fetched theories for so simple a thing as a stroll out of doors on a night like this? I am not surprised that you, at any rate, should wish to visit the place where that delightful picture sprang into being. It was my exceeding good fortune that you happened to be close at hand when I needed help. I must explain that——"

"My explanation comes first," he broke in. "I saw you crossing the park. A second time in the course of one day I had to decide whether to remain hidden or make a bolt for it. Again I determined to stand fast; for had you seen and heard a man vanishing among the trees you would certainly have been alarmed, not only because of the hour but owing to today's extraordinary events. Moreover, I felt sure you were coming to the lake, and I did not wish to stop you. That was a bit of pure selfishness on my part. I wanted you to come. If ever a man was vouchsafed the realization of an unspoken prayer, I am that man tonight."

Trenholme had never before made love to any woman, but lack of experience did not seem to trouble him greatly. Sylvia, however, though very much alive to that element in his words, bethought herself of something else which they implied.

"Then you heard what my cousin Robert said?" she commented.

"Every syllable. When the chance of an effectual reply offered, I recalled his disjointed remarks collectively."

"Did you hit him very hard?"

"Just hard enough to stop him from annoying you further tonight."

"I suppose he deserved it. He was horrid. But I don't wish you to meet him again just now. He is no coward, and he might attack you."

"That would be most unfortunate," he agreed.

"So, if you don't mind, we'll take a roundabout way. By skirting the Quarry Wood we can reach the avenue, near the place where we met this evening. Do you remember?"

"Perfectly. I shall be very old before I forget."

"But I mean the place where we met. Of course, you could hardly pretend that you had forgotten meeting me."

"As soon would the daffodil forget where last it bloomed.

"Daffodils,
That come before the swallow dares, and take
The winds of March with beauty.

"Not that I should quote you 'A Winter's Tale,' but rather search my poor store for apter lines from 'A Midsummer Night's Dream':

"I know a bank whereon the wild thyme blows,
Where ox-lips and the nodding violet grows;
Quite over-canopied with luxurious woodbine,
With sweet musk roses, and with eglantine:
There sleeps Titania.

"Believe me, I have an excellent memory—for some things."

They walked together in silence a little way, and dreamed, perchance, that they were wandering in Oberon's realm with Hermia and Lysander. Then Sylvia, stealing a shy glance at the tall figure by her side, acknowledged that once she filled the rôle of Titania in a schoolroom version of the play.

"We had no man," she said, "but the masks and costumes served us well. After a day's study I could be a Fairy Queen once more.

"I pray thee, gentle mortal, sing again; Mine ear is much enraptured of thy note——"

She stopped suddenly. The next lines were distinctly amorous. He laughed with ready appreciation of her difficulty, but generously provided a way out.

"Poor mortal!" he tittered. "And must I wear an ass's head to be in character?"

A loud report, and then another, brought them back rudely from a make-believe wood near Athens to a peril-haunted park in an English county. For the second time that night Sylvia knew what fear meant. Intuitively, she shrank close to the strong man who seemed destined to be her protector; and when an arm clasped her again, she cowered close to its sheltering embrace.

"Oh, what is it?" she wailed in terror.

"It is hard to say," he answered quietly, and the confidence in his voice was the best assurance of safety he could have given. "Those shots were fired from some sort of rifle, not of the same caliber as that which was used this morning, but unquestionably a rifle. Perhaps it is one of these modern pistols. I don't wish to alarm you needlessly, Miss Manning, but there is some probability that the police have discovered the man who killed Mr. Fenley, and there is a struggle going on. At any rate, let us remain out here in the open. We shall be as safe here as anywhere."

Sylvia, who had not been afraid to venture alone into the park at midnight, was now in a quite feminine state of fright. She clung to Trenholme without any pretense of other feeling than one of unbounded trust. Her heart was pounding frantically, and she was trembling from head to foot.

The police whistles were shrilling their insistent summons for help, and Trenholme knew that the commotion had arisen in the exact part of the Quarry Wood whence the murderous bullet had sped that morning. He was unarmed, of course, being devoid of even such a mildly aggressive weapon as a walking-stick, but there was doubt in his mind that the best thing to do was to stand fast. He was not blind to the possibility of imminent danger, for the very spot they had reached lay in a likely line of retreat for any desperado whom the police might have discovered and be pursuing. Naturally he took it for granted that the criminal had fired the two shots, and the fact that the whistles were still in full blast showed that the chase had not been abandoned.

Still, the only course open was to take such chances as came their way. He could always shield the girl with his own body, or tell her to lie flat on the ground while he closed with an assailant if opportunity served. Being a level-headed, plucky youngster, he was by no means desirous of indulging in deeds of derring-do. The one paramount consideration was the safe conduct of Sylvia to the house, and he hoped sincerely that if a miscreant were trying to escape, he would choose any route save that which led from the wood to Roxton village.

"Don't hesitate if I bid you throw yourself down at full length," he said, unconsciously stroking Sylvia's hair with his free hand. "In a minute or two we'll make for the avenue. Meanwhile, let us listen. If any one is coming in this direction we ought to hear him, and forewarned is forearmed."

Choking back a broken question, she strove submissively to check her distressed sobbing. Were it not for the hubbub of thousands of rooks and pheasants they would assuredly have caught the sounds of Hilton Fenley's panic-stricken onrush through the trees. As it was, he saw them first, and, even in his rabid frenzy, recognized Sylvia. It was only to be expected that he should mistake Trenholme for his brother, and in a new spasm of fright, he recollected he was carrying the rifle. Robert Fenley, of course, would identify it at a glance, and could hardly fail to be more than suspicious at sight of it. With an oath, he threw the telltale weapon back among the undergrowth, and, summoning the last shreds of his shattered nerves to lend some degree of self-control, walked rapidly out into the open park.

Sylvia saw him and shrieked. Trenholme was about to thrust her behind him, when some familiar attribute about the outline of the approaching figure caused her to cry—

"Why, it's Hilton!"

"Yes, Sylvia," came the breathless answer. "You heard the firing, of course? The police have found some fellow in the wood. You and Bob make for the avenue. I'm going this way in case he breaks cover for the Roxton gate. Hurry! You'll find some of the men there. Never mind about me. I'll be all right!"

He was running while he talked, edging away toward the group of cedars; and, under the conditions, it was not for Trenholme to undeceive him as to the mistake in regarding the artist as Robert Fenley. In any event, the appearance of Hilton from that part of the wood seemed to prove that the man whom the law was seeking could not be in the same locality, so Trenholme did not hesitate to urge Sylvia to fall in with her "cousin's" instructions.

For the time, then, they may be left to progress uninterruptedly to safety and not very prompt enlightenment; the flight of the self-confessed murderer calls for more immediate attention. Probably, after the first moment of suspense, and when he was sure that escape was still not utterly impracticable, he intended to cross the park to the northwest and climb the boundary wall. But a glimpse of the black line of trees daunted him. He simply dared not face those pitiless sentinels again. He pictured himself forcing a way through the undergrowth in the dense gloom and failing perhaps; for the vegetation was wilder there than in any other portion of the estate. So, making a détour, he headed for the unencumbered parkland once more, and gained the wall near Jackson's farm about the time that Trenholme and Sylvia entered the avenue.

He was unquestionably in a parlous state. Bare-headed, unarmed, he could not fail to attract attention in a district where every resident knew the other, nor could he resist capture when the hue and cry went forth. What to do he knew not. Even if he managed to reach the railway station unchallenged, the last train of the day had left for London soon after eleven, and the earliest next morning was timed for five o'clock, too late by many hours to serve his desperate need.

Could he hire a motor car or bicycle? The effort was fraught with every variety of risk. There was a small garage at Easton, but those cunning detectives would be raising the countryside already, and the telephone would close every outlet. For the first time in his life Hilton Fenley realized that the world is too small to hold a murderer. He was free, would soon have the choice of a network of main roads and lanes in a rural district at the dead hour of the night, yet he felt himself securely caged as some creature of the jungle trapped in a pit.

Crossing Jackson's farmyard, not without disturbing a dog just quieting down after the preceding racket, he hurried into the village street, having made up his mind to face the inevitable and arouse the garage keeper. By the irony of fate he passed the cottage in which Police Constable Farrow was lying asleep and utterly unaware of the prevalent excitement, to join in which he would have kept awake all that night and the next.

Then the turn of Fortune's wheel befriended Fenley again. Outside a house stood Dr. Stern's car, a closed-in runabout in which both the doctor and his chauffeur were sheltered from inclement weather. The chauffeur was lounging on the pavement, smoking a cigarette, and Fenley, of course, recognized him. His heart leaped. Let him be bold now, and he might win through. A handkerchief wiped some of the blood off his face where the skin had been broken by the trees, and he avoided the glare of the lamps.

"Hello, Tom," he said, "where is the doctor?"

"Inside, sir," with a glance toward an upper room where a light shone. "What's happened at The Towers, sir? Was it shooting I heard a while since?"

"Yes. A false alarm, though. The police thought they had found some suspicious character in the grounds."

"By jing, sir, did they fire at him?"

Fenley saw that the story was weak, and hastened to correct it.

"No, no," he said. "The police don't shoot first. That was my brother, Robert. You know what a harebrained fellow he is. Said he fired in order to make the man double back. But that is a small matter. Can I have one word with Dr. Stern?"

"I'll see, sir," and the chauffeur went to the house.

Furneaux had estimated Hilton Fenley correctly in ascribing to him the quality of cold-bloodedness. Ninety-nine men among a hundred would have appropriated the motor car then and there, but Fenley saw by waiting a minute and displaying the requisite coolness he might succeed in throwing his pursuers off the trail for some hours.

Stern came. It chanced that he was watching a good patient through a crisis, and would be detained until daybreak.

"Hello, Hilton," he cried. "What's up now, and what's the racket in the park?"

Fenley explained, but hurried to the vital matter.

"My car is out of action," he said. "I was going to the Easton garage to hire one when I saw yours standing here. Lend it to me for a couple of hours; there's a good fellow. I'll pay well for the use of it."

"Pay? Nonsense! Jump in! Take Mr. Fenley where he wants to go, Tom. Where to first, Hilton?"

"St. Albans. I'm exceedingly obliged. And look here, Stern, I insist on paying."

"We can settle that afterwards. Off with you. I'll walk home, Tom."

Away sped the car. Running through Easton, Fenley saw two policemen stationed at a cross-road. They signaled the car to stop, and his blood curdled, but, in the same instant, they saw the chauffeur's face; the other occupant was cowering as far back in the shadow as possible.

"Oh, it's Dr. Stern," said one. "Right, Tom. By the way, have you seen anything of——"

"Go on, do!" growled Fenley, drowning the man's voice. "I'm in a vile hurry."

That was his last real hairbreadth escape—for that night, at any rate, though other thrills were in store. The chauffeur was greatly surprised when bidden to go on from St. Albans to London, and take the High Barnet road to the City; but Fenley produced a five-pound note at the right moment, and the man reflected that his master would not hesitate to oblige a wealthy client, who evidently meant to make good the wear and tear on the car.

In about an hour Fenley alighted on the pavement opposite the firm's premises in Bishopsgate Street. If a policeman had chanced to be standing there the fugitive would have known that the game was up, but the only wayfarers in that part of the thoroughfare were some street cleaners.

Now that he saw a glimmer of light where hitherto all was darkness, he was absolutely clear-brained and cool in manner.

"Wait five minutes," he said. "I sha'n't detain you longer."

He let himself in with a master key, taken from his dead father's pockets earlier by Tomlinson. Going to the banker's private office, he ransacked a safe and a cabinet with hasty method. He secured a hat, an overcoat, an umbrella and a packed suitcase, left there for emergency journeys in connection with the business, and was back in the street again within less than the specified time.

His tongue clave to the roof of his mouth when he found a policeman chatting with the chauffeur, but the man saluted him with a civil "Good morning!"

In the City of London, which is deserted as a cemetery from ten o'clock at night till six in the morning, the police keep a sharp eye on waiting cabs and automobiles between these hours, and invariably inquire their business.

This constable was quite satisfied that all was well when he saw Mr. Hilton Fenley, whom he knew by sight. In any event, the flying murderer was safer than he dared hope in that place and at that time. The Roxton telephonic system was temporarily useless in so far as it affected his movements; for a fire had broken out at The Towers, and the flames of the burning roof had been as a beacon for miles around during the whole of the time consumed by the run to London.

CHAPTER XVI
THE CLOSE OF A TRAGEDY

Winter was in the Quarry Wood and feeling his way but trusting to hands and feet when he heard, and soon saw, Furneaux and the two constables coming toward him. The little detective held the electric torch above his head, and was striding on without looking to right or left. The bitterness of defeat was in his face. Life had turned to gall and wormwood. As the expressive American phrase has it, he was chewing mud.

The Superintendent smiled. He knew what torment his friend was suffering.

"Hello, there!" he said gruffly, and the three men jumped, for their nerves were on edge.

"Oh, it's you, Napoleon," yelped Furneaux. "Behold Soult and his army corps, come to explain how Sir John Moore dodged him at Corunna."

"You've lost your man, then?"

"Botched the job at the moment of victory. And all through a rope end."

"Tush! That isn't in your line."

"Must I be lashed by your wit, too? The rope was applied to me, not to Fenley."

"You don't mean to say, sir," broke in one of the astounded policemen, "that you think Mr. Hilton killed his own father!"

"Was it you who got that punch in the tummy?"

"Yes, sir."

"Well, save your breath. You'll want it when the muscles stiffen. *'Cré nom d'un pipe!* To think that I, Furneaux of the Yard, should queer the finest pitch I ever stood on."

"Oh, come now, Charles," said Winter. "Don't cry over spilt milk. You'll catch Fenley all right before the weather changes. What really happened?"

Aware of the paramount necessity of suppressing his personal woes, Furneaux at once gave a graphic and succinct account of Fenley's imminent capture and escape. He was scrupulously fair, and exonerated his assistants from any share of the blame—if indeed any one could be held accountable for the singular accident which precipitated matters by a few vital seconds.

Had Fenley reached the ground before the torch revealed the detective's presence, the latter would have closed with him instantly, throwing the torch aside, and thus taking the prisoner at the disadvantage which the fortune of war had brought to bear against the law. Furneaux was wiry though slight, and he could certainly have held his man until reënforcements came; nor would the constables' lamps have been extinguished during the *mêlée*.

"Then he has vanished, rifle and all," said Winter, when Furneaux had made an end.

"As though the earth had swallowed him. A thousand years ago it would have done so," was the humiliated confession.

"None of you have any notion which direction he took?"

"*I* received such a whack on the skull that I believe he disappeared in fire," said Furneaux. "My friend here," turning to the policeman who had voiced his amazement at the suggestion that Hilton Fenley was a murderer, "was in the position of Bret Harte's negro lecturer on geology, while this other stalwart thought he had been kicked by a horse. We soon recovered, but had to grope for each other. Then I called the heavens to witness that I was dished."

"That gave us a chance of salvage, anyhow," said Winter. "I 'phoned the Roxton Inspector, and he will block the roads. When he has communicated with St. Albans and some other centers we should have a fairly wide net spread. Bates is coming from the lodge to take charge of a search party to scour the woods. We want that rifle. He must have dropped it somewhere. He'll make for a station in the early morning. He daren't tramp the country without a hat and in a black suit."

Winter was trying to put heart into his colleague, but Furneaux was not to be comforted. The truth was that the blow on the head had been a very severe one. Unfortunately, he had changed his hard straw hat for a soft cap which gave hardly any protection. Had Fenley's perch been a few inches lower when he delivered that vindictive thrust, Scotland Yard would probably have lost one of its most zealous officers.

So the Jerseyman said nothing, having nothing to say that was fit for the ears of the local constabulary, and Winter suggested that they should return to the mansion and give Bates instructions. Then he, Winter, would telephone Headquarters, have the main roads watched, and the early Continental trains kept under surveillance.

Furneaux, torch in hand, at once led the way. Thus the party was visible before it entered the avenue, and two young people who had bridged months of ordinary acquaintance in one moment of tragedy, being then on the roadway, saw the gleam of light and waited.

"Good!" cackled the little detective when his glance fell on them. "I'm glad to see there's one live man in the bunch. I presume you've disposed of Mr. Robert Fenley, Mr. Trenholme?"

"Yes," said the artist. "His affairs seem to be common property. His brother evidently knew he was out of doors, and now you———"

Furneaux woke up at that.

"His brother! How can *you* know what his brother knew?"

"Mr. Hilton Fenley saw Miss Manning and myself, and mistook me for———"

"Saw you? When?"

"About five minutes ago, on the other side of the wood."

"What did he say? Quick!"

"He told us that the shooting was the outcome of your efforts to catch some man hiding among the trees."

"Of my efforts?"

"He didn't mention you by name. The words he used were 'the police.' He was taking part in the chase, I suppose."

"Which way did he go?"

Trenholme hesitated. Not only was he not quite conversant with the locality, but his shrewd wits had reached a certain conclusion, and he did not wish to be too outspoken before Sylvia. Surely she had borne sufficient for one day.

Thereupon the girl herself broke in.

"Hilton went toward the cedars. He may be making for the Easton gate. Have you caught any man?"

"Not yet, Miss Manning," said Winter, assuming control of the situation with a firm hand. "I advise you to go straight to your room, and not stir out again tonight. There will be no more disturbance—I promise you that."

Even the chief of the C. I. D. can err when he prophesies. At that instant the two lines of trees lost their impenetrable blackness. Their foliage sprang into red-tinted life as if the witches of the Brocken had chosen a new meeting-place, and a crackling, tearing sound rent the air.

"Oh!" screamed Sylvia, who chanced to be facing the mansion. "The house is on fire!"

They were standing in a group, almost where Police Constable Farrow had stood at ten minutes past ten the previous morning. Hence they were aware of this addition to the day's horrors before the house servants, who, headed by Tomlinson, were gathered on and near the flight of steps at the entrance. Every female servant in the establishment was there as well, not outside the door, but quaking in the hall. MacBain was the first among the men to realize what was happening. He caught the loud clang of an automatic fire alarm ringing in his room, and at once called the house fire brigade to run out the hose while he dashed upstairs into the north corridor, from which a volume of smoke was pouring.

"Good Heavens!" he cried, on reaching the cross gallery. "It's in Mr. Fenley's rooms!"

Mr. Fenley's rooms! No need to tell the horrified staff which rooms he meant. A fire was raging in the private suite of the dead man!

The residence was singularly well equipped with fire-extinguishing appliances. Mortimer Fenley had seen to that. Hand grenades, producing carbonic acid gas generated by mixing water with acid and alkali, were stored in convenient places, and there was a plentiful supply of water from many hose pipes. The north and south galleries looked on to an internal courtyard, so there was every chance of isolating the outbreak if it were tackled vigorously; and no fault could be found with either the spirit or training of the amateur brigade. Consequently, only two rooms, a bedroom and adjoining dressing-room, were well alight; these were burned out completely. A sitting-room on one side was badly scorched, as was a spare room on the other; but the men soon knew that they had checked the further progress of the flames, and were speculating, while they worked, as to the cause of a fire originating in a set of empty apartments, when Parker, Mrs. Fenley's personal attendant, came sobbing and distraught to Sylvia.

"Oh, miss!" she cried. "Oh, miss! Where is your aunt?"

"Isn't Mrs. Fenley in her room?" asked the girl, yielding to a sense of neglect in not having gone to see if Mrs. Fenley was alarmed, though the older woman was not in the slightest danger. The two main sections of the building were separated by an open space of forty feet, and The Towers had exceedingly thick walls.

"No, miss. I can't find her anywhere!" said the woman, well aware that if any one was at fault it was herself. "You know when I saw you. I went back then, and she was sleeping, so I thought I could leave her safely. Oh, miss, what has become of her? Maybe she was aroused by the shooting!"

All hands that could be spared from the fire-fighting operations engaged instantly in an active search, but there was no clue to Mrs. Fenley's disappearance beyond an open door and a missing night light. The electric current was shut off at the main at midnight, except on a special circuit communicating with the hall, the courtyard, and MacBain's den, where he had control of these things.

High and low they hunted without avail, until MacBain himself stumbled over a calcinated body in the murdered banker's bedroom. The poor creature had waked to some sense of disaster. Vague memories of the morning's horror had led her, night light in hand, to the spot where she fancied she would find the one person on earth in whom she placed confidence, for Mortimer Fenley had always treated her with kindness, even if his methods were not in accord with the commonly accepted moral code.

Presumably, on discovering that the rooms were empty, some further glimmering knowledge had stirred her benumbed consciousness. She may have flung herself on the bed in a paroxysm of weeping, heedless of the overturned night light and the havoc it caused. That, of course, is sheer guesswork, though the glass dish which held the light was found later on the charred floor, which was protected, to some extent, by a thick carpet.

At any rate, she had not long survived the husband who had given her a pomp and circumstance for which she was ill fitted. They were buried in the same grave, and Hertfordshire sent its thousands to the funeral.

Soon after her fate became known, Winter wanted Furneaux, but his colleague was not in the house. The telephone having broken down, owing to the collapse of a standard, and the necessity of subduing the fire having put a stop to any immediate search being made in the park, Winter thought that the pair of them would be better employed if they transferred their energies to the local police station.

He found Furneaux seated on the lowermost step at the entrance; the Jerseyman was crying as if his heart would break, and Trenholme was trying to comfort him, but in vain.

"What's up now?" inquired the Superintendent, thinking at the moment that his friend and comrade was giving way to hysteria indirectly owing to the blow he had received.

Furneaux looked up. It was the darkest hour of the night, and his chief could not see the distraught features wrung with pain.

"James," he said, mastering his voice by a fierce effort, "my mad antics killed that unfortunate woman! She was aroused by the shots. She would cry for help, and none came. Heavens! I can hear her now! Then she ran for refuge to the man who had been everything to her since she was a barrack room kid in India. I'm done, old fellow. I resign. I can never show my face in the Yard again."

"It'll do you a world of good if you talk," said Winter, meaning to console, but unconsciously wounding by cruel sarcasm.

"I'll be dumb enough after this night's work," said Furneaux, in a tone of such utter dejection that Winter began to take him seriously.

"If you fail me now, Charles," he said, and his utterance was thick with anger at the crassness of things, "I'll consider the advisability of sending in my own papers. Dash it!" He said something quite different, but his friends may read this record, and they would repudiate an exact version with scorn and disbelief. "Are we going to admit ourselves beaten by a half-bred hound like Hilton Fenley? Not if I know it, or I know you. We've got the noose 'round his neck, and you and I will pull it tight if we have to follow him to——"

"Pardon the interruption, gentlemen," said a voice. "I was called out o' bed to come to the fire, an' took a short cut across the park. Blow me if I didn't kick my foot against this!"

And Police Constable Farrow, who had approached unnoticed, held out an object which seemed to be a rifle. Owing to his being seated Furneaux's eyes were on a level with it, and he could see more clearly than the others. He struck a match; then there could be no doubt that the policeman had actually picked up the weapon which had set in motion so many and such varied vicissitudes.

But Farrow had more to say. It had been his happy lot during many hours to figure bravely in the Fenley case, and he carried himself as a valiant man and true to the end.

"I think I heard you mention Mr. Hilton," he went on. "I met Dr. Stern in the village, an' he tol' me Mr. Hilton had borrowed his car."

Furneaux stood up.

"Continue, Solomon," he said, and Winter sighed with relief; the little man was himself again.

"That's all, gentlemen, or practically all. It struck me as unusual, but Dr. Stern said Mr. Hilton's motor was out o' gear, an' he wanted a car in a desp'rit hurry."

"He did, indeed!" growled Furneaux. "You're quite sure there is no mistake?"

"Mistake, sir? How could there be? The doctor was walkin' home. That's an unusual thing. He never walks a yard if he can help it. Mr. Hilton borrowed the car to go to St. Albans."

"Did he, indeed? Just how did he come to find the car waiting for him?"

"Oh, that's the queer part of it. Dr. Stern is lookin' after poor old Joe Bland, who's mighty bad with—there, now, if I haven't gone and forgotten the name; something-itis—and Mr. Hilton must have seen the car standin' outside Bland's house. But what was he doin' in Roxton at arf past twelve? That's wot beats me. And then, just fancy me stubbin' my toe against this!"

Again he displayed the rifle as if it were an exhibit and he were giving evidence.

"Let's go inside and get a light," said Winter, and the four mounted the steps into the hall. Robert Fenley was there—red-faced as ever, for he had helped in putting out the fire, but quite sober, since he had been very sick.

Some lamps and candles gave a fair amount of light, and Robert eyed Trenholme viciously.

"So it was you!" he said. "I thought it was. Well, my father and mother are both dead, and this is no time for settlin' matters; but I'll look you up when this business is all over."

"If you do, you'll get hurt," said Winter brusquely. "Is that your rifle?" and he pointed to the weapon in Farrow's hands.

"Yes. Where was it found?"

"In the Quarry Wood, sir, but a'most in the park," said the policeman.

"Has it been used recently?"

Fenley could hardly have put a question better calculated to prove his own innocence of any complicity in the crime.

Winter took the gun, meaning to open the breech, but he and Furneaux simultaneously noticed a bit of black thread tied to one of the triggers. It had been broken, and the two loose ends were some inches in length.

"That settles it," muttered Furneaux. "The scoundrel fixed it to a thick branch, aimed it carefully on more than one occasion—look at the sights, set for four hundred yards—and fired it by pulling a cord from his bedroom window when he saw his father occupying the exact position where the sighting practiced on Monday and Tuesday showed that a fatal wound would be inflicted. The remaining length of cord was stronger than this packing thread, which was bound to give way first when force was applied.... Well, that side of the question didn't bother us much, did it, Winter?"

"May I ask who you're talking about?" inquired Robert Fenley hoarsely.

"About that precious rogue, your half brother," was the answer. "That is why he went to his bedroom, one window of which looks out on the park and the other on the east front, where he watched his father standing to light a cigar before entering the motor. He laid the cord before breakfast, knowing that Miss Manning's habit of bathing in the lake would keep gardeners and others from that part of the grounds. When the shot was fired he pulled in the cord———"

"I saw him doing that," interrupted Trenholme, who, after one glance at the signs of his handiwork on Robert Fenley's left jaw, had devoted his attention to the extraordinary story revealed by the detectives.

"You *saw* him!" And Furneaux wheeled round in sudden wrath. "Why the deuce didn't you tell me that?"

"You never asked me."

"How could I ask you such a thing? Am I a necromancer, a wizard, or eke a thought reader?"

Trenholme favored the vexed little man with a contemplative look.

"I think you are all those, and a jolly clever art critic as well," he said.

Furneaux was discomfited, and Winter nearly laughed. But the matter at issue was too important to be treated with levity.

"Tell us now what you saw, Mr. Trenholme," he said.

"When the shot was fired, I recognized it as coming from a high-velocity rifle," said the artist. "I was surprised that such a weapon should be used in an enclosed park of this nature, and looked toward the house to discover whether or not any heed would be given to the incident there. From where I was seated I could see the whole of the south front, but not the east side, where the brass fittings of the automobile alone were visible, glinting through and slightly above a yew hedge.

"Now, when Miss Manning returned to the house and entered by way of a window on the ground floor, I noticed that no other window was open. But after the report of the gun, I saw the end window of the first floor on the southeast side slightly raised—say six inches; and some one in the room was, as I regarded it, gesticulating, or making signs. That continued nearly half a minute and then ceased. I don't know whether the person behind the glass was a man or a woman, but some one was there, and engaged in the way I have described. If your theory is correct, the motions would be precisely those you suggest, similar to those of a fisherman reeling in a line."

"Your simile happens to be exact," said Winter. "While Hilton Fenley and my friend here were having a dust-up in the Quarry Wood I searched his rooms; and among other things I came upon a salmon reel carrying an exceptional quantity of line. So our case is fairly complete. I'm sorry to have to inform you, Mr. Fenley, that not only did your half brother kill your father, but he tried his level best to put the crime on your shoulders.

"He overreached himself in sending for Scotland Yard men. We have seen too much of the seamy side of life to accept as Gospel truth the first story we hear. The very fact that Hilton Fenley was attacking you in your absence prejudiced us against him at the outset. There were other matters, which I need not go into now, which converted our dislike into active suspicion.

"But it is only fair that you should understand how narrow was your escape from arrest. Had the local police been in sole charge I am bound to say you would have passed this night in a cell. Luckily for you, Mr. Furneaux and I set our faces against the notion of your guilt from the beginning. Long before we saw you, we were keeping an eye on the real criminal. When you did appear, your conduct only confirmed our belief in your innocence."

"I told you why, you will remember," piped Furneaux.

But Robert Fenley said no word. He was stunned. He began to feel ill again, and made for his room. Sylvia had not been seen since she heard of Mrs. Fenley's death. The detectives collected their belongings, which with the gun and a bag packed with various articles taken from Hilton Fenley's suite—the reel, for instance, a suit of clothes bearing marks, possibly of moss, and the leather portfolio of papers—were entrusted to Farrow and another constable for safe conveyance. Accompanied by Trenholme, they walked to Easton. On the way the artist supplied sufficient details of his two meetings with Sylvia to put them in possession of the main incidents. Furneaux, though suffering from a splitting headache, had recovered the use of a vinegary tongue.

"I was mistaken in you," he chuckled. "You're a rank impressionist. Indeed, you're a neo-impressionist, a get-busy-and-do-it-now master of art.... But she's a mighty nice girl, isn't she?"

"Meaning Miss Manning?" said Trenholme coldly.

"No. Eliza."

"Sorry. I misunderstood."

"*'Cré nom!* You've got it bad."

"Got what bad?"

"The matrimonial measles. You're sickening for them now. One of the worst symptoms in the man is his curt refusal to permit anybody else to admire one bright particular star of womanhood. If the girl hears another girl gushing over the young man, she's ready to scratch her eyes out. By Jove! It'll be many a day before you forget your visit to Roxton Park this morning, or yesterday morning, or whenever it was.

"I'm mixed. Life has been very strenuous during the past fifteen hours. If you love me, James, put my poor head under a pump, or I'll be dreaming that our lightning sketch performer here, long John Trenholme, late candidate for the P. R. A., but now devoted to the cult of Hymen, is going to marry Eliza, of the White Horse, and that the fair Sylvia is pledged to cook us a dinner tomorrow night—or is it tonight? Oh, Gemini, how my head aches!"

"Don't mind a word he's saying, Mr. Trenholme," put in Winter. "Hilton Fenley hit him a smack with that rifle, and it developed certain cracks already well marked. But he's a marvelously 'cute little codger when you make due allowance for his peculiar ways, and he has a queer trick of guessing at future events with an accuracy which has surprised me more times than I can keep track of."

Trenholme was too good a fellow not to put up with a little mild chaff of that sort. He looked at the horizon, where the faint streaks of another dawn were beginning to show in the northeast.

"Please God," he said piously, "if I'm deemed worthy of such a boon, I'll marry Sylvia Manning, or no other woman. And, when the chance offers, Eliza of the White Horse shall cook you a dinner to make your mouth water. Thus will Mr. Furneaux's dream come true, because dreams go by contraries!"

CHAPTER XVII
THE SETTLEMENT

Winter tried to persuade his mercurial-spirited friend to snatch a few hours' rest. The Police Inspector obligingly offered a bed; but short of a positive order, which the Superintendent did not care to give, nothing would induce Furneaux to let go his grip on the Fenley case.

"Wait till the doctor's car comes back," he urged. "The chauffeur will carry the story a few pages farther. At any rate, we shall know where he dropped Fenley, and that is something."

Winter produced a big cigar, and Trenholme felt in his pockets for pipe and tobacco.

"No, you don't, young man," said the big man firmly. "You're going straight to your room in the White Horse. And I'll tell you why. From what I have heard about the Fenleys, they were a lonely crowd. Their friends were business associates and they seem to own no relatives; while Miss Manning, if ever she possessed any, has been carefully shut away from them. The position of affairs in The Towers will be strained tomorrow. The elder Fenleys are dead; one son may be in jail—or, if he isn't, might as well be—and the other, as soon as he feels his feet, will be giving himself airs. Now, haven't you a mother or an aunt who would come to Roxton and meet Miss Manning, and perhaps help her to get away from a house which is no fit place for her to live in at present?"

"My mother can be here within an hour of the opening of the telegraph office," said Trenholme.

"Write the telegram now, and the constable on night duty will attend to it. When your mother arrives, tell her the whole story, and send her to Miss Manning. Don't go yourself. You might meet Robert Fenley, and he would certainly be cantankerous. If your mother resembles you, she will have no difficulty in arranging matters with the young lady."

"If I resemble my mother, I am a very fortunate man," said the artist simply.

"I thought it would be that way," was the smiling comment. "One other thing: I don't suppose for a minute that Miss Manning is acquainted with a reputable firm of solicitors. If she is, tell her to consult them, and get them to communicate with Scotland Yard, where I shall supply or leave with others certain information which should be acted on promptly in her behalf. If, as I expect, she knows no lawyer, see that she takes this card to the address on it and give Messrs. Gibb, Morris & Gibb my message. You understand?"

"Yes."

"Finally, she must be warned to say nothing of this to Robert Fenley. In fact, the less that young spark knows about her affairs the better. After tonight's adventure that hint is hardly needed, perhaps; but it is always well to be explicit. Now off with you."

"I'm not tired. Can I be of any service?"

"Yes. I want you to be ready for a long day's work in Miss Manning's interests. Mr. Furneaux and I may be busy elsewhere. Unquestionably we shall not be in Roxton; we may even be far from London. Miss Manning will want a friend. See to it that you start the day refreshed by some hours of sleep.'"

"Good-by," said Trenholme promptly. "Sorry you two will miss Eliza's dinner. But that is only a feast deferred. By the way, if I leave Roxton I'll send you my address."

"Don't worry about that," smiled the Superintendent. "Our friend the Inspector here will keep tab on you. Before you're finished with inquests, police courts and assizes you'll wish you'd never heard the name of Fenley.... By Jove, I nearly forgot to caution you. Not a word to the press.... Phi-ew!" he whistled. "If they get on to this story in its entirety, won't they publish chapter and verse!"

So Trenholme went out into the village street and walked to his quarters in the White Horse Inn. It was not yet two o'clock, but dawn had already silvered the northeast arc of the horizon. Just twenty hours earlier an alarm clock had waked him into such a day as few have experienced. Many a man has been brought unexpectedly into intimate touch with a tragedy of no personal concern, but seldom indeed do the Fates contrive that death and love and high adventure should be so closely bound, and packed pellmell into one long day.

Only to think of it! When he stole upstairs with the clock to play a trick on Eliza, he had never seen Sylvia nor so much as heard her name spoken. When he sang of love and the dawn while striding homeward through the park, he had seen her, yet did not know her, and had no hope of ever seeing her again. When he worked at her picture, he had labored at the idealization of a dream which bade fair to remain a dream. And now by some magic jugglery of ordinary events, each well within the bounds of credibility, yet so overwhelmingly incredible in their sequence and completeness, he was Sylvia's lover, her defender, her trusted knight-errant.

Even the concluding words of that big, round-headed, sensible detective had brought a fantasy nearer attainment. If Sylvia were rich, why then a youngster who painted pictures for a living would hardly dare think of marrying her. But if Sylvia were poor—and Winter's comments seemed to show that these financiers had been financing themselves at her expense—what earthly reason was there that she should not become Mrs. John Trenholme at the earliest practicable date? None that he could conceive. Why, a fellow would have to be a fool indeed who did not know when he had met the one woman in the world! He had often laughed at other fellows who spoke in that way about the chosen one. Now he understood that they had been wise and he foolish.

But suppose Sylvia—oh, dash it, no need to spoil one's brief rest by allowing a beastly doubt like that to rear its ugly head! One thing he was sure of—Robert Fenley could never be a rival; and Fenley, churl that he was, had known her for years, and could hardly be pestering her with his attentions if she were pledged to another man. Moreover he, John, newly in love and tingling with the thrill of it, fancied that Sylvia would not have clung to him with such complete confidence when the uproar arose in the park if——Well, well—the history of the Fenley case will never be brought to an end if any attempt is made to analyze the effects of love's first vigorous growth in the artistic temperament.

About a quarter past three Dr. Stern's little landaulet was halted at the same cross-road where a policeman had stopped it nearly three hours earlier.

"That you, Tom?" said the constable. "You're wanted at the station."

"What station?" inquired the chauffeur.

"The police station."

"Am I, by gum? What's up?"

"The Scotland Yard men want you."

"But what for? I haven't run over so much as a hen."

"Oh, it's all right. You're wanted as a witness. Never mind why. *They*'ll tell you. The doctor is there, smoking a cigar till you turn up."

"I left him at Joe Bland's."

"Joe Bland has left Boxton for Kingdom Come. And The Towers is half burnt down. Things haven't been happening while you were away, have they?"

"Not half," said Tom.

"No, nor quarter," grinned the policeman to himself when the car moved on. "Wait till you know who you took on that trip, and why, and *your* sparkin'-plug'll be out of order for a week."

It was as well that the chauffeur had not the slightest notion that he had conveyed a murderer to London when he began to tell his tale to his employer and the detectives. They wanted a plain, unvarnished story, and got it. On leaving the offices in Bishopsgate Street, Fenley asked to be driven to Gloucester Mansions, Shaftesbury Avenue. Tom had seen the last of him standing on the pavement, with a suitcase on the ground at his feet. He was wearing an overcoat and a derby hat, and was pressing an electric bell.

"He tol' me I needn't wait, so I made for the Edgware Road; an' that's all," said Tom.

"Cool as a fish!" commented Furneaux.

"Well, sir, I didn't get hot over it," said the surprised chauffeur.

"I'm not talking about you. Could you manage another run to town? Are you too tired?"

The mystified Tom looked at his employer. Dr. Stern laughed.

"Go right ahead!" he cried. "I'm thinking of buying a new car. A hundred and twenty miles in one night should settle the matter so far as this old rattletrap is concerned."

"Of course we'll pay you, doctor," said Winter.

"That's more than Hilton Fenley will ever do, I'm afraid."

Tom tickled his scalp under his cap.

"Mr. Hilton gemme a fiver," he said rather sheepishly. There was something going on that he did not understand, but he thought it advisable to own up with regard to that lordly tip.

"You're a lucky fellow," said the doctor. "What about petrol? And do you feel able to take these gentlemen to London?"

Tom was a wiry person. In five minutes he was on the road again bound for Scotland Yard this time. As a matter of form a detective was sent to Gloucester Mansions, and came back with the not unforeseen news that Mrs. Garth was very angry at being disturbed at such an unearthly hour. No; she had seen nothing of Mr. Hilton Fenley since the preceding afternoon. Some one had rung the bell about two o'clock that morning, but the summons was not repeated; and she had not inquired into it, thinking that a mistake had been made and discovered by the blunderer.

Sheldon was brought from his residence. He had a very complete report concerning Mrs. Lisle; but that lady's shadowy form need not flit across the screen, since Robert Fenley's intrigues cease to be of interest. He had dispatched her to France, urging that he must be given a free hand until the upset caused by his father's death was put straight. Suffice it to say that when he secured some few hundreds a year out of the residue of the estate, he married Mrs. Lisle, and possibly became a henpecked husband. The Garths, too, mother and daughter, may be dropped. There was no getting any restitution by them of any share of the proceeds of the robbery. They vowed they were innocent agents and received no share of the plunder. Miss Eileen Garth has taken up musical comedy, if not seriously at least zealously, and commenced in the chorus with quite a decent show of diamonds.

London was scoured next morning for traces of Hilton Fenley, but with no result. This again fell in with anticipation. The brain that could plan the brutal murder of a father was not likely to fail when contriving its own safety. Somehow both Winter and Furneaux were convinced that Fenley would make for Paris, and that once there it would be difficult to lay hands on him. Furneaux, be it remembered, had gone very thoroughly into the bond robbery, and had reached certain conclusions when Mortimer Fenley stopped the inquiry.

In pursuance of this notion they resolved to watch the likeliest ports. Furneaux took Dover, Winter Newhaven and Sheldon Folkestone. They did not even trouble to search the outgoing trains at the London termini, though a detailed description of the fugitive was circulated in the ordinary way. Each man traveled by the earliest train to his destination and, having secured the aid of the local police, mounted guard over the gangways.

Furneaux drew the prize, which was only a just compensation for a sore head and sorer feelings. He had changed his clothing, but adopted no other disguise than a traveling-cap pulled well down over his eyes. He took it for granted that Fenley, like every other intelligent person going abroad, was aware that all persons leaving the country are subjected to close if unobtrusive scrutiny as they step from pier to ship. Fenley, therefore, would have a sharp eye for the quietly dressed men who stand close to the steamer officials at the head of the gangway, but would hardly expect to find Nemesis hidden in the purser's cabin. Through a porthole Furneaux saw every face and, on the third essay, while the fashionable crowd which elects to pay higher rates for the eleven o'clock express from Victoria was struggling like less exalted people to be on board quickly, he found his man in the thick of the press.

Fenley had procured a new suit, a Homburg hat, and some baggage. In fact, it was learned afterwards that he hired a taxi at Charing Cross, breakfasted at Canterbury, and made his purchases there at leisure, before driving on to Dover.

He passed between two uniformed policemen with the utmost self-possession, even pausing there momentarily to give some instruction to a porter about the disposition of his portmanteaux. That was a piece of pure bravado, perhaps a final test of his own highly strung nerves. The men, of course, were not watching him or any other individual in the hurrying throng. They had a sharp eye for Furneaux, however, and when he nodded and hurried from his lair one of them grabbed Fenley by the shoulder.

At that instant a burly German, careless of any one's comfort but his own, and somewhat irritated by Fenley's halt at the mouth of the gangway, brushed forward. His weight, and Fenley's quick flinching from that ominous clutch, loosed the policeman's hold, and the murderer was free once more for a few fleeting seconds.

The constable pressed on, shoving the other man against the rail.

"Here. I want you," he said, and the quietly spoken words rang in Fenley's ears as if they had been bellowed through a megaphone. Owing to his own delay, there was a clear space in front. He took that way of escape instinctively, though he knew he was doomed, since the ship's officers would seize him at the policeman's call.

Then he saw Furneaux, whose foot was already on the lower end of the gangway. That, then, was the end! He was done for now. All that was left of life was the ghastly progress of the law's ceremonial until he was brought to the scaffold and hanged amidst a whole nation's loathing. His eyes met Furneaux's in a glare of deadly malice. Then he looked into eternity with daring despair, and dived headlong over the railing into the sea.

That awesome plunge created tremendous excitement among the bystanders on quay and ship. It was seen by hundreds. Men shouted, women screamed, not a few fainted. A sailor on the lower deck ran with a life belt, but Fenley never rose. His body was carried out by the tide, and was cast ashore some days later at the foot of Shakespeare's Cliff. Then the poor mortal husk made some amends for the misdeeds of a warped soul. In the pockets were found a large amount of negotiable scrip, and no small sum in notes and gold, with the result that Messrs. Gibb, Morris & Gibb were enabled to recover the whole of Sylvia Manning's fortune, while the sale of the estate provided sufficiently for Robert Fenley's future.

The course of true love never ran smoother than for John and Sylvia. They were so obviously made for each other, they had so determinedly flown to each other's arms, that it did not matter tuppence to either whether Sylvia were rich or poor. But it mattered a great deal when they came to make plans for a glorious future. What a big, grand world it was, to be sure! And how much there was to see in it! The Continent, America, the gorgeous East! They mapped out tours that would find them middle-aged before they neared England again. Does life consist then, in flitting from hotel to hotel, from train to steamship? Not it. German Kultur took care to upset that theory. John Trenholme is now a war-worn major in the Gunners, and Sylvia has only recently returned to her home nest after four years' service with the Red Cross in France.

But these things came later. One evening in the Autumn, Winter and Furneaux took Sheldon over to Roxton and dined with Dr. Stern and Tomlinson at the White Horse. Tomlinson had bought the White Horse and secured Eliza with the fixtures. Of course, there was talk of the Fenleys, and Winter told how Hilton Fenley's mother had been unearthed in Paris. She was a spiteful and wizened half-caste; but she held her son dear, as mothers will, be they black or white or chocolate-colored, and it was to maintain her in an establishment of some style that he had begun to steal. She had married again, and the man had gone through all her money, dying when there was none left. She retained his name, however, and Fenley adopted it, too, during frequent visits to Paris. Hence he was known there by a good many people, and could have sunk his own personality had he made good his escape. The mother's hatred of Mortimer Fenley had probably communicated itself to her son. When she was told of Hilton's suicide and its cause, she said that if anything could console her for his death it was the fact that he had avenged her wrongs on his father.

"What was her grievance against poor Mortimer Fenley?" inquired the doctor. "I knew him well, and he was a decent sort of fellow—rather blustering and dictatorial but not bad-hearted."

"His success, I believe," said Winter. "They disagreed, and she divorced him, thinking he would remain poor. The whirligig of time changed their relative positions, and to a jealous-minded woman that was unforgivable."

"The affair made a rare stir here anyhow," went on the doctor. "The people who have taken The Towers have not only changed the name of the place, but they have commissioned a friend of mine, an architect, to alter the entrance. There will be two flights of steps and a covered porch, so the exact spot where Fenley fell dead will be built over."

"Gentlemen," said Tomlinson, "talking is dry work. I haven't my old cellar to select from, but I can recommend the brands you see on the table. Mr. Furneaux, I'm sure you have not forgotten that Château Yquem?"

Then, and not until then, did the ex-butler hear that the detectives had never tasted his famous port. His benign features were wrung with pain, for it was a wine of rare "bowket," and hard to replace.

But Furneaux restored his wonted geniality by opening a parcel hitherto reposing on the sideboard.

"I never sent you that bottle of Alto Douro," he cried. "Here it is—a crusted quart for your own drinking. Lest you should be tempted to be too generous tonight, I've brought another. Now—a cradle and a corkscrew!"

So, after a dirge, and before the world shook in war, the story ends on a lively note, for what is there to compare with good wine and good cheer, each in moderation? And one bottle among five is reasonable enough in all conscience.